Barabbas
& the
Sword of Sacrifice

A Zealot's Journey To God

A NOVEL
by John Marcus Tompkins

Copyright © 2003 by John Marcus Tompkins

Barabbas & The Sword Of Sacrifice
by John Marcus Tompkins

Printed in the United States of America

ISBN 1-591608-59-7

All rights reserved. No part of this publication may be reproduced or transmitted in any form or by any means without written permission of the publisher.

Unless otherwise indicated, Bible quotations are taken from King James Version.

Xulon Press
www.XulonPress.com

Xulon Press books are available in bookstores everywhere, and on the Web at www.XulonPress.com.

Dedication

*To my Savior and Lord—Jesus Christ,
my supportive wife Tammy
and our sons—John Titus and Marcus Elijah.*

Contents

1. The Dream 9
2. Pharisees, Sadducees, & Pagans 15
3. Caiaphas Conspiracy 23
4. Fugitive—Race for Life 47
5. Pilate & Herod Antipas 73
6. Love & Lust 89
7. Zealots & Shepherds 109
8. Passing Over the Sacrifice 125
9. John Baptist—Dance of Death 151
10. Prisoner of Freedom 177
11. Essene Monastery—Qumran 197
12. Men & Miracles 221
13. Revelation: God or Man 239

1
The Dream

Fear escorts me into the courtroom. Then he shoves me into my seat at the table of defense. As I look about the court, I am optimistic because I have no accuser and a judge who does not know me. But as I turn, I see twelve peers who know me too well—the jury: Sexual Immorality, Impurity, Idolatry, Witchcraft, Hatred, Discord, Jealousy, Self-Ambition, Drunkenness, Rage, Murder, and Pride. Still, I feel that I will be vindicated. Where there is no accuser, there is no transgressor.

The judge calls the court to order as I notice something is missing—the counsel for my defense. After I inquire about my right to have an advocate, to my surprise the prosecution informs me that I refused the appointed defense attorney who is now the presiding judge. Hearing that lie, I realize something is wrong with this trial: someone is being set up—me. I did not refuse an advocate!

Only a few moments ago, I felt I was going to get a fair trial, and now my case looks bleak. The jurors hate me because I have abused them in the past. The judge, I surmise, wants revenge because he thinks I spurned him. The bloodthirsty prosecutor looks well studied and prepared. My defense—there is none.

Suddenly the courtroom doors fly open, and my worst nightmare materializes. My accuser, Sin, has found me. He takes the witness stand and exposes the overt, covert, and imaginary details of every immoral deed I have done, every evil thought, and selfish attitude I have possessed. Sin's testimony strips me of all privacy and dignity. In conclusion, he explains that guilty is the only verdict for me.

After Sin speaks, the prosecution calls Justice to the witness stand. My countenance brightens, for I feel that Justice will defend me. He surely knows that I am not getting a fair trial. But to my dismay, Justice eloquently delivers a philosophical reasoning that calls for my prosecution. Moreover, he says he will not be satisfied unless I receive the sentence of death.

Hearing Justice's argument for the death penalty, I plead for Mercy, but he is not present. Realizing Mercy's absence, my mind and body play tricks on me. I cannot keep the proceedings sorted in my mind, for Fear clutches my temples. Nauseated, I feel I am going to lose consciousness. Then Fear restricts my breathing as my heart beats in my throat. My only hope is that, in my despair, the jurors will sympathize with me.

Just when I think things cannot get worse, Satan makes his grand entrance, manifesting himself as the head prosecutor. He is well groomed and handsome, eloquent, and unerringly rational. He logically eradicates any sympathy for me and enables the jury and court spectators to focus their attention on my sins. This accuser not only reveals my sins but also portrays them as flagrant and egregious. "Justice must be served!" he demands.

Lucifer wants no room left for sympathy in this trial. To

ensure a guilty verdict, he employs a double-edged tactic: he exploits the ugliness of my sin and then portrays the virtue and beauty of Justice. "Without Justice," he says, "the free become slaves, the righteous become corrupt, the pure in heart become tainted, the merciful become ruthless, the peacemakers become dissenters, the meek become mockers, and the innocent become victims. Furthermore, if Justice is not satisfied, we forsake ourselves."

Satan's charisma overwhelms the court. Even I realize Satan is right. Then, as if he were fastening the dogs at the corners of my coffin, he asks the jury to consider that most of my sins were premeditated. Using incriminating, factual evidence, Satan demands that I deserve a horrible, torturous, and macabre death.

Hearing Satan's closing argument, the jury deliberates and Fear continues to torment me. Only a minute passes before the jury reaches its decision. Having asked the court to stand, the bailiff announces the name of the judge.

That name—I know that name—I have heard it many times. Although I never met this judge, I have friends who tried to introduce him to me. In fact, I recall the times when this judge sent me invitations to know him, but I never found time.

The foreman of the jury, Pride, stands to announce the verdict. He stares down his long, condescending nose at me and heralds, "Guilty! Guilty as charged!"

The verdict pierces my soul yet it satisfies Justice, the jury, and Satan. And me? I am numb. Fear paralyzes me as if I were a kitten caught in the teeth of a vicious wolf. Emotions rage, yet I am unable to express my feelings. I am a dead man.

The courtroom is silent and motionless as all eyes turn to the judge who prepares to pronounce my sentence. For the first time, I look closely at the judge's face. It is majestically illuminated. Though all eyes are on the regal judge, he appears unshaken and confident. His facial expression radiates his goodness. His patient, gentle brow expresses long-suffering. And his eyes—his concerned, compassionate eyes—tell a story of great love. As the goodness of the judge permeates the courtroom, Fear subsides. The judge tells the bailiff, Love, and the corrections officer, Power, to stand next to me. Surrounded by Love and Power, my mind calms. As long as I keep my eyes on the majestic judge, the situation seems bearable. I have hope. I am unable to explain how or why I become optimistic as I focus on the judge's appearance. His visage shines and warms my soul.

The time arrives for my sentencing. The jury, spectators, and Satan seem to scream silently, "Death!" Pressure mounts; the judge, I think, wants to free me, but he knows that Justice must be satisfied. He must sentence me according to the guilty verdict, yet I still have confidence in him. But is everyone to be satisfied? How can Justice be appeased? How can I be extricated? The answer lies between the lips of the judge. Will his words be sufficient?

The judge's eyes settle on me. I look at him as a child in trouble looks to his father for help. The judge pronounces, "To satisfy Justice and the verdict—guilty of negligent and premeditated sin—I sentence the defendant to death. This execution shall be administered according to the desires and satisfaction of the jury and the prosecutor." Satan and the jury leap and cheer triumphantly.

I am stunned by the judgement. The words of the judge resound like an echo in a bottomless pit. Fear reattaches. My knees buckle as my heart fails. How can this be? The judge appears so loving and gentle! How could one so merciful sentence me with a torturous death? Surely this is revenge.

In my hopelessness I no longer worry about death, but I am terrified of the method Satan and his jury will prescribe. As I kneel on the floor with my head down and my eyes closed in darkness, I wish Satan would simply take his sword and cut off my head. I can barely move or think. My situation seems worse than death. Fear crushes my mind while others celebrate the sentence.

The pandemonium of the court ceases at the sound of footsteps. Involuntary curiosity lifts my head and eyes toward the silence-making of the judge. Then, with a voice like the sound of many waters, the judge speaks. He proclaims to the world, "If the defendant accepts my conditions of love, I give myself for full payment, and I am ready to serve the sentence for him." With these words, the judge takes off his majestic robe. Stripped of his judicial raiment, he appears as any ordinary man.

Satan's thundering laughter makes the court explode in joyous celebration. The jurors and audience dance in triumph. Being saved by the judge, I am happy too. Then Satan silences the courtroom with his contemptuous accost. "Judge, I knew you were too compassionate to let this worthless defendant serve his sentence. And I knew your jurisprudence would make you satisfy Justice. I devised the whole action of this court to lure you into death. My master plan deceived the Master of Plans. Your tender, compassionate heart—your weakness, love for mankind—cost your life."

The courtroom disintegrates into pandemonium as the participants beat the judge unmercifully; then I, Barabbas, leave the scene, the cross, with my Savior hanging upon it.

2
Pharisees, Sadducees, & Pagans

Barabbas rolls over in his bed at the knock on the door. His dark brown eyes open with the realization that he was dreaming. He rises and brushes his fingers through his tangled black hair and stretches his well-proportioned body. "Some dream or nightmare," he mutters to himself. *I wonder what it means.* The knocking at the door becomes louder as he pulls on his blue mantle over a cream-colored tunic. "I'm coming. I'm coming!" he shouts. Half dressed, without a sash or sandals, Barabbas jerks the door open.

Javan, a young messenger, apologizes, "I'm sorry, Barabbas. I didn't know you were asleep. I'm looking for your father."

"That's all right; I had a nightmare—a bloody crucifixion. I'm glad you woke me."

"Why were you in bed so early?"

"I am to carry orders to Joppa and Caesarea early in the morning for Sir Joktan, the merchandiser. I wanted to sleep while I had the opportunity."

Javan, intrigued with places beyond his home of Jerusalem, asks, "What are Joppa and Caesarea like?"

"Well, both are beautiful seacoast cities that import and export. Joppa is smaller than Caesarea, but closer."

"Tell me more."

Willing to appease and impress his friend, Barabbas relishes the details. "Joppa, called the gateway of Jerusalem, is built on a tall, rocky knoll jutting deep into the Mediterranean. It forms a small, beautiful cape with a breakwater formed of gigantic rocks. The water is deep enough for ships to anchor in the harbor, but the size of the harbor and the great, perilous rocks make many captains prefer to dock at Caesarea. It's to Joppa that the cedars of Lebanon were sent for the construction of Solomon's temple." Then with disgust Barabbas comments sarcastically, "And it's there that the educated Greeks of intellectual renown believe that Andromeda was chained to be eaten by a sea monster to pacify Poseidon, only to be rescued by Perseus. Ugh!"

"Barabbas, you despise Hellenism, don't you?"

In self-righteous anger Barabbas blurts, "Hellenism is paganism and I detest it!"

"Calm down, Barabbas. You are too emotional. I don't like the beliefs of the Greeks either, but I don't lose my head over polytheistic mythology."

Barabbas admits his hostility. "You're right, Javan, but the belief in many gods heats my blood. For four thousand years God has taught us Israelites that there is but one God."

"Barabbas, I'm your best friend and I know you. You're headstrong, and I appreciate your belief. But as your friend, I'm telling you your anger is going to get you into serious trouble if you don't learn to control it. So . . . if you think you can hold your anger, tell me about Caesarea."

Barabbas, still irritated but not wanting to show it, explains, "Caesarea is a great commercial center and seaport. Herod named the city after Caesar Augustus, and it was so well constructed by Herod the Great that it came to be called little Rome."

The mention of Herod spurs Barabbas to elaborate, "Herod the Great was the ruler who murdered all the babies in Bethlehem almost thirty years ago. And Herod was also the one who murdered his wife and some of his own children. Even Caesar admitted that he had rather be Herod's hog than one of Herod's children."

Incensed at the thought of Herod the Great, Barabbas spits, "The city was not only built by a murderer, but also named after a pagan Roman ruler in return for political favors. This hypocrisy makes me sick!" Forgetting his friend's reprimand, Barabbas again voices resentment. "I suspect our religious leaders are involved with foul Roman politics. It's detestable!"

"Yes, Barabbas," Javan chuckles "you definitely have a problem."

Realizing he has shown his bitterness again, Barabbas stops himself, then laughs with Javan. "Javan, my zeal, not anger, is ever present when I hear or see any philosophy contrary to the scriptures, the ancient writings, the words of our fathers: *The Lord our God is one Lord, and thou shalt love the Lord thy God with all thine heart, and with all thy soul, and with all thy might.*"

"Amen," affirms Javan. "Now . . . I must be about my mission. Do you know where I may find your father? I have a message for him."

"*I* don't know where he is, but my mother should know. She said she was going to the Hinnom Valley."

"Well, since I am this close to the water tower, I'll look for her. I will see you later. Thanks . . . Barabbas."

"Wait, Javan," Barabbas implores with some embarrassment. "I was wondering if you would help me."

"Help you with what?" asks Javan, pretending he does not know.

"I know you're not supposed to . . . but will you tell me the message?"

"Why not . . . you know the business." Javan mockingly speaks with pretentious pomp, "Your majesty, High Priest Caiaphas, demands the presence of the temple treasurer, your father."

"Why?"

"I don't know. The high priest did not lower himself to extend his confidentiality to a slave. Ha! But I will say this, Barabbas. I have never seen Caiaphas as angry as when he summoned me to find your father. I quote Caiaphas, 'Javan, find Rabba and bring him to me. I don't care how long it takes. You find that rebellious, religious fanatic and bring him here. Now!'"

No longer hiding his resentment, Barabbas vehemently states, "You know as well as I that Caiaphas is a thief and a hypocrite! For my father to share the same beliefs with Caiaphas is incomprehensible. Both men believe in the same God. They fast, tithe, sacrifice, pray, and observe the strictest rules of their faith; yet one is good and the other, I think, is evil."

"Well, Barabbas, you know that both Rabba and Caiaphas truly believe in only one God. Yet, Rabba is a Pharisee, and Caiaphas is a Sadducee. You know that Sadducees don't believe in the resurrection of the dead or a future life. They don't believe in angels, demons, or the idea of a spiritual world. If you embrace this view, how can one believe in punishment in the hereafter? But—on the other hand, let's not forget who has the greater education, social status, religious position, *and* favor of the Romans."

"Cursed are the Romans—pagans!" snaps Barabbas.

"Barabbas watch yourself. Don't forget that our belief as Pharisees calls us to be subjected to those in authority. To think of our rulers, whether they are religious or governmental, in any other way than with reverence is a sin. We must bless them. And any injustices they perform will be judged by God. God is our avenger."

"Javan, I have been taught that all my life, and it makes me sick. I think it's time to do something about these pagans and hypocrites."

"You talk like a Zealot."

Seeing the displeasure on Barabbas' face, Javan speaks to change the subject, "When the Messiah comes, He will judge all."

"I may be the one to crush these serpents. If a messiah is needed, then I may be the messiah for the job."

Javan jokes, "You can't be the Messiah. Jesus claimed that position when he started his ministry."

"Aw, Jesus has miracles and strange teachings, but a real messiah will come with a sword to set his people free. I don't have a sword, but I do have the desire to be free of Roman rule."

"Your talk is big." Javan laughs, then sobers. "But I see potential in you, Barabbas. I believe you *are* different. Maybe God has great plans for you." They are silent for a moment, then Javan smiles and says, "Well, I must go now. I am a messenger who delays not. Ha! I am sure of the urgency of this message. Caiaphas probably wants your father to appropriate money for something."

As Javan leaves, Barabbas ponders the words of anger from the High Priest. *Maybe Javan is right about the levity of Caiaphas' summon; but to be safe, I will be present when Father graces the presence of the High Priest. It's Caiaphas' anger that worries me.*

"Hey, Javan, wait! Let me help you find Mother. I'll race you to the tower at the Water Gate and look in the Hinnom Valley for her. Let's go!"

The two young men race to the tower. Barabbas reaches

the top with Javan not far behind. Gasping for air, Barabbas snorts at the putrid and nauseating stench. "Phew! It stinks up here!"

"Yes, the south wind brings the smoke and that awful stench up here. I don't know which one is worse, the rotten carcasses or the burning garbage. You know—if it didn't stink, Hinnom would be a beautiful valley."

Looking at the terrain, Barabbas replies, "Javan, this will never be a beautiful valley. The Canaanites worshiped Baal and Molech, the fire-god, by throwing their children in a fire that burned continuously. Moreover, two kings of Judah—Ahaz and Manasseh—practiced human sacrifice here. I thank God that King Josiah defiled this valley to stop the atrocities."

"Barabbas, I know that you think you know everything, but let me teach you something about the valley of Hinnom. This valley is like Hell." Javan speaks words with didactic authority: "'Their worm dieth not, and the fire is not quenched. There will be wailing, weeping, and gnashing of teeth.' Have you heard that before?"

"The first part of that is from the book of Isaiah. Go ahead. Explain yourself."

"Look into the valley and see the deterioration of the carcass' remains: the maggot dies not. Smell the smoke of the burning city garbage. Even through the night, the fire continuously smolders. From time to time an executed criminal's body is thrown out there. His family weeps and wails. And as you can see and hear, in the far distance wild dogs howl and gnash their teeth as they fight over the garbage. That is what Hell is like."

"Where did you learn this strange but plausible teaching, Javan?"

"Jesus."

"I should have known," Barabbas says with disgust. "Come, Javan, let's look for Mother."

"Barabbas, I still think the view from here is just *beautiful*. To the east of Jerusalem is the deep ravine of the Kidron Valley running past the Temple with the Gihon Spring on one side and the Garden of Gethsemane and the Mount of Olives on the other. To the west is the Tyropoen Valley dividing the City of David and the Upper City. And here at our feet is the Pool of Siloam."

"And to the south is the stench of the Hinnom Valley and my mother approaching the Water Gate. Javan, have you forgotten about the message for Father?"

Climbing down the tower, Barabbas greets his mother: "Javan has a question for you."

"Hello, Mary. How are you?" Javan greets Barabbas' mother.

"Fine, thank you, except for this smell."

"Where is Sir Rabba? I have a message for him."

"He is at blind Bartimaeus' house. Bartimaeus is moving from his upstairs apartment to the one below. Rabba is helping him move. I helped them clean out the old apartment. There was so much junk in there! That's why I came here. I carried a load of trash from Bartimaeus' apartment to the fire. If you are going there, will you tell Rabba that I will have dinner ready in about an hour—around sundown?"

"Yes, I will be glad to . . . I must hurry along and give Sir Rabba the message."

"Thank you. It was good to see you. Tell your family I said Shalom. May God bless you."

"Goodbye, Javan," says Barabbas.

"Goodbye, Barabbas. I'll see you later."

As Barabbas and his mother walk toward home, all seems well in the city of Jerusalem.

Ten miles north of Jerusalem, in the ruins of the city of Ai, a four-thousand-year-old curse crawls across the sand. Camouflaged with cryptically colored blotches of white, yellow and brown, an ill-tempered desert horned viper gains traction with the heavily keeled scales on his belly. The viper throws its broad, spade-shaped, horned head and body forward at an angle in the direction of travel. Eating the filth and dust of the ground, the cursed sidewinder seeks for a strategic location.

The serpent relies not on his sight or hearing because both are poor. The viper's vision is hampered by the dust on his transparent eyelids, which protect his vertical pupils. It has no eardrums or external cavities; however, the serpent employs his most powerful weapon—the tongue. He masterfully flicks his retractile forked tongue, picks up particles of scent from the air and pulls them to the openings in the roof of his mouth. The particles enter the openings that lead to an organ that is lined with sensitive cells that transmit findings to the brain, then to the olfactory duct. Using the olfactory duct to smell, the viper recognizes this as the place where animals and humans have been.

The serpent slithers among the rocks in the ruins near the shade of a tamarisk tree. It lowers and rotates its maxilla ninety degrees by muscular action to expose his large venom glands and tubular fangs. It prepares a mixture of haemotoxins and anti-coagulants, which will destroy kidney and liver cells and break down blood cells to cause internal and external bleeding. It can hardly wait to inject fiery venom into unsuspecting victims. Its victims will suffer severe swelling, dizziness, vomiting, and convulsions followed by a painful death. Shuffling itself into the sand between two rocks, the viper is completely submerged, hidden except for the two horns growing out of the top of its head.

3
Caiaphas Conspiracy

On the narrow cobblestone streets of the lower City of David, Javan considers the surroundings. A sweet aroma tainted with the smell of smoke fills the air as the residents begin to cook on open fires. Some remove bread from their brick ovens. Javan observes the residents as they open huge pottery jars and remove dried fruits and grains. The evening meal approaches. *What a beautiful sight: God's chosen people living in harmony even under the rule of the Romans.*

Walking across the strategic Mount Zion, or Hill of Ophel as the Jebusites knew it, Javan recalls the history. Joshua defeated the Jebusites but did not drive them from this mount. Later, to conquer this strongly fortified Canaanite hill surrounded on three sides by deep valleys and ravines, King David proclaimed that whoever attacked the Jebusites first would be chief and captain. Joab climbed up into the city by way of an underground water shaft to conquer them.

Though the buildings in the lower part of the city are older, Javan appreciates them more than the newer ones in the upper city of Jerusalem. The houses here crowd together; some share a common wall. They are made of bricks, irregular stones, or plaster. The roofs are made with beams and branches covered with layers of clay, strong enough to support people or another room for the house. Outdoor staircases give easy access to the roofs on which the residents dry fruits and grains. More than a shelter, the roofs channel rainwater to the cisterns beneath during the rainy season.

The pleasant weather allows open doors and shutters so Javan can see inside the homes. He notices curtains separating the interior rooms and floors of packed clay or plaster. Most of the interior walls are whitewashed plaster, which brightens the rooms. The furnishings consist mainly of tables, chests, framed bed mats, oil lamps, and water jars. These water jars are unglazed to seep water, which evaporates to cool the jar and its contents.

Leaving the lower city of Mount Zion through an arched tunnel with a building above it, Javan stops to view Mount Moriah before him. This Mount Moriah was annexed to the city by King Solomon, who built the House of the Lord. It was once the threshing floor of Araunah, a Jebusite also called Ornan. King David purchased this threshing floor from Araunah for fifty shekels of silver. Araunah offered to give the mount to David, but David refused because he wanted to build an altar of sacrifice. David said, "I will surely buy it of thee at a price: neither will I offer burnt offerings unto the LORD my God of that which doth cost me nothing." Not only did David make sacrifices to the Lord on Mount Moriah, but Abraham also came here to sacrifice his son, Isaac. Isaac was spared: God provided himself a lamb. While considering the cost of sacrifice, Javan catches sight of Bartimaeus' abode just short of the Temple.

About two hundred yards from the Temple, Javan finds

Rabba helping blind Bartimaeus move his belongings from an antiquated upper level apartment to one along the street. Javan greets the two men, "Hello, Sir Bartimaeus and Sir Rabba."

"Hello, Javan," answers Rabba.

Bartimaeus asks, "How are Nicodemus and the rest of the family?"

"Fine. Thank you." Without hesitating, Javan states his business, "Sir Rabba, I'm sorry to hinder you, but Caiaphas requests your immediate presence."

"Did he say what he needed, Javan?"

"No, Sir."

Rabba turns to Bartimaeus. "I'm sorry, Bartimaeus. I must go and see Caiaphas, but afterward I will be back to help you arrange your furnishings. The sun is about to set, but I will be back tonight before you sleep."

"Don't trouble yourself to come back tonight. I'll be all right. I appreciate your help, Rabba, my friend."

Rabba gently grasps the hand of Bartimaeus. "I shall not leave this house undone. I must see what Caiaphas wants, and I must then go lock the accounting office in the Temple. From the Temple, your house is on my way home. I'll be back tonight."

In the upper city of Jerusalem, near the southwest corner of the city walls, Barabbas stops at a block's distance to survey Caiaphas' house. This modern house, not built into the wall itself or attached to any other dwelling, stands by itself. Barabbas notices that the sloped Roman roof covered with clay tiles will not allow him to observe the meeting from the ventilation ports on the upper side of the house. However, if the roof were flat, the two guards at the ornate front door would probably be up there. *I guess I can't have everything.* Studying the layout of the house, Barabbas notices an area from which he can secretly observe the meeting of Caiaphas and his father.

Barabbas knows that the High Priest Caiaphas and his father, Rabba, would never let anyone who is not a member of the Sanhedrin attend a Temple business meeting. Yet, Barabbas is not sure this meeting will be business; therefore, he justifies eavesdropping. Considering the rudeness and the anger of Caiaphas, Barabbas considers eavesdropping on his father his duty as a son.

As night falls, only two porters guard the front door, so Barabbas makes his move toward the side of the house near the service area. Inconspicuously, holding his head down, he walks to the firewood stack. He quietly removes the wood near the hatch and places them to hide his back. As he surreptitiously pulls the hatch open slightly to look inside, he bumps the wood stack and a couple of logs fall.

One of the guards at the door says to the other, "Did you hear that?"

"Hear what?"

"A noise at the side of the house."

"I didn't hear anything, but I wasn't listening."

"I heard something, and I'm going to check it out. I think it came from the wood pile."

In the darkest shadowed corner beside the huge wood box, Barabbas squats with two logs lying on his shoulders and one leaning across the side of his face.

The guard comes to the woodpile in front of the hatch and looks around. Not knowing what to do, Barabbas prays for God to hide him in the darkness. Then the guard picks up a piece of the wood that fell and places it back on the stack. Grabbing another piece of wood, he throws it in the dark corner where Barabbas hides. Not a sound comes from him. As the doorkeeper returns to his post, Barabbas knows that God answers prayer.

The porter who waited by the door asks of the returning porter, "Did you find your ghost?"

"Yes. A couple of pieces of fire wood fell off the stack."

Back in position, Barabbas looks through the crack in the hatch to see beautiful rugs on flagstones and a breathtaking mosaic floor. The walls have wood panels and ivory inlays. Barabbas' eyes soak up the elaborate glasswork of the oil lamps and the gold and silver trimmings of the furniture. *Evidently the position of the high priest is a lucrative one.*

The tall but overweight Caiaphas walks into view from another room. He is wearing the blue, purple, scarlet ephod with threads of pure gold—the vest of the high priest. On the shoulders of the ephod are two onyx stones in settings of gold. These stones have the names of the twelve tribes of Israel engraved upon them. The "breastplate of judgement" is attached to the front of the vest by two golden chains and a blue cord. On the breastplate are twelve precious stones engraved with the names of the twelve tribes of Israel. The robe of the ephod has pomegranate figurines and bells attached to its hem.

I can't believe the audacity and disrespect of Caiaphas! I thought the high priest was supposed to leave the holy garments in the Temple. Look at him! He's wearing the ephod! With the exception of the holy crown of gold with "Holiness to the Lord" engraved on it, he is wearing all the holy attire. To look at him, you would think that today is the Day of Atonement!

One of the men on the porch opens the door slightly and announces that Rabba is coming. Caiaphas' graying hair shines in the light of the oil lamps, and his face hardens. *Caiaphas acts as though he gained his position as high priest by some noble or God-ordained means. Ha! By means of political favoritism, the Roman procurator, Valerius Gratus, appointed him!*

Anak, Caiaphas' personal guard, goes to stand by the door. Caiaphas waits as the silence is broken by a knock on the door.

Anak, a gigantic man with a face like a hawk and a

droopy stature like a vulture, opens the door and addresses Rabba. "The High Priest Caiaphas is waiting for you in the forum room." Escorting Rabba to the open room, the warrior-like Anak gravely announces, "Rabba has arrived."

At this moment, Barabbas is deeply troubled. Without anyone saying a word, anger overcomes him. *I'll get even with anybody who harms my father, especially those hypocrites!* Restraining himself, he listens as the wrinkled-browed Caiaphas begins to speak.

"Rabba, I'll skip all the small talk and get to the point. You probably know why I have summoned you."

"No, sir."

Like a prosecuting attorney, Caiaphas interrogates, "Rabba, isn't it true that you went to work for Sadoc, the money lender, as a part-time auditor?"

"Yes, sir."

"Rabba, you have worked at the Temple as head accountant for how long?"

"Twelve years, sir. I have served the Temple with the best of my ability as unto the Lord."

"Have you been paid sufficiently?"

"Yes, sir. God has been good to me."

"Well, why have you taken a second job?"

"Well, uh—my son, Barabbas, needed three horses to run his mail and message service from Jerusalem to Joppa and Caesarea. Barabbas and I went to Sadoc to borrow the money for the horses. In need of an auditor, Sadoc offered me a job. With my part-time earnings and Barabbas' earnings, we paid for the horses. Barabbas paid the major part of the loan. And the tithes on the earnings were paid by both of us."

"Rabba, let me be more blunt. Sadoc told me you asked questions about Governor Pilate's withdrawals."

Realizing that Caiaphas knows something, Rabba tries to find out how much. "What do you mean, sir?"

Caiaphas retorts, "Don't play dumb. You asked Sadoc how it is possible that Pilate can make withdrawals on someone else."

"Well . . . uh . . ." Rabba realizes that he is cornered by the insistent questions of the subtle Caiaphas. In frustration, Rabba concedes, "I assume you are going to discover my suspicion sooner or later."

In a more pleasant tone, Caiaphas interrupts, "Your silence will be rewarded."

Rabba rebuts, "I don't want a reward! I want what is right in the eyes of the Lord. My eternity is at stake."

"Don't be a fanatic! Rabba, your pharisaical beliefs make you a fool!" Calming himself and lowering his voice, Caiaphas asks, "Now, what are you going to do with your information—blackmail us?"

Rabba emphatically states his intentions: "Tomorrow, I will go before the rulers and elders of the Sadducees, Pharisees, and Scribes—the seventy-one of the Sanhedrin over whom you preside. I will tell them what I have found."

Fearing that Rabba will speak to the Sanhedrin, Caiaphas wishes to stop him. In a threatening tone Caiaphas insinuates with words of consequence, "I advise you not to do that, Rabba."

"Why not? I have nothing to hide," Rabba counters.

Caiaphas retaliates, "When I tell the Sanhedrin that you as treasurer are working for Sadoc, the high interest lender and arm-breaker, they will frown at you. And when I tell them that you as treasurer are responsible for the money you accuse me of misusing on political favors, they won't believe a word you are saying. The Sanhedrin will think you are trying to frame me. And you know that we Sadducees hold the power, wealth, and the majority."

"Caiaphas, may God forgive me for calling you despicable, but you are! However, tomorrow, I shall ask the elders to judge between you and me. Besides that, I have the proof—the insignias of all the parties on paper." With those incriminating words, the shaken Rabba lets his words rest.

Caiaphas curses. Anak lunges forward and grabs Rabba by the neck with his fist ready and asks, "May I strike him for irreverence?"

Barabbas almost faints with relief as Caiaphas instantly answers, "No!"

Pointing to the door, Caiaphas shouts, "Go! Rabba, go before I change my mind!"

Anak relinquishes his hold, and Rabba turns and goes out the door. Anger and the desire for revenge swell up in Barabbas as he watches Caiaphas and Anak. Anak, eager to go after Rabba and beat him, asks, "Do you want me to shut Rabba up?"

"No. *You* shut up, and let *me* think."

Barabbas wants to catch his father and find out what the high priest has been doing; but listening for Caiaphas' plan takes priority.

Caiaphas rises from his chair and paces the floor. Incensed at the lack of action from Caiaphas, Anak says, "If you don't need me to stop Rabba, may I go home?"

"Go! Please go! I must think before I act," exclaims Caiaphas as Anak leaves.

Still pacing the floor, Caiaphas mutters to himself and occasionally curses aloud. Barabbas impatiently waits, watches, and listens.

After half an hour of walking the floor, Caiaphas halts and shouts, "The insignia! It's on the ledger at the Temple!" Running out the door, Caiaphas orders the two porters to follow.

One street over, Barabbas runs toward the Temple as the short-winded Caiaphas slows to a brisk walk. "Run ahead and secure the temple treasury office," orders Caiaphas.

While the two guards race to secure the treasury door, the youthful, nineteen-year-old Barabbas races to secure an inconspicuous spot for espionage. *They may try to hurt my father.* Having farther to run, yet with much more to lose, Barabbas finally gets ahead of the two sentries just before reaching the Temple.

Reaching the corner of the royal porch of the Temple, Barabbas searches for Rabba. After crossing the porch, he moves over the Court of the Gentiles, where moneychangers and retailers do business in the daytime. Then he climbs the steps that lead three feet higher to the Sacred Enclosure. All Gentiles are forbidden to enter this place and trespassers are punished with the strictest penalty—death. Barabbas sees a few men bowed in prayer. At last, crossing the Sacred Enclosure and up the steps, he reaches his destination of the Court of Treasury.

In each of the four corners of the Treasury Court is a room. One of the two closest rooms to the ten feet of curved steps, which are called the Steps of the Degrees, is Rabba's office. By torchlight, Barabbas sees that the treasury office is bolted and locked.

Barabbas takes advantage of another opportunity to advance in the cat-and-mouse game. He joins the men praying on the steps of the degrees, which lead into the Court of Israel where only male Jews are allowed to enter. Positioning himself face down in prayer near the door of his father's office, Barabbas earnestly prays as he waits. "Holy God of Abraham, thank you for your guidance. Please protect my father and help me to rout these evil men. God, I need you!" Barabbas stops praying as he sees Caiaphas' two guards walk toward the treasury door. One of them tries the lock and finds it secure.

As these men stand at the door, the night custodian of the Court of Treasury approaches the two and asks if he may help them. One replies, "We have orders from Caiaphas."

A few moments later, Caiaphas enters the Treasury Court to find the accounting office locked. Caiaphas looks to the custodian. "Who locked this door?"

"Rabba came by earlier and locked it as he always does at the end of the day. Is there a problem?"

"Do you have the keys to the door?"

"Yes, sir."

"Open it," Caiaphas commands.

After the door is opened, Caiaphas goes inside and discovers that the ledger is gone. Looking to the custodian, Caiaphas asks, "Have you seen the temple ledger?"

"Yes, sir. Rabba took it with him. Strange . . . I've never seen him do that before."

Face flushed with impatience, Caiaphas and the two guards leave the treasury office and walk past Barabbas and the others praying. Then, climbing to the top of the ten feet of stairs onto the Court of Israel, the guards stop to wait as Caiaphas goes farther out of Barabbas' sight. He watches them anxiously as he waits.

Caiaphas crosses the Court of Israel and climbs up three feet higher to the Court of Priests, where only priests are allowed to enter. Finally, eight feet below the Holy Place and the Holy of Holies, Caiaphas looks for the sword used to sacrifice animals at the altar. Realizing the sword is gone, Caiaphas curses.

Hurrying down the steps of the degrees, Caiaphas speaks to the two door guards, "Come with me to the Roman barracks." Hearing Caiaphas' orders, Barabbas quietly stops his pretense of prayer and leaves behind them.

Barabbas' mind and legs race toward the fortress of Antonia, the praetorium, rebuilt by Herod the Great and named after Mark Antony. Realizing that Caiaphas as high priest will not enter the house of a pagan, Barabbas prays for an opportunity to eavesdrop on Caiaphas and Pilate.

Seeing the lights of the praetorium and the legionnaires on guard, Barabbas stops in the darkness. He wonders where the conspirators will talk. Suddenly, out of darkness, Caiaphas and the two door guards appear at the well-lit fortress gate. *The colonnade of the portico—that's where they'll talk. The colonnade is at the edge of darkness and out of the hearing of others. A conspiracy like this will not be discussed in the open.*

Crawling in the darkness, Barabbas reaches the colonnade as Marcus, the commander in charge when Pilate is absent, and his guards appear at the gate. Together, Caiaphas and Marcus walk toward the colonnade. Barabbas thanks God for this strategic spot to eavesdrop.

Barabbas hears Marcus say, "Pilate is at Caesarea and won't be back until tomorrow. In the meantime, I'm in charge. If the governor comes back and finds that you and I have let things get out of hand, he'll put us either in prison or to death."

"Yes—but Marcus, don't you think your action is too drastic?"

"Drastic?" he exclaims. "You're a fool! Thirty pieces of silver to save my neck! That's cheap! Caiaphas, you'd better think. It's Anak to whom I gave the money . . . so if he is caught, everyone will think you're behind it. He's *your* servant. You'd better hope that he's successful."

Disgusted, confused, and worried, Caiaphas pulls at his own hair as he follows Marcus out from the colonnade. Frustrated by the expression on Caiaphas' face, Marcus says with a villainous smile, "Thirty silver coins are nothing."

Almost out of range of their voices now, Barabbas barely hears the rebuttal of Caiaphas, "You know I am not talking about the value of the money. I'm talking about the value of life. You—not I—paid Anak to *murder* our temple treasurer."

"As if you cared," scoffs Marcus.

In horror Barabbas sickens as he realizes an oversight in his work of espionage—Anak is not here. *"Oh! My God, help me!"* Barabbas leaps up and sprints away from the colonnade toward home.

Racing down the street, Barabbas prays his father went straight home. *If Rabba went home immediately after leaving Caiaphas' house, surely he is safe at home with Mother: Nobody in his right mind would murder my father with someone else around as a witness.* Barabbas questions . . . as fear makes his legs run faster toward home.

Running in the darkness of the tunneled archway between Mount Moriah and Mount Zion, Barabbas trips over something in the street. Barabbas flies through the air landing in a sprawled manner and rolling to a stop on the rough pavement. Scraped and bruised, Barabbas staggers to his feet. His eyes focus on the silhouette of a man lying facedown on the cobblestone pavement. Barabbas approaches the thing he fears most—his father's death. Rolling the body over, Barabbas sees the Sword of the Lord stuck from the lower abdomen up into the upper torso piercing the vital organs. Removing the Sword of Sacrifice, used to sacrifice animals at the holy Temple, Barabbas runs to hide it in a crevice behind the monument of God's mercy, just outside the arched tunnel.

With an aching heart and an incredulous mind, Barabbas weeps. Sobbing and screaming, he proclaims the Shema, which all monotheistic Jews try to proclaim in their dying breaths: "Hear! O Israel! The Lord our God is one Lord: Thou shalt love the Lord thy God with all thine heart! With all thy soul! With all thy might!"

The public proclamation of the Shema awakens the lower city to discover the tragedy. Barabbas falls on his knees before his father and mourns as the residents gather around the body of Rabba.

Hours later, the body of Rabba is at the undertaker's, and Barabbas is at home with his mother, Mary. Neighbors and friends have left after expressing their condolences and their willingness to help the bereaved. Lazarus and Martha, Mary's brother and sister from Bethany, and Javan remain there at the request of the survivors. Lazarus and Martha kneel in prayer by Mary's bed. The neighborhood drifts to silence as Barabbas and Javan walk out on the porch. Painfully, Barabbas asks, "Javan, do you love me?"

"Yes, Barabbas . . . like a brother."

"Then swear to me you will not tell anyone what I'm about to tell you."

"I swear."

Barabbas jumps off the porch and runs to the Monument of Mercy, less than three blocks away. He pulls out the Sword of Sacrifice as Javan arrives behind him.

"The Sword of the Lord," whispers Javan, seeing it in Barabbas' hand.

Holding the sword in his left hand, Barabbas gazes at the fine gold and silver engravings. "There is no other sword like it," Barabbas proclaims. "It's a work of art. Beautiful gold and silver finish, but the point and edge are deadly. Just like the appearance of Anak and Marcus—murders! Marcus paid Anak to murder my father!" Taking his eyes off the sword to look Javan in the eyes, Barabbas boils with anger as he tells how Rabba was murdered.

Finally, Barabbas vows, "With the Sword of the Lord, I *will* avenge my father's death." Then, hiding the sword under his mantle, Barabbas looks for assurance in Javan's face. "Javan, nobody else knows about this. Swear your secrecy."

"I swear."

"Will you help me, Javan?"

Nervously Javan replies, "I can't kill anyone."

"I don't want you to kill anyone. I want your allegiance and confidence. All I ask is that you be loyal. The Sword of the Lord shall devour the wicked. I need you, Javan."

Javan embraces Barabbas and says, "I swear I will be

faithful to you as you are faithful to the Lord, the God of our fathers."

Barabbas is appreciative of Javan's loyalty but moves the conversation toward his present need. "Javan, can you get a horse?"

"My father will let me use his."

"Listen to me carefully. In the morning, ride your horse into the marketplace to Joktan's office. Tell him my father's funeral is today. Ask him to let you run the messages for me. He will give you the mail and invoices to carry to Joppa and Caesarea. Go west on the road to Joppa. At the entrance of the city is a stable with a gray, light-spotted stallion—he's spirited, so hold on. Take the gray and leave yours. Go to the dock and deliver the mail and invoices to Joktan's import-export office. Leave Joppa and go north along the coast to Caesarea. Caesarea also has a stable at the entrance of the city. A black Arabian stallion awaits you there. Then come straight home on the road through Samaria. It's a long ride, but Joktan pays well, and he is a good man. The business is yours for a while. I shall leave soon, so take care of my mother."

"What are you going to do, Barabbas?"

"There's no time for questions. Keep our secret, and wait to hear from me. Go get some sleep . . . you'll need it." The two embrace and depart for their homes.

At sunrise, after little sleep, forcing themselves to eat, Barabbas, Mary, Lazarus, and Martha face reality. They all know that according to Jewish tradition, Rabba must be buried before sundown. A messenger arrives to tell Mary and the family that Caiaphas wishes to see them. The four ready themselves.

As they walk to the royal porch of the Temple, Barabbas prays for help to restrain his anger. Arriving at the porch, Caiaphas greets the family with his condolences from a distance.

"You know that as a priest I cannot show grief for the dead, but I personally and confidentially tell you I am deeply sorrowful about the death of Rabba. He was a devout man who did his job unto the Lord. The Temple of the Lord suffers a great loss today. I wanted to come unto you, but as high priest I cannot come into the house of a dead man. And I am sorry that I cannot come to the funeral. I cannot become unclean, for I must offer sacrifices to the Lord. I hope you understand."

Caiaphas continues with his pretentious sorrow for the family and his personal concern, "I hate to mention this to you, but with Rabba gone, we cannot find the temple ledger or the Sword of Sacrifice. If you find these articles at your house or somewhere else, would you please return them?"

As a crowd gathers, Mary's voice breaks with restrained tears as she clears her voice the best she can and answers, "Certainly. Sir Caiaphas, I appreciate your grief." Mary's lips quiver for a moment; then she proceeds. "Yesterday, you were one of the last people to see Rabba. Did he give any clue as to why anyone would want to murder him?"

"Murder him?" Caiaphas pretends to be shocked. "A man with his reputation? He did not have an enemy in this world! Everybody respected him. He was a paragon! What a man should be! I can't dream of anyone wanting to murder him."

Mary is puzzled at Caiaphas' answer. She probes, "What do you mean, Caiaphas? What do you think happened to my husband?"

"Mary, I don't think we should discuss that right now."

Distraught, Mary cries aloud, "Tell me now! I have to know! I have to know!"

Barabbas becomes angry, so he prays for self-control. The crowd grows silent at the apparent tension. With great pretense, Caiaphas acts as if he doesn't want to answer her publicly.

"Mary, I suppose you will find out anyway," Caiaphas

sighs. "Yesterday, when Rabba came to me, he was very disturbed. He was depressed about his inability to live a sinless life. Of all people, you and I know that Rabba was more righteous than other men. I suppose that only such a devout, altruistic man as Rabba would think like this. He felt he was a failure. I know this is hard to believe, but you know how introspective he was. Well it seems that when he left my house, he went to the Temple, got the ledger, and apparently took the Sword of Sacrifice with him. The night custodian, the last man to see him alive, said he saw Rabba take the ledger. Rabba, overcome by depression while passing through that dark tunnel, I suppose, placed the sword on his lower abdomen and fell on it. Apparently someone came along and took the sword and ledger or someone misplaced them in the commotion of finding the body."

Clenching his fist, Barabbas jumps past Mary and yells across the distance of the unclean to the clean, "Caiaphas, are you saying that my father committed suicide?"

Hanging his head, Caiaphas sadly agrees, "I'm so sorry." He turns and walks away.

"That's a lie," Barabbas screams. "Rabba was murdered and you know it! I'll prove it and find justice for my father's murderer." Mary restrains Barabbas by placing her hands over his mouth.

The crowd disperses, whispering to those who did not hear. Mary, her siblings, and Barabbas turn toward home.

After a short walk, Barabbas breaks away, telling his mother that he is going to the stable to see about his black and white stallion. Mary knows that when Barabbas is troubled, he often goes to be with his closest companion—Logos, his first horse.

About two hours before the funeral is to begin, Barabbas arrives home with his horse fully saddled. Making his way through the mourners, he calls Mary into his room and tells her the truth about Rabba's death. Barabbas makes her swear that she will tell no one, for it may cost her life. "Mother, the missing ledger is the proof we need to incriminate Caiaphas, Anak, and the other religious leaders. The ledger also holds incriminating evidence about Pilate and Marcus. We need that ledger to prove Rabba was murdered. I don't know what Father did with the ledger, but I feel sure that he put it in a safe place. If you find it, keep it safe for me." With tears in his eyes, Barabbas hesitates to gain his composure. "Mother, I'm leaving for a while after the funeral. Don't worry—I'll be fine, and I'll be back. I promise."

"First I lose my husband, and now my son is . . . . Don't go," she begs.

"I must."

Mary weeps.

Someone knocks on the door and says, "Joktan is here to see you." Opening the door, Barabbas sees his best client, Joktan, carrying two black garments of the finest material and needlework.

Seeing Mary's swollen, tearful face, Joktan apologizes. "I'm sorry—I did not mean to interrupt."

"You haven't. Mother and I are just making plans." Pointing to Mary, Barabbas makes the introduction. "Mother, this is my patron, Sir Joktan. Sir, this is my mother, Mary." Joktan's eyes stare on Mary, for she is a beautiful lady. Her olive complexion, shiny black hair, and shape mesmerize Joktan.

"It's a pleasure to meet you, Mary. You have a fine son. He's the best."

"Thanks. And thank you for giving him a job."

Being considerate and showing compassion, not wanting to take up too much of their time, Joktan gives his condolences and states his reasons for coming. "Listen . . . I brought these garments for you two. If I can be of any assistance, please let me know. Barabbas, your friend Javan came by this morning and told me the tragic news. You take the time you need. Until then, I will use Javan. Here are two weeks' wages. I must go."

"Thank you, Joktan. May God bless you for your kindness."

In the upper city of Jerusalem, Joseph of Arimathea directs the funeral procession. He leads the pallbearers. Following the bier, Barabbas and Mary are accompanied by Lazarus and Martha. Behind them the mourners are followed by a long procession of monotheistic dignitaries and acquaintances. And by request the last follower is Eber, younger brother of Javan, son of Nicodemus.

After passing through the Judgment Gate, the passageway in the northwest wall of Jerusalem, Barabbas sees the burial sites of the wealthy: tombs made from natural caves, those hewn out of rock, and sarcophaguses made of limestone. Noticing the rocks piled on the shallow graves of the poor, he weeps because his altruistic father deserves better. *My father lived for God, and all he got from man was murdered. And some believe he committed suicide. My father has been disgraced! God, give me the strength and the opportunity to take vengeance!*

Reaching the burial site south of Golgotha, the followers congregate around the grave. The immediate family gathers on one side of the bier, religious dignitaries on the other, and Nicodemus at the head. Dressed in his long black robe, Barabbas slyly steals a look at the place where Anak stands at the front, on the opposite side near Nicodemus. As the sound of the mourners recedes to silence, Nicodemus, Rabba's closest friend, delivers a comforting eulogy. In closing, he announces that Barabbas has requested to pray. Moving slowly to the head of the coffin to pray, Barabbas locates Eber standing with his horse, Logos. Nicodemus moves to stand at Mary's side.

Barabbas speaks: "Let us bow on our knees to God." Standing and watching to see that everyone kneels, Barabbas prays, "Great and wonderful God of Abraham and our fathers, blessed be thy name. Holy art thou and worthy to be praised. I thank thee for the breath of life." As Barabbas prays he slips his left hand through his robe to the inside of his right leg. Then in a louder voice Barabbas prays, "God, I thank you for your judgment!" As he heralds that statement, he draws the Sword of Sacrifice and strikes Anak on the back of the neck, sending his head rolling in the dirt.

As the crowd screams and runs in terror, Barabbas turns and runs to his horse. Mary faints. Barabbas mounts the horse, pulls the reins back, and kicks, making Logos stand on his back legs. At that moment, he holds the bloody Sword of Sacrifice in the air and proclaims, "The Sword of the Lord has given me vengeance!"

Racing back toward the Jerusalem Judgment Gate on the Joppa Road, Barabbas passes the terrified crowd. At the gravesite, some stand astonished and sickened at the gore before their eyes, and some of the more calm, analytical bystanders are puzzled at Barabbas' choice of escape. The only thing back in Jerusalem for Barabbas is an indictment of premeditated murder and Roman imprisonment until a trial is conducted.

Barabbas figures that on horseback with two hundred yards to the Judgment Gate, three hundred yards through the city from the Judgement Gate to the portico of the Temple, and turning north two hundred yards more to the gate of the Fortress Antonia, he will lead the terrified funeral attendants by no more than two minutes. *Oh! God, You have been so merciful. Please help me one more time. Jehovah, I am ready to complete my mission. I ask not for my life—but for the opportunity . . . .* Barabbas stops praying as he approaches the gate of the Roman praetorium. The guards at the gate give attention to Barabbas as he vociferates, "MURDER! MURDERRRR! HELPPPP! MURDER!" Barabbas knows the success of his plan depends on his ability to be heard and his ability to stay on his horse until the right time.

The bloodcurdling screams bring legionnaires from the fortress and religious Jews from the portico of the Temple running toward Barabbas. The two groups converge. On the right side of the horse stands a throng of Jews; on the left stands a throng of legionnaires. A Roman sergeant commands the legionnaires to push back the Jewish crowd. Barabbas reminds himself to stay on the horse so that the soldiers cannot search him. The sergeant grabs the bridle of the horse and commands Barabbas to dismount. *Oh, God! What do I do now?*

Suddenly the screams and wails of terror from the funeral procession capture Barabbas' attention. The sergeant sees the black-dressed mourners approaching. Some of them come within three blocks of the fortress. *My plan is failing! If I dismount, they'll find the sword. My accusers are arriving. God, show me the way!* Looking toward the fortress gate, Barabbas sees Marcus quickly coming. "Sir Marcus!" yells Barabbas desperately. The sergeant looks to Marcus for instruction as he holds the horse by the bridle. Barabbas realizes that Marcus will order him to dismount when he comes close enough. *Now for a diversion!* With that thought, Barabbas looks to Marcus and makes a public exclamation. "It's Anak, Sir! Anak has been murdered! At the funeral of Rabba, the temple treasurer, Anak has been murdered!"

With that proclamation, Marcus stops about ten feet away from the sergeant-held horse as two young men dressed in black approach from less than two blocks away. With hardly any time left before the two mourners arrive to expose Barabbas, he takes his chance: Straight-legged, Barabbas climbs off his horse. Seeing that assuring gesture,

Marcus asks, "When and where did this happen?"

Pointing toward the cemetery, Barabbas exclaims, "Just two minutes ago in the Jewish cemetery, Barabbas, the son of Rabba, cut off the head of Anak."

Distracted by the shouts and actions of Barabbas, Marcus isolates himself from the immediate help of the Roman soldiers. Pointing to the legionnaires between the fort and himself, Marcus gives orders to the sergeant holding the horse: "Villus, take these soldiers and go arrest this Barabbas."

Barabbas notices four guards at the praetorium gate. The other legionnaires leave with Villus while the rest hold the Jewish people on the portico of the Temple. The two young men dressed in black robes are stopped thirty yards short of reaching Marcus by two of the portico soldiers.

The two black-robed young men try to come forward by protesting the portico soldiers. Presuming that the two young men offer the same information as Barabbas, Marcus demands of Barabbas, "How was Anak murdered?"

"The temple treasurer's son, Barabbas, took the Sword of the Lord and . . . ." Quickly drawing the Sword of Sacrifice, Barabbas pierces the mid-section of the astonished Marcus. Grabbing the Roman's robe with his right hand and shoving the sword with his left hand until the hilt will go no farther, Barabbas looks Marcus in the eye and says, "I'm Barabbas and *this* is the Sword of the Lord!"

As Marcus falls to the cobblestone pavement, Barabbas swings up on Logos and sheathes the sword. Barabbas never expected to be alive beyond this point. Now he acts to make the best of it.

The legionnaires at the portico run to aid the dying Marcus. Barabbas races toward the north wall gate just one hundred yards west of the Fortress of Antonia. Villus and the soldiers come running. The four guards of the praetorium gate are the only ones close enough to try to stop him. The fastest of the guards runs to intercept Barabbas at the north wall gate. This legionnaire raises his spear toward the approaching Barabbas. At the last moment, holding to the saddle horn, Barabbas drops off the left side of Logos, and then bounces back up in the saddle. *Thank You, Lord. Surely, You have routed my enemies!*

Fifteen miles northeast of the fleeing Barabbas, a shepherd named Rosh keeps a wary eye on his sheep grazing near the Jordan River just outside Jericho. Wearing a robe made of sheepskin with the fleece still intact, Rosh carries a sling made of goat's hair and leather, a light tent for the nights he cannot find a cave, a rod sheathed in his robe, and a six-foot staff with a crook at one end.

The sheep graze without fear because they know that Rosh is watching over them. They know he will find water when they are thirsty and shelter when there is a storm. They know he will search for them if they become lost and protect them from predators. The sheep know their shepherd's voice.

The sheep graze on grass and shrubs as Rosh leads them toward the cave in the side of the mountain that overlooks Jericho. The loving shepherd looks at the dark clouds coming toward him and gives his unique, guttural call to the sheep. They raise their heads and give attention to Rosh. Again Rosh gives his call. The rams and ewes are first to come to the mouth of the cave. Rosh points his rod to count his sheep as they enter the sheepfold. Recognizing each sheep by name, Rosh speaks to some of them. He appraises each sheep as it passes beneath his rod.

Rosh takes a special look at Keseb, the best-looking lamb of the flock. *Keseb will be the lamb my family will sacrifice next month. There is no other like him. He is less than a year old and without spot or blemish.* Longing for someone to talk to, Rosh speaks to the lamb. "Keseb, sacrificing you is not an easy thing to do. You are the best-looking lamb that I have, but the LORD deserves my best."

Noticing that two of his sheep are missing, Rosh eyes scan the mountainside. *Ah, there she is, always lagging behind with her five-month-old suckling lamb, Pasah. Pasah needs to be weaned, but he is so dependent upon his mother.* As the two sheep reach the cave entrance, Rosh grabs Pasah and gently rubs him. "Pasah, you're the most loving lamb of all." Pasah relaxes securely in Rosh's lap.

"Pasah, look over at the city of Jericho. After Joshua destroyed the city, he placed a curse on the man who would rebuild it. The scriptures record that Joshua said the man who rebuilds the foundation will lose his firstborn son and whoever sets up its gates will lose his youngest son. Many years later, Hiel the Bethelite was cursed. When he laid the city's foundation, it cost Abiram, firstborn of Hiel, his life. When Hiel set up the gates, Segub, the youngest son of Hiel, died. Pasah, we should take note of the power of the Lord. When people don't heed the Lord, they perish. Bless the name of the Lord."

The loving shepherd lies in the entrance of the cave. He places his body between the predatory beasts and his sheep. Nothing can get to the sheep without first passing the shepherd. The good shepherd risks his body as a sacrifice for his sheep.

In the ruins of Ai, the serpent waits.

4

Fugitive—Race for Life

With his heart racing as fast as the legs of his horse, Barabbas lies streamlined on the back of the stallion. The rhythmic pounding of hooves behind him is no match for the adrenaline pumping through Logos. Barabbas takes a decisive lead. *Oh, God, if I ever needed you—I need you now! Calm yourself, Barabbas, and think. God, help me!* Logos seems to sense the pursuing danger. He speeds on as Barabbas tries to devise a plan, but a plan never comes. The trailing danger follows relentlessly as fear rides in the saddle with the fleeing youth. Logos knows the road well, for he travels it often with the mail. With less than an hour before sundown, Barabbas holds tight to the mane of his salvation.

Adjusting his speed to keep a safe distance from the pursuing soldiers, Barabbas begins to calm himself from the fear of the stalking legionnaires. He slows to give Logos a rest. *I have to stay ahead of the soldiers, yet I must not run Logos to death.* Barabbas turns and is astonished to see three Roman horsemen riding quickly toward him. In the distance behind the three cavalrymen, another group of legionnaires on horseback follows. *I know what they are trying to do. The three horsemen are going to risk riding their horses to death in hopes that my horse falls first. Just in case these three fail, the slower ones behind will take up the pursuit. I don't stand a chance. Logos could survive if I get off the main road, but the legionnaires would surely surround me. If I stay on the road, I have a chance, but is my horse able to endure?*

Passing through the burned ruins of Bethel where Abraham and Jacob once built altars to the Lord, Barabbas encourages himself. Remembering it was at Bethel that Jacob once had a dream about the angels of God ascending and descending on a staircase to heaven, Barabbas prays. *God, give your angels charge to help me. Save me or not—I give you thanks and all my praise.* In spite of his prayer, Barabbas notices that Logos' pace has slowed and his stride has shortened. He encourages Logos, but heat and exhaustion gain the upper hand.

Discouragement and fear hound Barabbas toward the dark pit of despondency when suddenly a ray of hope shines through in the form of a dark cloud. It moves over the landscape. This cloud produces enough shade to give higher spirits to Logos. Barabbas thanks God for the cloud, which not only cools Logos but also causes darkness to come sooner as the sun sets. Logos gallops into the darkness, which causes the stalking legionnaires to stop for the night. *If that cloud had come any later, I would be a dead man!*

The legionnaires camp near one of the villagers who has food and water, and Barabbas walks northward in the darkness. Barabbas wants to reach Sychar, where he stops to rest when he runs the mail route from Caesarea. He longs for the thirst-quenching water of Jacob's well.

Scared and spent, Barabbas reaches a stable. It is operated by a stocky man, a Pharisee named Lud, and his wife Sarai. Chickens roost and animals are in the barn. Lud's house, the stable, and a guestroom are all connected. Lud comes from his house, which is built onto the stable. In desperation Barabbas declares, "Hello, Lud! I need provisions."

Lud takes the reins and leads Logos into the stable. "Barabbas, what are you doing here this time of night?" he asks, opening the door to the stall.

"Lud, please don't ask questions now. Take care of Logos first."

By the tone of Barabbas' voice, Lud suspects something is very wrong. "All right, Barabbas. Go to the house and help yourself to some food. Tell Sarai to prepare a cot for you."

After preparing the stall for Logos, the rugged Lud goes into the house, folds his callused hands on the table, and watches Barabbas eat. As Barabbas takes his barley bread filled with cheese and sops up the last bit of gruel, Lud expresses his concern, "Barabbas, I can tell something is wrong."

Barabbas stops chewing, swallows, and then pauses. His silence seems to herald bad news. With tears in his eyes and a tremble in his voice, Barabbas chokes, "Rabba is dead."

"What?"

Trying to gain his composure, Barabbas whispers, "Anak murdered Rabba for a price that was furnished by Marcus."

"That's unbelievable. Why?"

"To cover up the lies and treachery of Caiaphas and Pilate."

"No!"

In shock, Sarai whispers, "I'm—I'm so sorry." She grabs Barabbas by the hand.

Lud rages. "The Romans and these ungodly religious leaders are corrupt! Now start from the beginning, and tell me the whole story."

Barabbas recounts the whole story of Rabba's death. Then he tells of his revenge.

Hesitantly, Lud asks, "Barabbas, would you like to join the Zealots?"

"I don't think so—not at this time. I have something else to do."

"They can help you. As a fugitive, you don't stand a chance. The Romans will not stop looking for you. What else can you do?"

"First I am going to get away from the jurisdiction of Pilate until things calm down. I need to go to the region of Galilee, which is under the rule of Herod Antipas, for a time. As you know, Pilate and Herod are both Romans, but they don't like each other. I don't think that Herod is going to help Pilate find me. Second, I shall come back and get the truth from Pilate even if I have to kill him."

"Barabbas, you can't get near him. It would take a group of Zealots to assassinate Governor Pilate."

"I don't want to assassinate him. I want the truth about my father's findings. Then I might kill him because of the truth. Right now I just want to stay alive. I need rest. May I sleep in the stable?"

"Sleep in the house, Barabbas."

"Thanks, Lud, but if the Romans found me in here, you and Sarai would be in serious trouble."

Embracing his friends, Barabbas goes to the stable and climbs up on the hay. Opening the large double doors of the loft to see the moonlight, he views the silhouette of the two mountains facing each other—Mount Ebal and Mount Gerizim. Ever imaginative, he pictures the historical scene of Joshua reading the curses of the law to six tribes of Israel on Mount Ebal and the blessings of the law to the other six tribes of Israel on Mount Gerizim. Barabbas can almost hear Joshua reading the curses and the blessings and both mountains responding with an "Amen." *Joshua was determined that the children of Israel would never forget the laws of God. I am determined to save the beliefs of my fathers.*

By the moonlight, Barabbas notices that no trees grow on Mount Ebal. Looking toward Mount Gerizim, he notices a light move underneath the canopy of trees of this flourishing mountainside. *I wonder who is climbing up there at this time of night.* Giving in to exhaustion after the good meal, he lies down to sleep facing the east so the sun will awaken him early next morning.

Later in the night after climbing Mount Gerizim, Lud meets with a band of Zealots. The group of men consists of farmers, shepherds, fugitives, and others from the area. At the campsite under a canopy of giant terebinth, elm, and oak trees, Lud reports the story of Barabbas. The leader, Jair, holds the clandestine meetings here because it is close enough to reach Jerusalem and far enough away not to be disturbed by the Romans. Does Barabbas want our help?" asks Jair.

"No. He has a mission of his own. He is going to assassinate Pilate, but not before he gets some answers." The group laughs at the idea.

"This mere boy is going to assassinate the well-protected, cautious governor of Judea and Samaria?" laughs Jair. "If he could do that, I would make him commander of this group!"

The next morning Barabbas awakens as Lud calls, "Barabbas, it's almost dawn. It's dark, but you need to go. The legionnaires will come this way soon. I have put some food in your saddlebag. Come and let's draw some water from Jacob's well."

Barabbas takes his wineskin to the well and fills it with water. "I could have used this water yesterday," says Barabbas. "This water is the best. I only wish that its thirst-quenching power could last forever."

"Barabbas, you must go now."

Barabbas & The Sword of Sacrifice

The first spark of dawn lights the roadway for Barabbas. This road, called the way of Shur, leads from Egypt through Jerusalem to intercept the King's Highway, which leads to Damascus. By traveling this route, Barabbas thinks he can travel fast enough to sidetrack the cavalrymen and be within the jurisdiction of Herod Antipas. Barabbas knows the legionnaires, out of fear of Pilate's anger, will not stop chasing him until they completely lose him or capture him.

Along this trade route Barabbas keeps a wary eye on the commuters he passes. Most of them are families, shepherds or independent merchandisers. Although the news of the murders is behind him, Barabbas does not want to run into trouble. He calculates that walking to Sychar the night before gives him at least a ten-mile lead. He feels that the posse's plan by now is to track him, not chase him.

Meanwhile, back in Sychar, the Roman soldiers abruptly arrive. Exum, the commander of the Roman cavalry, and his troops go from door to door asking questions about Barabbas. The doors that are not immediately opened are kicked open. The hostile soldiers waste no time with the frightened citizens. One legionnaire drags a middle-aged man by his hair out into the street before Exum. The legionnaire says, "This man says he saw a young man ride out from the stable early this morning."

"To the stable," orders Exum. All twelve legionnaires mount their horses and ride toward the stable.

Hearing the thunder of horses' feet pounding the earth, Lud runs into his house. Boarding and bracing the door behind him, Lud grabs his sword. Sarai begins to scream in terror. Two of the legionnaires ram the door. It flies open, and two other troops protected by their shields knock the sword-wielding Lud down as if he were a fly. Sarai screams as a fist strikes her face, knocking her unconscious. Thrown into the yard before Exum, Lud looks up to hear a question: "Where's Barabbas?"

"I don't know what you are talking about," growls Lud. "Liar!" Exum explodes. The soldiers kick Lud. Pressing the interrogation further, Exum demands, "Where did Barabbas, the young man who stayed here last night, go?"

Clutching his side and groaning, the undaunted Lud avows, "Sir, my wife and I were here alone last night." At the nod of Exum's head, the troops beat Lud unconscious. The cavalrymen mount their horses and ride northward on the trade route as the middle-aged man in town had motioned. Exum realizes he is farther behind than he thought. With this setback, he resolves to kill Barabbas when he finds him.

Twenty miles into the day's journey and fifty miles away from Jerusalem, Barabbas crosses the ridge of mountains called Gilboa. He remembers that this 1640 foot Mount Gilboa is the place where King Saul committed suicide after losing three of his sons, including the noble, loving Jonathan. The Philistines crushed Saul's army on this mount. Barabbas despises the thought of Saul wasting time trying to kill King David. *David truly loved King Saul. If Saul had directed his aggression toward the real enemy, God would not have rejected him.*

On the trade route coming from the Gilboa ridge, Barabbas sees a beautiful sight—the junction of the valley of Jezreel and the valley of Jordan. This paradise of grasslands and gardens of fertile ground flourishes because of the waters of the Jordan River and the abundance of natural springs. In the middle of the junction, Barabbas sees the city of Scythopolis sitting on a large mound. Barabbas notices that from north to south or east to west, Scythopolis is the intersection for Palestine.

Barabbas approaches Scythopolis with enthusiasm. The ruins of the walls that once surrounded the city please him. *This is a privilege to enter the city freely. Joshua would have loved to have done this at the time when this city was called Beth Shan. Joshua failed to capture this city when it was under Egyptian rule. The iron chariots mentioned in the Book of Joshua were invincible.* Passing the ruins of the walls, Barabbas remembers the shame brought to King Saul when the Philistines owned the city. *The Philistines fastened Saul's body to the wall of Beth Shan and put his armor in the temple of Ashtaroth. What a disgrace!*

Barabbas begins the first phase of his plan. He makes a stir as he races into the city. Nearly running over some merchandisers in the street, Barabbas shouts, "Where is the stable?" The inhabitants look at Barabbas with disdain. Finally, an elderly man gives direction to Barabbas. Barabbas races to the stable, flips a silver coin to the owner and orders, "Care for my horse right now while I get something to eat. I must leave as soon as possible."

Astonished and delighted at the silver coin, the stable owner politely asks, "Where are you headed?"

"That's none of your business," Barabbas curtly replies.

After getting something to eat and drink, Barabbas returns to the stable in haste. "Where's my horse?"

Brushing Logos, the owner of the stable calls: "Over here, Sir. Fed, watered, brushed, and ready to go. Come back any time, and I'll give you service."

Barabbas mounts his horse and scatters the people in the street again as he races out of the city. The eyes of many follow the direction of Barabbas' departure. Barabbas wants to make sure that the pursuing Roman soldiers follow him; that is, he wants them to follow him where he is not.

In Jerusalem at Pilate's palace, Villus tells Pilate about the murders committed by Barabbas. Pilate expresses his regret about the foolish mistake made by Marcus—isolating himself with a murderer. Villus tells Pilate of the suicide or murder of Rabba, the temple treasurer. This news of the temple treasurer's death raises a question in Pilate's mind. Pilate raises his eyebrows and orders a soldier to bring Caiaphas to the tribunal in front of the palace. Turning to Villus, the concerned Pilate asks, "What did you do about capturing this murderer named Barabbas?"

"I sent our best cavalrymen and Exum to capture or kill him."

Pilate looks at Villus intently. "They must catch him. I'm going to make an example of him. These stinking Jews are not going to kill Roman citizens, and especially not my commanders. You understand me, Villus?"

"Yes, sir," Villus answers with fear in his voice.

"Come with me." An entourage of protection, the praetorian, follows Pilate and Villus to the Gabbatha, the mosaic pavement in front of the palace. Upon arriving, the enraged Pilate orders the legionnaires to secure the streets and man the walls. "From this moment, there is a curfew in Jerusalem. Arrest anyone on the streets one hour after sundown. I'm going to teach these religious rebels a thing or two." The infuriated Pilate shouts an order to a group of soldiers: "Bring Caiaphas here in the next hour or you will be incarcerated for a week! The soldier I sent earlier to find Caiaphas will be flogged for lack of expediency." At those orders, the soldiers move with attentive haste.

As Pilate paces and shouts orders to the legionnaires coming and going into the streets, the attention of the praetorian band is interrupted by the twelve legionnaires pulling Caiaphas by his sleeves in a halftime pace. Two of the praetorian tie and whip the soldier Pilate first sent to get Caiaphas. Approaching with dread, Caiaphas greets Pilate: "Let me explain!"

"You'd better explain quickly before I try you for treason."

Caiaphas says, "Wait! Things aren't as bad as you think. Everything is under control!"

"Under control?" Pilate mocks, his voice rising. "What about this Barabbas? What does *he* know?"

"Nothing! Really nothing. He is to be feared only because he is a murderer. He knows nothing about our dealings. Honestly, he knows nothing! You're jumping to conclusions."

"I need to talk to our contact. I think I will call for him."

"I wouldn't," warns Caiaphas. "He will not come. He doesn't want to be seen with you."

"He'll come if I send my troops after him!" retorts Pilate, with authority.

"Come, Governor. You know you don't want to do that. After all, our contact is looking out for your best interests. With his help, you will be wealthy and powerful. His influence reaches the throne of Caesar Tiberius! Remember how he saved your neck when you first came to Jerusalem? Had it not been for his plan, you would have been banished by the Emperor. Don't be hasty—everything is under control. Our contact assured me he has his dagger on the heartbeat of the situation."

Following Pilate as he walks to his tribunal seat, Caiaphas calms Pilate by trivializing what happened to the temple treasurer. He persuasively assures Pilate but fails to mention the missing ledger. *He thinks a later time will be more appropriate.* "Only Rabba knew about the clandestine dealings. But with Rabba dead, all is well. The only thing of concern is this series of murders. And I'm not worried about that because I know you have that under control. I have never seen anyone stand up to you, Governor Pilate." These words soothe the anger and strengthen the ego of Pilate. He is appeased for now.

About two hours before sundown, Barabbas reaches the split in the road at the ford of the Jordan River. At the ford, the commuters may either cross the Jordan to travel on the east side of the Sea of Galilee or stay on the west side following the road to Tiberias. Barabbas rides Logos into the shallow water to ford the river. Dismounting and letting Logos drink, Barabbas rinses his fatigued horse by throwing water on him.

Along the shoreline, villagers sell food and fodder to the commuting merchants camping for the night. Barabbas eats and then feeds Logos. Nobody pays close attention to him because many pass by here. After the scene he made at Scythopolis, Barabbas wants the pursuing soldiers to know which way he takes but doesn't want it to look obvious.

After refreshing himself, Barabbas tries to encourage Logos by speaking to him: "Logos, if you can travel a little farther, we will have the posse sidetracked." Barabbas climbs on his friend and rides east across the river toward the trade route called the King's Highway, which leads to Damascus. After riding out of sight of the campers, he climbs off Logos to give him a rest. Barabbas prays. *God, I need a convincing witness of the direction of my travel before I backtrack to cross the river. However, God of Israel, if nobody comes my way, I praise you for . . .*

Barabbas' prayer is interrupted by the appearance of something coming toward him. *God, you are too good to me.* Barabbas leaps on his horse to trot him toward the approaching caravan. As if playing a guessing game, Barabbas uses his talent of analytical observation to scrutinize the group. *This caravan has one owner because everybody has a group of animals to lead except the man up front who wears a leather belt for his sword and a sash for his money. I see some mules in the caravan; therefore, these people are not Israelites. Since mules are a crossbreed, most Jews don't use them because crossbreeding is outlawed in the Book of Leviticus. Next, I see donkeys which doesn't tell me much . . . except that the owner of this caravan is smart. These small animals carry great weight and require only a fraction of the fodder as a horse needs.*

Barabbas continues the guessing game. *Aha—the camel—the spitting, griping, ill-mannered camel . . .. He holds his head in the air as if he were a king. Here it comes the egotistical, conceited, haughty-headed camel, which is actually not arrogant at all because he is only holding his head in that manner to see out from under his bushy eyebrows.*
Enthralled by God's provision for the camel, Barabbas notes the camel's makeup. *God gave the camel bushy eyebrows for protection from the sun, and tight-closing nostrils and lips to protect him in sandstorms. Given three stomachs that hold five gallons of water each, a camel can go weeks or even months without water.*
Within speaking distance to the man leading the caravan, Barabbas makes his last observations. *This tough-footed, low-perspiring, heavy-insulated camel is indigenous to hot sands—the desert. I say this man is headed past Jerusalem through the desert to Egypt. There are no oxen-pulled carts in this caravan. This non-Jewish, single proprietor who is tough enough to cross the Sinai Desert has to be an Ishmaelite from the wilderness of Paran—a descendant of Ishmael, Abraham's first son.*
Only steps away from the man leading the caravan, Barabbas pulls back on the reins and asks, "Where is home for you, Sir?"
"Paran," answers the man as Barabbas grins.
Barabbas moves along as if he were through dealing with the proprietor. Looking for just the right conversation piece, Barabbas waits because he wants to be conspicuously inconspicuous with his motive. He watches donkeys and camels loaded with cloth, clothes, and perfumes pass by. Then items made of glass, stone, wood, clay, gold, copper, tin, bronze, and brass pass until Barabbas spots his opportunity for a conversation that will later sidetrack the pursuing posse. Seeing a camel loaded with armor, Barabbas calls out to the proprietor, "Sir! Wait a minute!"

The proprietor turns and stops in the road. "What do you want?"

Barabbas says nonchalantly, "I see that you carry armor."

"Would you like to buy a piece?" asks the proprietor.

Barabbas shakes his head. "No. But since I am low on money, I was wondering if you would like to buy my sword."

"Young man, I buy only swords of precision or ornament," the proprietor apologizes.

Barabbas draws the Sword of Sacrifice. "What about this?"

The proprietor carefully looks at the sword and says, "That is the most unusual sword I have ever seen: a little longer than a dagger, pointed on the tip for piercing and sharp on both edges for slashing." The proprietor looks at the gold and silver ornamentation. "Where did you get this sword?" With that question, Barabbas sheathes the sword. The proprietor declares, "I thought you wanted to sell it."

Barabbas replies, "You talked me out of it. I still have some money—enough to get me to Damascus. Goodbye." Barabbas mounts and races toward the King's Highway. Riding out of sight of the caravan, Barabbas turns around to follow the caravan back to the Jordan River. He is careful not to be seen. The slow walk back gives Logos a rest while Barabbas calculates the time necessary to sidetrack the pursuing soldiers.

When the caravan reaches the river, it stops to make camp for the night. Barabbas gets off the road and leads Logos through the forest to camouflage his approach to the river. Here the forest is thick, but Barabbas leads Logos through the underbrush until they stop six hundred yards upstream. *Well, God, I need your help again. Whether we drown or reach the other side, I still love you.* "Logos, come on. We can make it with God's help." With those words, Barabbas jumps into the water, pulling the reins. Logos follows. The river is narrow and deep here compared to the ford downstream. The current is strong, but the will of Barabbas and Logos is stronger.

Reaching the other side unseen, Barabbas crawls out on the bank, exhausted from the dangerous swim. *Thank you, God, for letting me backtrack and cross the river without being caught by the Romans.* Barabbas consoles his horse. "Logos, let's go through the brush to get on the road to Tiberias. Nobody suspects that an orthodox Jew will go there. We can rest there. It's only seven miles away. Then we can rest for the next week if we like."

Meanwhile, two miles short of reaching the ford of the Jordan River, Anthony asks Exum, "Where do you think Barabbas is going?"

"Well, I'm not sure, but I think he's going to Damascus. It's a busy city."

"Why not Tiberias?" questions Anthony.

"Religious Jews will not go to Tiberias."

"Is it because the city is named after Emperor Tiberius Caesar or is it because Herod Antipas resides there?" Anthony questions again.

"Neither. Barabbas will not go to Tiberias because the city is said to be built over a graveyard. Orthodox Jews consider the city unclean." Looking puzzled, Exum discloses his concern. "You know, there is something that bothers me about this chase."

"What, sir?"

"I know this Barabbas is smart, yet look at the obvious trail he left at Scythopolis. I think Barabbas may be leading us astray. We'll have to be careful. Remember that none of us know for sure what he looks like. All we can identify is his horse and the Sword of Sacrifice. And all we have now is his trail. That makes me more determined to catch him."

Approaching the camp at the ford, Exum orders the soldiers to freshen up as he tries to gather information about

Barabbas. Exum finds out from one of the villagers that Barabbas did not make an ostentatious show of fording the river. Then Exum crosses the river to inquire about Barabbas. The Ishmaelite proprietor of the caravan tells Exum about meeting Barabbas down the road. Exum asks, "How long ago did you meet him?

"About a half hour ago," answers the proprietor.

Fooled by Barabbas' backtracking, Exum calls his men. "Men, Barabbas is only a half hour ahead. I want two men to go with me, and the rest of you pursue Barabbas. Anthony, I must go to Tiberias and inform Herod Antipas that we are in pursuit of a murderer. I don't want to do anything in the jurisdiction Galilee without Tetrarch Antipas knowing about it. Then I must go through Caesarea Philippi to inform Tetrarch Herod Philip that you are chasing Barabbas through his Batanea jurisdiction. I'll meet you in Damascus. I hope you will have Barabbas with you—dead or alive. I don't care which."

Some soldiers and Anthony ride northeast on the trade route in pursuit of Barabbas as Exum and his two escorts ride northwest on the opposite side of the Sea of Galilee toward Tiberias.

As the sun begins to set, Barabbas and Logos take their time going to Tiberias. *Nobody will think of looking for a religious Judean in Tiberias.* Hearing galloping horses on the road behind him, Barabbas turns to look. *Oh, my God! Where did they come from? What are they doing on this road?* Barabbas sees Exum and the two legionnaires coming down the road toward him. Barabbas mounts his horse and tries to ride inconspicuously off the road toward the Sea of Galilee, only one mountain away.

Exum focuses his eyes on the black and white stallion ahead. "Stop that rider!"

Barabbas realizes a tragic stroke of bad luck has cornered him. Logos runs as fast as he is able as the pursuing trio gains ground.

The exhausted Barabbas and the enervated Logos know that the Roman soldiers will catch them this time. Barabbas decides his only chance is to stop and fight. *Three legionnaires against me—I don't stand a chance.* Barabbas picks his spot—the top of the mountain. *If I can just make it to the top, I'll have the advantage. There is no need to run any farther. I can't escape.* Barabbas approaches the sandy mountaintop, which overlooks the Sea of Galilee. *Deliver me or not . . . ..* Barabbas proclaims aloud the Shema—the last and dying words of the orthodox Jew—"Hear, O Israel: The LORD our God is one LORD: And thou shalt love the LORD thy God with all thine heart, and with all thy soul, and with all thy might!"

As Logos takes the last step over the top, Barabbas is startled at what he sees before him. Hundreds and hundreds of people are between him and the Sea of Galilee. Logos lunges forward, left then right, jumps and stumbles to miss the people. Barabbas catapults through the air, landing on his face. Fear makes the breathless, bruised prey—Barabbas—get up and run through the crowd as the Roman soldiers appear on the mountaintop.

A hand grabs Barabbas' outer garment and jerks him around as Exum calls from the peak of the inclined mountain, "Where is he?"

"Who?" asks the man nearest Exum.

"The boy who rode that black and white stallion here," answers Exum, pointing to Logos. The people look among themselves, saying nothing. Barabbas' heart races as the firm hand holds him by his mantle. Puzzled by the multitude, Exum asks, "Why are all of you congregated?"

"We have come to see Jesus," many voices answer.

Hoping to find someone in charge, Exum asks, "Where is he—this Jesus?"

"He is not here yet," answers one. "We are expecting him

to come by sea."

Observing that the people before him are religious Jews, Exum loudly explains, "The man who rode that horse here murdered the high priest's confidant. So for your religion's sake, tell me where to find the owner of the black and white stallion."

Feeling the hand grasping his mantle tighten, Barabbas knows he is in grave trouble. The eyes of the crowd turn toward Barabbas as the man directly in front of him says, "I did not see."

The words "I did not see" ricochet, reverberate, and echo through the crowds on the mountainside.

"Curse you, Zealots! Herod Antipas is going to hear about you anti-Roman, Jesus people." Angry and humiliated, Exum orders the two legionnaires to seize the black and white stallion. Taking Logos with them, the Roman trio rides north toward Tiberias.

The group of men surrounding Barabbas stare at him as their leader greets him. "Hello, Barabbas. I'm Tola."

"How do you know my name?" asks Barabbas.

"I was sent news about you as you slept in Sychar. Jair sent word that you were headed for my region. He said you have the makings of a great Zealot. If I had not received the news about you, I would have turned you over to the Romans. What great luck you possess."

"Not luck—the hand of God," Barabbas affirms. "I appreciate your help very much, but I must get some answers—answers that might exonerate me and incriminate the Roman Governor Pilate. Without these answers, I can never live a normal life, and you may never galvanize the Israelites against the Romans. So tell me, what are you doing among these followers of Jesus?"

"Well, as you know, we Zealots believe that to pay tribute to Caesar is to be a traitor to God. To make matters worse, a corrupt tax collector in the city of Nain was extorting money, so our organization rectified the situation. Now, Herod Antipas' troops are on the prowl. Congregating with the multitudes that follow Jesus is cover for us until things cool down. Jesus has an ability of being where Antipas is not. Whether this is deliberate or coincidental, I don't know. Judea, Galilee, Gaulanitis, or Perea—in which of these regions Jesus will next appear, I don't know. All I know is that Jesus offers refuge to all his followers."

"Tola, do you have something for me to eat and drink? I have to go to Tiberias tonight."

"Certainly, Barabbas. I even will have one of my men give you a ride to the city, but he will not go into Tiberias."

Staring across the gold and silver trim of the ivory inlaid table, Herod Antipas and his wife, Herodias, listen to Exum recount the story about Barabbas' escape. Then Exum advises them that the followers of Jesus should be dispersed.

Hearing the comment about Jesus and the Jews, Antipas defends his philosophy of rule. "Exum, there are two philosophies to consider. One is the philosophy of force. For example, my brother, Tetrarch Archelaus, used force and shed the blood of many Judeans and Samaritans. Tetrarch Philip and I complained to Rome about Archelaus, and he was banished. I should have been made king at that time, but Caesar appointed Pilate to be governor. If Caesar had not decided to make Judea and Samaria a royal province, I could be their king.

Even my father, Herod the Great, who once ruled all four regions of the tetrarchs, used ruthless force to secure his throne. He murdered one of his wives, three sons, mother-in-law, brother-in-law, uncle, and many others. If he thought that someone was a threat to his throne, he murdered him. He also tried to destroy this transient Jesus as a baby. Using force, he was successful only in murdering the infants in the Bethlehem region. I'm more subtle and intelligent than my father. With diplomacy and politics, Judaism can be diluted, which will eradicate the Zealots and the Jews' belief in God."

"Well, Herod, I admit that nobody knows the Jews like you."

"I should be king for several reasons. First of all, I am accepted by the Jews because I am blood kin to the Jews. And . . . my wife is Jewish. Herodias is the daughter of Simeon, a former high priest. Although she has renounced the Jewish religion, her genealogy satisfies the religious Jews. Second, I pledge my allegiance to Rome because the Jews are weak and prejudiced toward all others' races and religions. They think they are the only race to have a god's favor. They make Herodias and me ill with their esoteric ideology."

Not wanting to stir the anger of Antipas, Exum reiterates, "Nobody knows the Jews like you."

"I know the Jews because I am Edomite stock and an Idumean—a descendant of Esau. Esau, my forefather, was tricked by Jacob, the orthodox Jew's forefather. Now, I, a descendant of Esau, will take back what Jacob stole—our inheritance. With the exception of my Jewish wife and my stepdaughter, Salome, I detest the Jews. That is why I built Tiberias, my Galilee headquarters, over a graveyard. I don't want these despicable Jews here to remind me that I am not king over Jerusalem. I know that Pilate is your commander, but he does not want to be governor of Jerusalem. He spends nearly all his time in Caesarea because he has interest in Rome. Now, he and Claudia Procula, his wife, have to live in Palestine, which is like a prison to them."

"Well, Antipas, I know all this makes a strained relationship between you and Pilate, but maybe things will be different one day. Right now, if you will help us catch Barabbas, Pilate would be in your debt. As for tomorrow, I must leave to meet my men in Damascus. We must go home to face the failure of not capturing Barabbas. I'll take his horse and be on my way in the morning."

Extending a friendly hand, Antipas says, "Exum, I'll try to capture this murderer for you and Pilate."

Exum shakes Antipas' hand. "Good night, Herod. Good night, Herodias."

Herod Antipas and Herodias go to lie down for the night. On the way through the palace they see Salome, Herodias' teenage daughter, looking out the window as the candle and moonlight shine through her night garment. Herod's eye seduces the five-foot-six, maturely shaped body of his stepdaughter. Her olive complexion, the youth of her soft skin, the shine of her coal-colored hair, the rosy red of her lips, the symmetrically honed nails, the curve of her body, and the seductively tantalizing sparkle in her eye will not leave Herod alone. As Herod memorizes every part of her body, Salome uncomfortably asks, "What news did Exum bring?"

Herodias speaks as she watches Salome cross her arms to conceal her body. "Oh, nothing much, except for the news of a nineteen-year-old murderer who outsmarted a group of Rome's best legionnaires. He was last seen about five miles from here. So *you* be careful. Goodnight, my darling."

Taking his last surveying gawk at Salome, Herod says, "Good night."

"Mother, may I talk to you for a minute?"

"Yes, certainly." Herod goes to his chambers, leaving Herodias and Salome to talk alone.

"Mother, I can't stand the way he looks at me."

"Salome, he's a man. That is their nature. Use that knowledge for your benefit. If you understand the male, you can own him."

"Sometimes you sicken me."

"Salome, you're angry because I left your father. I recognize an opportunity when I see one. Philip the First is a loser; he rules no territory. I was smart enough to marry his brother, though."

"Exactly. Mother, you married my uncle—my father's brother. What does that say for you?"

"It says I know how to manipulate a man to my advantage. One day, if you become anything, you will use this art too. You're young. You'll learn after your chaste heart is broken by a man. You'll learn."

"I'll never do what you have done!"

Realizing that her lecture did not appeal to her daughter, Herodias goes to the royal bedroom. After undressing, she climbs into bed with Antipas. Herod pays her no attention as he looks toward the ceiling in a contemplative stare. The sensitive Herodias asks, "What's on your mind, my love?"

"Barabbas."

"What is so important about Barabbas that lures you away from me?" she asks as she wraps her arms around him.

"He may have the key to Jerusalem."

"What do you mean by 'the key to Jerusalem'?"

"Something tells me that this Barabbas who murdered the confidant of the ruling Roman governor and the confidant of the High Priest holds the missing link that ties the ruling to the religious. There is something crooked here. Caiaphas is doing something wrong, and Pilate is doing something wrong. I just know it. What relationship could these two have?" Antipas pauses to ponder. "If Caiaphas is caught, he will be stoned. If Pilate is caught, he will be banished or crucified. And I would be king of Jerusalem. It is just too much to hope for."

"My darling, I didn't think of that. That is what I love about you—your insight."

"Well, let me think. Nobody would expect a Pharisee to come to Tiberias. Apparently, this analytical young man backtracked and was coming this way before Exum saw him. I respect this Barabbas because he is a thinker. And I love him because he may be a threat to Pilate. Now, considering that he is a boy, I can imagine that . . ."

In the semitropical humidity of the night, Barabbas keeps surveillance on Antipas' stables. Two of Herod's guards stand at the barn's entrance, and another takes care of the horses. Every hour two other guards come by to check the stable. There are barracks for the soldiers and the caretakers at one end of the stable. Barabbas is glad the guards are on duty. He reasons that if they were not guarding the horses, then this situation probably would be a trap. Barabbas knows the tetrarch's stables are always guarded, so he is sure the guards are not expecting him. Fatigued and irritable from riding, swimming, running, winning, and losing, Barabbas speaks softly to himself. "All this reasoning does not get Logos back. I need to rest, but Logos will be gone forever if I don't retrieve him tonight. I need a plan."

After the midnight watch and the changing of the guards, Barabbas puts a plan into action. One stone at a time and one foot at a time, he keeps his eye on the goal—the top wall on the two-story barracks. Some of the stones protrude from the mortar less than an inch. Wedging his fingers and toes in between and on top of the stones, he risks an injurious fall that would give notice to the guards.

Reaching the apex of the wall atop of the two-story barracks, Barabbas peeps over and stares in fright at the soldiers sleeping on the flat roof. *Now that is something I did not think about.* Looking at the ground twenty-four feet below and then at the five sleeping soldiers, Barabbas shudders. *I don't have enough strength to climb down, and I'm not stupid enough to climb on over this wall.* Looking down again at the ground, he sees the two surveillance guards walking around the corner to the back of the barracks. Pulling up, Barabbas lies flat on top of the wall until the two guards leave. *Well, that settles that. I didn't climb down, and I didn't climb over. I'll walk this narrow wall to the Roman-sloped rooftop of the barn.*

In infantile progression—the stomach, the knees, and then the feet—Barabbas minces toward the barn roof, which connects the barracks. *The only choice is straight ahead, and it is not a good one.* With a fall on the left and sleeping soldiers on the right, he reaches the barn roof. *I hope this humidity has not brought soldiers to sleep in the loft of this stable tonight. I've had all the excitement I can stand for one day. And I'm still not through.*

With his sandals in his mantle, the barefoot Barabbas quietly walks over the incline of the stable roof. Walking to the peak of the incline on the front of the barn, he sees the two guards at the stable door. *Now where is the third? I can't go into the stable if he is in there.* Barabbas waits impatiently. After what seems like eternity, the third soldier strides out to talk to the two guards at the barn door.

Barabbas takes his sword out of his belt and throws it into the hay inside the loft. He takes his belt and loops it over the brace of the hook and pulley. *Here goes.* Looking at the brace, the belt, and the shutter, not the ground below, Barabbas slides off the roof and down the belt. Then he steps into the window. Leaving his belt, picking up his sword, and putting it in his sash, Barabbas looks outside the loft window. *Thank God. They are still there. I must hurry.*

Crawling through the hay to the place where the hay is kicked into the mangers, Barabbas looks for Logos. *There he is!* Barabbas slides off the hay hatch on his stomach, drops down arm's length, hangs by his fingers, and drops to the ground on his catlike bare feet, making two of the horses shudder. The guard at the door turns and takes a glance inside but never breaks the fluency of his speech to the two porters. Barabbas hugs Logos and strokes him as he looks for a bridle. *Evidently they lock the bridles up. I can ride Logos out of here with just this halter, but a bridle would make it easier. I am sure that as soon as we run to escape, those two guards will immediately follow. I need a bridle.* Looking about the stable, Barabbas sees something that brings a smile. *There is one they missed.* A supporting post with hay stacked against it almost conceals the bridle. As he reaches over the hay, a blur of fist catches the corner of his eye and his temple.

After the excitement in Tiberias, miles away and hours later, just before dawn, Rosh awakens to the bleating of his sheep. His flock is awake and ready to go. He gets up from the cave entrance to lead his flock to the stream that flows into the Jordan River.

In the early morning darkness, Rosh carefully walks down the mountain, calling his sheep as he goes. As he reaches the bottom of the valley, he senses something wrong; the area is too quiet. *There is a predator, an enemy, in the area.* Rosh pauses, scans the area, hears a desperate bleat, a growl, and then, a bleating cry crushed short of a full breath.

"No!" screams Rosh as he runs up the mountainside toward the source of the fracas. With his staff in his hand, breathing deeply, the shepherd approaches the place where a struggle apparently took place. Looking to his left, he sees Pasah caught in a briar patch. Rosh looks at the blood-splattered ground. With his eyes following the trail of blood to an underground den, Rosh knows that Pasah's mother is dead. *The enemy devours the sheep that stray.*

The loving shepherd is pleased to see a huge round rock so strategically placed near the entrance of the den that recedes into the earth. *God provides the rock.* Rolling the rock over the den of darkness, the shepherd hears the gnashing of teeth as the enemy brutally rips the stray apart.

Realizing he is trapped in his own black pit, the family-breaking enemy roars like a lion seeking freedom to devour more. The rock secures the sheep and imprisons the enemy in the abyss.

In the ruins of the city of Ai, the horned viper waits.

5

Pilate & Herod Antipas

The light of dawn breaks through the delirium caused by the whirlwind of Pilate's anger displayed during the night. The lightning bolt of Pilate's threat and the thunder of the legionnaire's lash kept most of the inhabitants awake for the night. The capricious, tumultuous storm of Roman authority struck the city without a warning. Without sufficient rest, the city of Jerusalem winces at the light coming from the east over the Temple of God. The residents try to guess what brought the curfew. The religious Jews reason that their disobedience brought divine judgment upon them. The legionnaires on the city walls and in the streets believe that the Roman god Jupiter is angry about the death of Marcus.

Javan breaks the silence of the city as he runs down the street and knocks on Mary's door. "It's Javan," he cries out.

Mary quickly opens the door and says, "Come in. It's dangerous out there."

Javan looks at the swollen face and the red eyes of the worn and weary Mary. "It's safe on the streets," he assures her. "Caiaphas came by and told my father that the curfew is withdrawn. Caiaphas said that Pilate wanted to remind the Jews that the Romans control Jerusalem. And that is just what he did, wouldn't you say?"

"Yes, he certainly did. Well, Javan, what brings you here this early in the morning?"

"Father told me to come and make sure that you are all right."

"Nicodemus is a thoughtful man and a dear friend. Tell him I appreciate his concern."

"Wait, Mary, that's not all. Here is your money from the mail service. I paid all the stable fees on your horses, and this is half the profit. One-half for me and one-half for you."

"Javan, you deserve more. You do all the work."

"No, Mary, this is your mail service. This business will be an income for you."

"Many thanks, Javan, for looking after my well-being."

"Oh, yes . . . I have something else for you." Javan pulls out a small bag and gives it to Mary.

She opens the bag. "It's more money. Where did it come from?"

"Joktan," whispers Javan. "He sends his condolences again."

With tears in her eyes, Mary struggles to speak. "He is a kindhearted man, but I can't keep it. I shall return it. I need to carry back the funeral robes also." Mary pauses, then adds, "You know, three days ago I had the perfect family—a devoted husband and a respected son. And now my husband is dead and my son a notorious fugitive." Mary breaks down and sobs bitterly.

After knocking on the door, Martha, Mary's sister, walks inside. As Martha comforts Mary, Javan excuses himself.

In the breakfast room that overlooks the Sea of Galilee, Antipas, Herodias, and Exum wait for Salome to come downstairs to eat breakfast. Exum admires the four columns that support the three arches, which is open to the rear of the palace on the cliff above the sea. The base, shaft, capital, and entablature are artistically ornamented. Exum looks out at the Sea of Galilee and makes a philosophical conclusion. "You know, the finest sculpture in the world is no comparison to natural beauty. The grooved shaft and the design carved on the frieze before us are no match in splendor to the sea before us."

Herod agrees and elaborates, "Yes, art doesn't do justice to natural beauty. This commanding view of the Sea of Galilee cannot be captured on canvas or stone. A view like this must be experienced. However, the picturesque sea can be very ugly, too. The mountains on the east side rise 2700 feet. When cool winds rush down their slopes toward the humidity of the sea, violent storms occur suddenly. Even on this thirteen-by eight-mile lake, the waves caused by a storm can be dangerous. That reminds me. I heard that Jesus calmed an awful storm on this sea by speaking to it."

"Preposterous," laughs Exum.

The interrupting sound of Salome coming down the stairs arrests the attention of the three seated at the table. With her black hair draped to one side of the Mediterranean-shellfish-red dyed tunic, Salome enters the room. Looking attentively at Salome, Exum remarks, "Herod, as you were saying, natural beauty cannot be captured on canvas or stone."

With lustful eyes for Salome, Herod leans forward and whispers risqué words to Exum so that Herodias cannot hear. "Natural beauty must be experienced."

"Good morning," greets Salome.

"Serve us!" Herod commands the servants.

A pain caused by the shackles on Barabbas' wrists awakens him. He looks around to see stone walls surrounding him with the exception of the door of bars on one side and a small porthole for a window on the opposite wall. *Well, I can see that I'm not in prison, but these shackles tell me that I'm not free to go.* Barabbas stands to his feet and looks out the porthole. *It's a long way down. There's the sea. Just as I suspected, I'm in the dungeon beneath the palace. Oh, God, the legionnaires are going to carry me back to Jerusalem. God, what am I going to do?* Barabbas calls, "Guards, help me!" The guards ignore him. Fear tries to crowd the cell, but Barabbas sings every hymn he knows about the deliverance of God. He encourages himself as he meditates on the one true God.

As Exum and the two legionnaires ride out of Tiberias with Logos, Antipas and Herodias watch them disappear out of sight. "Where is he?" Herodias asks. "In the prison?"

"No, he's in the dungeon. I didn't want anyone to know. If word got back to Pilate, would I be in trouble. Let's go see him."

Antipas and Herodias hurry to the dungeon and wait in the execution room. The keeper of the dungeon interrupts the meditation of Barabbas by opening the cell door. Two troops march inside and grab Barabbas by the back of his shackled arms and escort him down the corridor to the execution chamber. The executioner steps back as Barabbas is shoved to his knees and pushed forward so that his neck is parallel with the floor across the chopping block. The executioner steps forward again to position himself to make a clean lop.

The massive, muscular executioner swings the curved wide blade, mounted on tamarisk wood, behind him and focuses on the target—Barabbas' neck. The executioner gives a heave and swings forward until Antipas shouts, "Stop!" The momentum of the blade is broken in midair and diverted to the neighboring chopping block. "Do you have any last words?" asks Antipas.

Facing the floor, Barabbas utters, "Hear—" The guard behind him interrupts by jerking Barabbas by the hair to make him face Herod. Barabbas starts again, "Hear, O Israel: The LORD our God is one LORD: And thou shalt love the LORD thy God with all thine heart, and with all thy soul, and with all thy might. Although the fig tree shall not blossom, neither shall fruit be in the vines; the labour of the olive shall fail, and the fields shall yield no meat; the flock shall be cut off from the fold, and there shall be no herd in the stalls: Yet I will rejoice in the LORD, I will joy in the God of my salvation."

Antipas yells, "Curse God and live, Barabbas!"

Barabbas voluntarily lowers his head to the chopping block and waits for the executioner.

Antipas looks at Herodias and grins. "Omar!" he calls.

"Yes, sir," replies Omar, Antipas' confidant.

"Give me the sword." Omar hands Antipas the Sword of Sacrifice. Herod motions the guard to raise the head of Barabbas again. On his knees, hands shackled, neck arched backward by the hair-grasping guard, Barabbas feels the Sword of Sacrifice press against his throat. "If my subjects were as loyal to me as you Pharisees are dedicated to your God, I would be king. Your devotion to Jehovah is admirable, commendable, and even noble. It is a *shame* you have to die. Your head will gain me favor from Pilate and notice from Tiberius Claudius Nero Caesar for a job well done." In a monologue, Antipas continues to toy with Barabbas: "If only you had something to trade for your neck. Your horse, perhaps? No, he was taken by Exum and the two legionnaires who chased you yesterday. They don't know that I have captured you. I saved you from them. Now, if you had something to trade for your life, you would not have them on your trail. Perhaps you would like to trade this sword? No, I have to confiscate it, for it is the murder weapon. This is the Sword of Sacrifice, and you are the sacrifice unless you have something to give me. You will surely die by this sword."

"I have nothing, sir."

In a teasing higher tone Antipas mimics, "Oh, yes, you do! If you didn't have something I wanted, you would be on your way back to Jerusalem with Exum. I saved your life. Now, you owe me. And I'm going to collect what you know or your head. Either way, I win. Now, talk . . .. I want to know why you killed the confidant of the high priest and of the governor."

It dawns on Barabbas what Herod wants—incriminating evidence that might cost Pilate his Jerusalem jurisdiction, which Antipas covets. Barabbas' countenance brightens as a brilliant plan pieces together in his mind. "Sir, four days ago. . . " Barabbas tells his story from the beginning of his espionage on Caiaphas to his arrival in Tiberias. At the end of his story, Antipas claps his hands. Omar orders the guards to take Barabbas as Antipas and Herodias leave the execution chamber with the Sword of Sacrifice.

Omar escorts Barabbas to the palace bath and removes the shackles. He commands, "Bathe yourself, for you will dine with Herod tonight. I will get a razor and clean clothes for you." Barabbas pulls off his clothes and enters the bathing room. The twelve-foot Greco-Roman tub with an island in the middle is a welcome sight for Barabbas. He scrubs and then relaxes.

About two hours before sunset in Jerusalem, Mary tries to break the obsession of questions that plagues her mind. Seeing her sister's misery, Martha suggests that Mary go for a walk. Facing the fear of passing through the arched tunnel, Mary agrees, "I need to take back the money and the funeral clothes that Joktan loaned me."

Martha says, "I'll go with you."

"Martha, I must go alone. I want to be alone when I pass

through the arched tunnel between Mount Zion and Mount Moriah."

"If you think you will be all right, I understand."

Mary leaves her house and walks toward the Temple. The walk helps Mary to see her anxieties in their proper perspective. *If Rabba were here, he would tell me to rejoice in the Lord. Then he would support his advice with sound reasoning: "If your happiness is dependent upon Caiaphas and the way he treats you, then you are dependent upon Caiaphas for your happiness. If you are angry with Caiaphas, then, your happiness is dependent upon him and what he does. Let Jehovah be your happiness." Rabba was a smart man. If he were here, he would tell me to forget about Caiaphas and concentrate on the important things. "Let the dead bury the dead." I need to focus my attention on Barabbas. How can I help Barabbas? I don't even know if he is alive. God, help me to help Barabbas!*

With a new perspective gleaned from her memory of Rabba's teachings, Mary reaches the arched tunnel and stops. *I'm strong because Rabba would want me to be. I am strong because Barabbas needs me to be. I am strong because Jehovah is with me.* Mary sets her eyes on the other end of the tunnel and takes the first step into the arched tunnel. She walks. *The LORD is my shepherd; I shall not want. He maketh me to lie down in green pastures: he leadeth me beside the still waters. He restoreth my soul: he leadeth me in the paths of righteousness for his name's sake. Yea, though I walk through the valley of the shadow of death I will fear no evil: for thou art with me; thy rod and thy staff they comfort me. Thou preparest a table before me in the presence of mine enemies: thou anointest my head with oil; my cup runneth over. Surely goodness and mercy shall follow me all the days of my life: and I will dwell in the house of the LORD for ever.*

Reaching the Holdah Gates of the Royal Portico, Mary

sees Joktan's office. She notices three men in the ornate stone office. Not wanting to disturb Joktan, she stops at his door and holds the robes and the small bag of money.

Noticing Mary at the door, Joktan responds. "Please wait. I'll be through in a minute." Joktan announces, "Gentlemen, we will finish this business tomorrow."

The gentlemen gather their belongings and leave. "Mary, I am pleased to see you. Won't you have a seat?"

"Well, I can't stay. I just came by to deliver these clothes and the money you sent me. I appreciate your thoughtfulness and your kindness, but I can't accept this money."

"Mary, I know you don't understand, but let me be kind to you. You and Barabbas deserve it. I ask nothing in return."

"Thank you, Joktan, but I can't accept these gifts."

"Mary, I'll take the clothes and the money back if that is what it takes to make you happy. But first, I ask you to grant me one favor. If you'll grant me that, then I'll do anything you ask of me."

"What is it—the favor?"

Mary looks at the begging eyes, the tanned skin, the small crows' feet, the square hairline, and the dimpled chin as Joktan pleads, "Will you listen to what I have to say? That's all I ask."

Slightly embarrassed and moved to compassion, Mary replies, "Yes."

Joktan begins, "Mary, all I know to do is to tell you the truth and how I feel."

"I appreciate truth."

Joktan begins, "I was born a Jew. My ancestors were Pharisees, members of the Hasidim that later joined in the revolt of the Maccabees against Antiochus IV. My great-great-great grandfather fled to the Island of Crete. There my family learned the merchandising trade at the harbor of Fair Havens. They began to order and ship goods to all the countries surrounding the Mediterranean. They became wealthy through the years, but I feel that they sacrificed something—something that is here in Jerusalem. I don't know what it is, but I hope you will help me find it."

Mary knows exactly what that something is but holds her thoughts to herself and listens as Joktan tells more.

"My family paid a great sum of money to buy Roman citizenship. This citizenship has given us many privileges, especially in trade. I am a friend with the Jews and friends with the Romans. Yet I am neither: I'm not Roman by blood or a Jew by belief. This Roman money has not bought me happiness. But there is something in the belief of the Jews that my spirit craves, whatever that is. I was not raised by Orthodox Jews; therefore, I am lost. I'm like a ship without a sail.

You are probably asking why now; that is, why am I hungry for Jewish belief at this time? Let me answer that. I know that Orthodox Jews believe in the one God. But, to my dismay, I don't know who He is. I didn't care to know until your husband died. Most of the Pharisees around the Temple make me sick. I classify them as hypocrites. However, I often watched your husband when I went to sell supplies to the Temple. He was an altruistic, philanthropic, God-fearing man. He stirred the heart of my emotion as I watched him pray. He humbly prostrated himself before God."

Tears flood Mary's eyes as Joktan talks. Joktan stops to apologize, "I didn't mean to upset you. This is probably not a good time to talk to you. I'm sorry. I'll stop."

"No. Go on and tell me. This blesses my soul to know that someone actually notices . . ."

"Well, that's about all I can tell you except . . ." Joktan stops without finishing.

"Tell me, Joktan," pleads Mary.

"I can't," he says with a tone of embarrassed regret.

"Why not?"

"The only other thing I know to tell you is that you would

think I am most immature and foolish if I told you how I feel about you." The room fills with silence as Joktan drops his head and Mary lifts hers to look at the pitiful man before her. Neither of them says a word for a time. As if someone has pulled a curtain on the sun, darkness falls.

Joktan breaks the sound of silence: "Mary, it's dark. You must go and rest. Come and I'll walk you home." With a solemn face, Mary bites her bottom lip and rises to leave. Joktan picks up the robes and the money and walks out the door with Mary. He walks her home, and neither of them speaks until she reaches her door.

Without looking Mary in the eyes, Joktan hands her the clothes and money. She does not refuse because if she did, she would have to speak. "Mary, when life comes back together for you, help me find mine." Mary goes into her house.

Antipas and Herodias sit in the chamber that overlooks the dining room. They watch as the kitchen steward sets the table with meat. The aroma of food spiced with mint, dill, anise, cummin, almond, and pistachio fills the room. Following the instruction of Herod, the steward makes sure the foods served are those considered clean by the Hebrews according to the law given by Moses.

The steward sets the table with fish that once possessed scales and fins, but he serves no fish classified as unclean such as catfish, lampreys, oysters, shrimp, eel, or shark. He serves no scavenger bird such as vulture and no predatory bird such as the eagle. In the clean fowl classification, he serves birds that flock—quail, dove, and chicken.

Divided-hoof, cud-chewing animals considered clean, such as cows, antelope, sheep, and goats, are used to provide the red meat for the table. The camel, which chews the cud and does not have the divided hoof, is not served; but camel's milk and cheese are set on the table. The pig, which has the divided hoof and does not chew the cud, is not served. Though Antipas loves to eat reptiles such as lizards, snakes, and turtles, the steward does not serve these foods.

In the clean insect classification, the steward sets the table with grasshopper, locusts, and some beetles. To the preferred cuisine of Herod, the insects are prepared three different ways: fried, dried, and succulently boiled. The fried insects surround the featured dish of mutton, the meat of mature sheep.

The steward sets the table with the "fruits of the earth" such as grains, fruits, and vegetables. In the grain family, the steward serves wheat, barley, and millet parched, roasted, cracked, or in the form of bread. He provides fruits and vegetables such as grapes, garlic, cucumbers, melons, leeks, onions, beans, lentils, squash, clusters of raisins, cakes of figs, and apricots. And last of all, the steward brings in the juice of grapes and sets it on the long, deep burgundy, gold and silver-trimmed, ivory inlaid table. With this accomplished, the steward lights the candles on the table and the lamps about the dining room to show Antipas that the meal is ready.

Antipas orders, "Omar, bring Barabbas and call Salome to dinner."

With a puzzled look on her face, Herodias questions Antipas, "Why are you giving a feast for a murderer? It doesn't make sense."

Antipas explains, "First of all, you're wrong: Barabbas is not a murderer. He only avenged the murder of his father, and that is commendable."

"You're right. I guess I would have done the same thing."

Antipas interrupts, "Second, Barabbas is going to get the ledger that is Pilate's demise and my hope of Jerusalem kingship."

"What makes you think that Barabbas will give the ledger to you?"

"Whom else can he give it to? Caesar? The emperor doesn't listen to people who aren't Roman citizens, especially those accused of murder. Barabbas needs me to present the incriminating ledger to Caesar for him. Barabbas knows he can trust me to do that because it is no secret that Jerusalem should be my jurisdiction. And he knows I am not fond of Pilate."

"Well, how do you know that there *is* a ledger? All you have is Barabbas' word."

"Why should he lie? But just to be sure, I sent word to Mizzah, my ambassador who oversees my Jerusalem palace. He is to check out the story and try to find the ledger."

That answer provokes Herodias to ask, "What if Mizzah finds the ledger before Barabbas does?"

Antipas slides his finger across his throat and says, "I'll dispose of Barabbas. I won't need him any more. I can't keep him around because he could prove my collusion. But right now, I need him, and he needs me. He may be the only one who can find this ledger."

"What do you think it will prove?"

"I suspect that Pilate is up to his usual tricks. Do you remember the time that Pilate took money from the temple treasury to build an aqueduct to Jerusalem?"

"Yes," Herodias sighs.

"Well, when the Jews learned that Pilate was taking their tithes, the Zealots revolted. Pilate and the legionnaires killed many of them. Caesar was displeased with Pilate for shedding blood in the incident. Remember the time when Herod Philip and I complained to Caesar about Herod Archelaus shedding Hebrew blood in Judea and Samaria? Our complaints followed by a Jewish delegation removed Archelaus from Jerusalem and banished him to Rome. I think that if Pilate is found guilty of stealing Jewish tithes, which could cause another bloody skirmish, he will be called back to Rome."

"My darling husband, tell me why does Rome listen to these insignificant Hebrews?"

"Historical superstition, I think . . . for the most part."

"What do you mean?"

"Something that started with Alexander the Great about three hundred years ago—it's an unusual story."

"I'd love to hear it. Unusual history fascinates me."

"Come, let's sit at the table, and I'll tell you the story."

As Antipas and Herodias sit at the table, Omar arrives with Barabbas. "Come and sit. I was about to tell the story of Alexander." Barabbas sits in the seat of honor, and Salome appears at the door. "Come, my darling Salome, and meet our guest, Barabbas. Salome, this is Barabbas, our guest. Barabbas, this is my stepdaughter, Salome, and my wife, Herodias." They all exchange greetings.

Barabbas knows that Salome is a pagan, but he cannot help noticing her beauty. And Salome remembers that Barabbas is accused of murder, but she cannot help noticing that he is handsome.

Herod says, "Now, what was I about to tell you?"

Herodias replies, "The unusual story about Alexander the Great."

"Oh, yes . . . Alexander. Jewish historians say that when Alexander and his soldiers came to seize the city of Jerusalem, the high priest, Jaddua, and all the other priests, dressed in their priestly attire, opened the city gates and walked out to greet him. When Alexander saw the priests walk out dressed in their fine white linen garments, he walked away from his troops and met them. Alexander saluted the priests and gave adoration to the name of God on Jaddua's miter. Alexander then went into the Temple and offered sacrifice according to the directions of the priests. Jaddua read to Alexander the prophecy in the Book of Daniel which says that a Greek was to destroy the Persian Empire."

Herodias looks at Antipas as he finishes the story and asks, "Do you believe that incredible story?"

Antipas shifts the question to Barabbas, "What do you think, Barabbas?"

"Uh . . ." Barabbas nervously hesitates to answer.

"Come . . . relax, Barabbas. I know you're an expert in Jewish history—you're orthodox, aren't you? Do you believe Alexander did that?" Antipas tries to make Barabbas feel comfortable. "Here, take your sword. I'll give you a horse and provisions when you decide to go. You're free to go, and you're free to stay here in the palace. But right now, relax. What do you think about the story? Is it true?"

Receiving the Sword of Sacrifice and the friendly gestures from Antipas, Barabbas gives his opinion. "Well, I believe every word of it."

"Why?" entreats Antipas.

"First of all, Alexander did not take Jerusalem by the sword. Second, he allowed the Jews to observe their own religious laws. On sabbatical years, he exempted them from tribute. He built Alexandria in Egypt and helped Jews settle there to enjoy privileges like the Greeks. In fact, in some ways, the Jews had more privileges than some Greeks. Alexander blessed the Jews and used the Jewish blessing."

Antipas attentively asks, "What Jewish blessing?"

"The blessing—whoever blesses the Israelites will be blessed, and whoever curses the Israelites will be cursed. Being a student of Aristotle, Alexander was taught Jewish history. A man smart enough to bring the Koine Greek language to the world, I think, was smart enough to figure out that God blesses the country that blesses Israel. Therefore, in some sense, I believe that God blessed Alexander because Alexander blessed the Jews."

"Do you believe what you say, Barabbas?"

"Yes, sir."

"Then, because of your plausible, cogent words, I believe

it too. In fact, I believe it so much that I am going to bless you. And you, therefore, will bless me. I'll give you what you need. You need me to present this incriminating ledger to Caesar when you find it. That would be a blessing to you, wouldn't it?"

"Yes, sir. I would be most grateful if you would." Barabbas thinks to himself. *You just want to get rid of Pilate so that you can rule over Jerusalem. That's all.*

Herod says, "Let's eat." The musician begins to play his harp in the side chamber as the servants pour the wine. Antipas and Herodias talk as Barabbas and Salome eye each other with bashful enthusiasm.

Finally Herod suggests, "Barabbas why don't you tell Salome about Jewish customs? She is inquisitive about how others live. And Salome, tomorrow, you may show Barabbas around the palace." With that introduction, the two begin to talk as they eat.

After dinner, Antipas leads Barabbas to the three arched windows that overlook the Sea of Galilee and talks privately with him. "Barabbas, I know that one day you will have to go back to Jerusalem to find the ledger. Right now, it is too dangerous to go back. All the Jews in Jerusalem know you, and I'm sure there'll be a reward for you. So you need to stay here in the palace for a while."

"Yes, sir. I thank you very much."

"Here in Tiberias, as you know, there are no Jews to recognize you. All I ask is that you don't give your identity to anyone. I would be in jeopardy with Caesar if he knew that I housed a fugitive who murdered a Roman. Understood?"

"Yes, sir."

"I have a palace in Jerusalem that houses my ambassador, Mizzah, who is to report to me in a few days. He will be helpful in choosing a good time for you to go back and search for the ledger."

"Thank you, Herod. You saved my life."

Pasah, the orphaned lamb, nestles cozily next to Rosh, the gentle shepherd. The orphan raises his head and cries out with a pitiful bleat.

"Oh, Pasah," Rosh sympathetically whispers, "you must quit crying. You break my heart. When I draped your trembling body over my shoulders and carried you from the scene of your mother's death, you bleated a heartbreaking cry. When I carried you to the stream for a drink of water, you sounded another heart-rending cry. When I carried you to the best grass in the pasture, you bleated another mournful whine. When I played with you, you bleated a call of distress. Even when I held the other milk-producing ewes so you could nurse, you moved me to tears with your whimpering cry for your mother."

Rosh's voice pleads as he speaks reassuring words. "Pasah, I am with you always. Stay near me, and I will protect you. Don't go astray. Listen to my call."

The shepherd of love gives cuddling comfort to the little one in the darkness.

In the ruins of Ai, the cursed serpent waits to spread his poison.

6

Love & Lust

Inside the stone walls, the garden is landscaped in layers to the center—first, the large almond trees, which produce pinkish-white blossoms; second, the balsam trees, which produce green flowers; and last an array of white-flowering myrtle. At the base of the trees are flowers and shrubs: irises, roses, tulips, anemone, lilies, hyacinths, narcissus, and juniper. The heart of the garden holds a small pool surrounded by palm trees. Interwoven between the palm trees and flowers are benches. On one bench sits beauty and innocence of adolescence—Salome, and on another sits strength and resolution—Barabbas. Salome's worldview floats in a wandering orbit. Barabbas' view of the world is forced out of a normal orbit because of the great gravities pulling on it. She longs for truth, and he longs to establish truth. Under the erroneous philosophy of using force, Barabbas wages a physical war that can be won only by the spiritual—a war that is humanly impossible to win—a war that is won by surrendering. But his actions are dictated by his belief. She does not know what the war is about, but wishes to find out in her own struggle to be free.

Her infatuated eyes, hemmed in by long, dark eyelashes, look at Barabbas with respect. "I have enjoyed showing you the palace today. Your presence is comforting, yet our friendship makes me apprehensive. I don't want to ruin our day by asking you something too personal, but I must. Please tell me about your belief."

Barabbas becomes enthusiastic to give a good answer about his God. "Salome, I'm glad you asked." Barabbas begins, "First of all, there is only one God."

"You mean just one numerical god. Why not many?"

"By definition, God is all-powerful—omnipotent. If there were more than one God, then one god would be subject unto another. Therefore, there is only one supreme God because all the others would be less powerful and more vulnerable to death—mortal and not God the all-powerful. If there were two gods then both could not claim all power. My God is the God of all power and beside him there is no other. Isaiah the prophet wrote: 'Before me there was no God formed, neither shall there be after me. I, even I, am the Lord; and beside me there is no savior. I am the first, and I am the last; and beside me there is no God. I am the Lord that maketh all things; that stretcheth forth the heavens alone; that spreadeth abroad the earth by myself. There is none beside me. I am the Lord and there is none else. There is no God else beside me; a just God and a Savior; there is none beside me. Look unto me, and be ye saved, all the ends of the earth: for I am God, and there is none else.'"

"But Antipas talks about Jupiter, the god of justice, and Liber, the god of wine and drunkenness. Mother often mentions Venus, the deity of love, particularly sexual love, and Cupid, the god of erotic attraction."

"Curse Jupiter, Liber, Venus, Cupid, and all the Roman Gods!"

"Barabbas, you aren't afraid to curse the gods?"

"Salome, I'm not afraid to curse the gods of the Romans or the Greeks. They are not gods at all. There is only one supreme God—the God of Israel."

"Well, who is your God?"

"His name is Yahweh or Jehovah as one might say."

"What do you mean?"

"Actually, the four consonants—Y H W H is His name. His name is not to be taken in vain. But for now, until God reveals his name to man, the redemptive name Jehovah is the name of my God."

"One god makes sense, now that I think about it."

"Sure it does. Since the beginning of the creation of Adam and Eve, God has taught man for four thousand years that there is only one God. Did God lie to us? Certainly not. We Jews recite and meditate on the Shema found in the Book of Deuteronomy. 'Hear, O Israel: The Lord our God is one Lord: And thou shalt love the Lord thy God with all thine heart, and with all thy soul, and with all thy might. And these words, which I command thee this day, shall be in thine heart: And thou shalt teach them diligently unto thy children, and shalt talk of them when thou sittest in thine house, and when thou walkest by the way, and when thou liest down, and when thou risest up. And thou shalt bind them for a sign upon thine hand, and they shall be as frontlets between thine eyes. And thou shalt write them upon the post of thy house, and on thy gates.'"

"What does it mean when you say bind them as frontlets between the eyes?"

"We Jews wear small leather boxes fastened by leather straps to our left hands and our foreheads during morning worship. These boxes, which are called phylacteries, contain the scripture that 'The Lord our God is one Lord.' This one precept God never wanted man to forget. I base all my belief in one God—the God of Israel."

"Barabbas, your God makes my gods to be superstition."

"Precisely." Barabbas gets up from his bench and walks over to sit by Salome. "Now that you have asked me a personal question, it's my turn to ask you one. Do I sense some friction between you and your father, Antipas?"

"How sensitive you are. Antipas is not my biological father: He's my uncle."

"I actually knew that. I'm sorry—I just couldn't resist hearing your response."

"Well, my ancestry is common knowledge, and I know that it is not something to be proud of. But—it doesn't bother me to tell the truth."

"If you don't mind, please tell me of your people," requests Barabbas.

"As you know, I am of the descendants of Esau, the brother of Jacob, the father of your ancestors. The father of your people and the father of mine were brothers. Julius Caesar appointed Antipater, my great-grandfather, procurator of Judea. Then, Antipater's son, Herod the Great, became governor and king over all Israel. He was a ruthless man—"

Barabbas interrupts to say, "Yes, he's the one that killed the babies in and around Bethlehem because some wise men told him about a king being born in there. Some say this king was Jesus."

Salome continues: "My grandfather, Herod the Great, was cruel to anybody who seemed to covet being king. Mariamne, one of his wives, and their two sons, Alexander and Aristobulus, were murdered because the Great Herod suspected them of collusion for the throne. The Great had other sons: Philip the first, my father; Philip the second, tetrarch over Iturea and Traconitis; Antipas, my uncle and stepfather, tetrarch of Galilee and Perea; and Archelaus, tetrarch of the coveted Judea, Idumea, and Samaria. Those are the notable sons that survived the viciousness of Herod the Great. Then there's my mother. Let's not forget the notable thing Herodias, my dear mother, did—she married her father's half brother, her uncle. Next, she left him to marry his brother, now my stepfather, Antipas. Don't mention any of this to Antipas; he is very tired of hearing about it, especially after John the Baptist spoke out against his immoral marriage." Salome shamefully admits, "No wonder I'm so mixed up. Trying to unscramble this inbreeding is impossible!"

Without thinking, Barabbas blurts what is in his heart, "But what a beautiful woman you are."

"*Woman*"—Salome takes note. *No one has called me a woman before. No one has ever made me feel like a woman before. What has come over me? I love this new warm sensation that I can't explain. Barabbas*—Salome adores him with her eyes.

After sharing their personal convictions, Barabbas and Salome relax in each other's company. Barabbas is mesmerized by the beauty and innocence of Salome. Throwing caution to the wind, Barabbas does what he thinks is improper and presumptuous: He embraces Salome and gives her an intoxicating kiss. With her heart racing and her spine tingling, she holds on to invite the intrusion.

The next evening in Jerusalem, Caiaphas arrives at the praetorium gate to meet Pilate. "Hello, Governor Pilate."

Impatiently, Pilate asks, "What do you want, Caiaphas?"

"Governor, I heard that Exum came back this afternoon without Barabbas."

"Yes. Exum's pursuit was thwarted by the followers of Jesus."

"Governor, what are you going to do about it?"

"About the disciples of Jesus or Barabbas?"

"Both."

"Well, this Jesus I'm not concerned about. He doesn't

even own a sword. Barabbas may show up again, and if he does, I'll arrest him."

"Governor Pilate, I have some bad news. I've known it for some time, and I am sorry I didn't tell you sooner. But before I tell you the bad news, I am glad to tell you I have put a foolproof plan in force to correct the situation. I beg you to hear me out before you react."

"Don't play games with me, Caiaphas."

Without hesitation, Caiaphas says, "Governor, the temple ledger is missing."

"Whaaaaat!" shouts Pilate.

"Wait, my lord, let me finish! I don't know that Barabbas has the ledger, but I *do* know that he stole the Sword of Sacrifice."

Pilate stops Caiaphas there by saying, "I don't care about this sword. I believe that Barabbas has that ledger. What about Sadoc's ledger? Without Sadoc's ledger, the temple ledger is no proof."

With a look of guilty displeasure, Caiaphas admits. "Well, Governor—"

"Oh! No! No, no, *nooo*! Tell me it's not true."

"Rabba worked for Sadoc part-time."

Pilate grits his teeth and then asks, "Does our contact know about this?"

"Yes, sir," answers Caiaphas, searching for words to soothe Pilate. "Our contact has a plan to catch Barabbas. And you are wrong about Jesus, the one who gives refuge to the Zealots. If there is to be an uprising, it will be with the Jews. He is the one who stirs up trouble with—"

"I don't care about this Jesus," Pilate interrupts. "You see to him. I want to know about our contact's plan to capture Barabbas."

"Governor, our contact and I have a plan to stop both."

"Just let me hear how our contact is going to help me capture Barabbas."

Caiaphas explains the plan, which brings satisfaction to Pilate's face.

Shortly before mid-day, hearing a knock on the door, Mary opens it and sees a big-eyed animal staring her in the face. She screams with joy, "Logos!" In excitement, she leaps and hugs the man holding the reins. Then she hugs Logos and says, "Logos, I'm so glad you're safe! If only you could talk!" Mary looks to Joktan and says, "Last night I heard that the soldiers came back without Barabbas, but nobody could tell me if he is safe or not. Have you heard?"

With an exuberant smile above his deeply dimpled chin, Joktan is pleased to announce, "He is safe."

"Please tell me . . ."

"Villus told me that about five miles from Tiberias, Barabbas rode into a camp of Jesus' followers who gave him refuge. The legionnaires took his horse and left when nobody would identify Barabbas. Isn't that wonderful? He's safe, Mary. He's safe!"

Mary grabs his hand. "Yes. Praise God! He's safe!"

Joktan puts the reins in Mary's hand, clasping hers with his. "Thank God . . . he's safe, and Logos is back where he belongs—with you. He's yours."

Mary looks to Joktan and asks, "How can this be?"

"After I heard that the legionnaires brought Logos back, I went to Villus and asked to purchase the horse. I supply goods to Villus and the Romans, you know. He agreed to sell the horse to me, and now he is yours."

"Oh, no. I must pay you for him."

"No, Mary. He is yours. I shall take no money from you."

"Thank you. I can't wait for Javan to get back and see Logos. He'll be so excited. I'll put Logos back on the mail route where he belongs."

"Mary, would you like for me to take Logos to the stable for you?"

"Yes. May I walk with you?"

"I would like that very much."

Mary and Joktan walk toward the stable, talking as they go. The light shines brighter and warmer along the way.

After a night of rest, Antipas lies in bed as Herodias looks out the south bedroom window, which overlooks the courtyard where Antipas makes judgements over his subjects. She sees Salome showing Barabbas the open courtroom. Salome points to the archway in the south wall that opens toward the soldier's barracks and the prison. Then she points to the archway that opens to the west from which the public may watch court proceedings.

Watching the two, Herodias says to Antipas, "Herod, have you noticed Salome and Barabbas?"

"What do you mean?"

"It has been nineteen days since Barabbas arrived. I have counted them. Salome's love for Barabbas grows greater every day."

With slight irritation in his tone, Antipas asks, "Does that bother you?"

"I don't know."

Antipas speaks further: "Mizzah should arrive here this evening. He will tell us the state of affairs in Jerusalem concerning Barabbas. I can stop him from seeing Salome at any point. Barabbas is helpful at this time, but after I get my hands on the ledger, he may be done away with."

Analyzing the situation, Herodias speaks some of her thoughts aloud for Antipas to hear. "Let nature take its course. It may be good that Salome is in love. Barabbas is a religious Jew, so I don't think he'll fall for her. She needs to have her heart broken. This will be a good lesson for her." Herodias pauses to think silently to herself: *Once this loser breaks her heart, she will be able to see clearly how to handle herself with men. She needs to be used once in order to learn the facts of life. Then she will accept the way of Venus and Cupid. In fact, the more I think about the situation, the more I like it. She could fall in love with an undesirable whom we could not remove from the picture.* However, Herodias again speaks the rest of her thoughts aloud to Antipas, "If Barabbas falls in love with her, he can be executed for his crimes."

"As you wish," Antipas replies.

Just before sundown, Barabbas and Salome arrive back at the palace for dinner. After spending the afternoon at the hot springs at the south end of the city, standing at the steps before the palace front door, Barabbas looks at the sun-kissed Salome and starts to say something when Omar opens the palace front door. "Barabbas, come quickly! Antipas wants to see you."

Walking swiftly to keep up, Barabbas and Salome follow Omar to find Herod. Salome squeezes Barabbas' hand and whispers, "What were you about to say before Omar came?"

"I can't tell you now—tomorrow in private."

Reaching the door of the tetrarch's study, Omar says, "Antipas wants to speak privately with you, Barabbas."

Barabbas opens the door and walks inside. Seated at a table is a man who looks familiar. *I've seen this man before . . . in Jerusalem.* Antipas introduces the two, "Mizzah, this is Barabbas. Barabbas, this is Mizzah, my ambassador in Jerusalem, the head of the Herodians."

"Barabbas, Mizzah informs me that Pilate offers a reward for your capture. From undisclosed sources, we learned that when Caiaphas told Pilate the ledger was missing, he offered the reward. Therefore, I conclude that the ledger is a definite threat to Pilate."

Mizzah takes up where Antipas stops. "Now is not a favorable time to go back to Jerusalem. Is there any information you can give me to help me to find the temple ledger? Or is there any place I need to look?"

Barabbas & The Sword of Sacrifice

Aware of the precarious situation and the possible deceit of Antipas and Mizzah, Barabbas says, "I feel I'm the only one who can find this ledger. In fact, there is a possibility someone is waiting for my return to give the ledger to me. You might be lucky and find it, but I doubt it."

Mizzah understands what Barabbas means, but he does not give up his pursuit of questions. "Barabbas, who could possibly have that ledger?"

Uncomfortable with Mizzah's persistence, Barabbas tries to get out of the interrogation by giving Antipas and Mizzah something else to think about. "Well, the night of my father's murder, it was Anak who stole the Sword of Sacrifice. Caiaphas lied in saying that Rabba took the Sword of Sacrifice and committed suicide. Anak stole the sword and murdered my father; then I took the sword. The ledger—the temple custodian saw Rabba take it."

"So?" questions Mizzah, not knowing where Barabbas is leading.

"So either I took the ledger from my father—which I did not—or Rabba hid it or gave it to someone. Or Anak stole it—and he is dead."

"I didn't think about that," confesses Antipas. "But none of this adds up."

"That's why you need me. I am a contact person. I admit that I cannot find the ledger from Tiberias, but when I get to Jerusalem, if the ledger is there, I will find it. I must go to Jerusalem."

"Not at this time—there are bounty hunters looking for you. Even your own people would hand you over for the reward. You wouldn't last an hour in Jerusalem. You need to wait until things cool down, and even then, you would need a cover—something like a holiday. Maybe . . . the Passover?"

"The Passover is two weeks away, but I suppose I can wait that long. I *would* like to be in Jerusalem for the Passover," replies Barabbas.

Antipas gives his decision: "We'll see how things go." He sits back in his seat to give orders more formally. "Mizzah, go back to Jerusalem tomorrow. Investigate what you can about the ledger. Keep a close watch on the affairs of Pilate and Caiaphas. Send me a message of any development." Antipas looks at Barabbas and says, "You will stay here until we see how things go."

Mizzah and Barabbas give their consent. Mizzah speaks up again, "Antipas, I have another incident that needs your attention."

"What?" questions Antipas.

"One of the Jerusalem palace servants has been stealing from you. Pilate would not judge him because his crimes are against the Herodian palace, so I brought him to you."

"I shall hold a court session in the morning for my subjects. Likewise, we have caught some thieves here in Galilee. The verdict is quite simple: If someone steals from me . . . . My subjects know the penalty—death." Antipas looks at Barabbas and Mizzah to see if there are any more questions. The two look content, so Antipas exclaims with excitement and optimism, "Let's dine and celebrate our future."

The next morning Herod's household, Mizzah, and Barabbas eat breakfast together. After they finish eating, Antipas orders Omar to inform the soldiers to prepare the court.

Upon receiving their orders, the soldiers bring the prisoners to the southern arch of the stone courtyard. The public gathers at the western arch to observe the proceedings. The arches are guarded by four guards on the inside and outside of each arch. Several troops stand along the inside and outside of the court walls. The floor near the front is open except for the two tables before the judgement seat of Antipas. In the back stands the ax-wielding executioner with his chopping block.

Antipas takes the judgement seat, which is at the north end

of the court, and Mizzah prepares to present the crimes of the servant who stole from the Herodian palace. Antipas calls the court to order. The court becomes silent. "Bring the accused." Two soldiers bring in the Herodian servant. His wrists are bound with leather straps. Mizzah clears his throat to speak. "Herod Antipas, this servant was caught stealing from your Jerusalem palace."
Antipas addresses the servant, "What is your name?"
"Elah," answers the servant.
"Elah, what do you have to say for yourself?"
"My brother is paralyzed. I took one of the idols to help him. He has three small children. I can't stand to see them hungry. I'm sorry, Sir."
Antipas proclaims his judgement. "The crime is stealing from the government. You steal from the people and me. This is the same as insurrection. Your sentence—you shall lose your head on the block."
The Herodian servant breaks down and cries. The two guards grab the servant and carry him toward the chopping block as he curses Herod aloud.

Still sitting at the breakfast table conversing with Salome, Barabbas hears the Herodian servant's curses. "Who is that cursing aloud?" asks Barabbas.
Salome replies, "This happens every time Antipas holds court. Somebody is displeased with his judgement. You can't please everybody."
"I see," says Barabbas. "May we watch the court proceedings?"
"Yes," answers Salome. "There is an arch in the eastern wall reserved for the guests of Antipas. I shall show you the place."
In the courtyard, the loud curses stop and silence falls as the Herodian servant's head falls to the ground.
"Next," calls Antipas.

The guards bring in a group of four men. A commanding sergeant stands to accuse the four. "Herod Antipas, these four men tried to steal the taxes from your collector in the city of Nain."

Antipas asks the four prisoners, "What are your names?"

The accused four give no answer. They know that if they give their names, Antipas will probably raid their homes and try to find Zealot propaganda.

Herod asks, "Sergeant, do you know their names?"

"No, sir. These men are not from Nain, so the citizens there did not know them. And they will not give their names."

"Well, stubborn Zealots, what do you have to say for yourselves?"

One of the four speaks. "Antipas, you know what's wrong. Your tax collectors are extortioners. They starve the poor. They take more than they are supposed to—"

Wasting no time, Herod interrupts, "Your crime is stealing from the government. You are insurrectionists. Your heads are required."

Barabbas and Salome arrive just in time to see twelve soldiers surround the four Zealots and escort them to the executioner, Hema. The four do not resist the soldiers or say a cross word because they know that the tetrarch grants the convicted one last testimony if they behave properly and calmly. This privilege is one the Jews do not want to forfeit.

Their hands tied with leather straps, all four volunteer to go first. The one closest to the executioner is pushed forward. Barabbas is stunned by what he sees—Tola, the Zealot who saved Barabbas from Exum on the Galilean mountainside. *I have to do something. Tola saved my life!*

As Tola places his neck across the chopping block, Barabbas yells out, "Wait, Herod!" Antipas looks at Barabbas and Salome standing in the eastern arch. Barabbas pleads, "Great Judge Herod Antipas, hear my plea before you execute these men."

Though Herod is angry about the interruption, he grants Barabbas a hearing. Pointing to Barabbas, Herod says, "Come before my judgement seat and we will speak privately."

As Barabbas approaches, Antipas thinks to himself. *I'm tired of this Barabbas. I'm tired of his courtship with Salome. In fact, if Salome were not present, I would not hear him. I want that ledger, but I'm not going to be pushed around. I'm going to be nice, but tomorrow, I'm sending him to Jerusalem to find that ledger. Surely I can be tolerant for one more day.*

Tola and the other three Zealots anxiously watch Barabbas approach Antipas. Salome steps inside the arch and waits while Barabbas converses with Antipas. "What is the meaning of this, Barabbas?" whispers Antipas.

In a low pleading voice, Barabbas implores, "Sir, I beg you not to execute these men. The one with his head at the chopping block is the man who saved me from Exum on the mountain. Please, Herod, I beg you."

"Barabbas, I am hospitable to you, but these proceedings do not concern you—these are governmental affairs. I have certain guidelines to follow. Now listen to me. You get out of this court before—" Antipas does not finish because he wants to appear friendly to Barabbas until the ledger is found.

Unwilling to give up, Barabbas importunes Antipas again. "Please, Antipas, put them in prison, but don't kill them."

Antipas wrinkles his forehead and gives stern words. "Barabbas, I have given my judgement, and that I cannot break. Once I have given my word—it is law. These men have stolen from the government and me. They will surely lose their heads. Now get out, or I'll have you taken out. I'll not hear another word from you. One more word from you and I shall have the guards take you out. Now go!"

Realizing that he cannot save Tola and the others, Barabbas faces something harder than dying—watching friends die. He turns and walks back toward the eastern arch. He lowers his chin as he walks past Tola and whispers, "I'm sorry. There's nothing I can do." Heartbroken, Barabbas' eyes cloud with tears. He takes Salome by the hand and exits. *There is nothing I can do. There are so many soldiers. Even if I pulled my sword—even if I killed a couple of the soldiers, Tola and his men would still die, and so would I. What would that accomplish? Here I am, helpless. My friends and comrades are dying. God, help them.*

Barabbas stops just outside the courtyard wall and leans against it. Salome holds him close to console him. Barabbas hears Antipas ask the convicted, "Do you have anything to say before you die?"

Placing his neck across the chopping block again, Tola begins the recitative rhythm of the Shema. "Hear, O Israel:" The other three Zealots join in harmony, "The Lord our God is one Lord: And thou shalt love the Lord thy God with all thine heart:" Hearing the first part of the Shema takes on a new meaning as Barabbas listens. *I must love God with all my heart!* Together the four recite, "and with all my soul" *All my soul!* Barabbas concentrates on the words. Even though Barabbas has heard and recited this passage of scripture thousands of times, he receives a new revelation. *I must love God more than anything or anyone—anyone!* With the four reciting the last phrase, Barabbas joins with them, "and with all thy might."

With that final word, Hema, the executioner, positions himself so that he will be able to make a clean lop at Antipas' cue. Barabbas receives a final revelation of the Shema. *With all my might! I will grab Salome by the hair and throw her past the guards at the eastern arch, pulling my Sword of Sacrifice, and pressing it to her throat.*

Salome screams as her face hits the cobblestone floor of

the judgement court. Barabbas' heart races as he realizes what he has done. He shouts to Antipas, "Stop! Stop, or I'll kill her—so help me God!" Salome weeps as Barabbas continues to speak. "Herod, I love her, but I'll kill her! The guards do not move. Hema, with his ax raised, waits for the signal from Antipas.

"Barabbas, let her go!" orders Antipas.

"I will kill her if you execute these men," swears Barabbas.

Using deceit in an attempt to get Barabbas to free her, Antipas says, "Barabbas, you can't hurt her. You love her."

"I cannot love her more than my God—with all my heart, soul and might." With those words, Barabbas twists his hand in Salome's hair for a firmer hold and pulls her neck tighter against his sword. Salome shrieks with pain. Antipas hesitates, so Barabbas presses his knee sharply on Salome's chest and pulls her hair again to position her neck for immediate, expedient decapitation. "Antipas, the choice for me is simple: I choose my God. For you, the choice is either for these four men or Salome. I've made my choice! What's yours?"

Watching the trickle of blood run down Salome's face as Barabbas puts more pressure on the bruised and pitiful, wheezing Salome, Herod concedes, "What do you want?"

"Five horses—your Arabian horses, your best—brought to this courtyard."

Antipas curses and yells to the soldiers, "Get them!" A group of soldiers runs quickly toward the stables. Antipas orders the soldiers to free the four Zealots.

Freed from their straps, Tola and the other three gather around Barabbas. Barabbas shouts to Antipas, "These four men are to leave alone with a horse each. After enough time for them to flee, I shall release Salome as I leave. Do you understand?" Antipas remains silent as the archers mount the walls. Then Barabbas says, "If an arrow hits me, I shall cut her throat, I swear to you before my God. If I do not see these four men reach the yonder mountaintop and give me a signal that they are not followed, I shall sacrifice Salome and myself. Do you understand? Answer or she dies!"

Antipas agrees, "It shall be as you say."

The soldiers arrive with five thoroughbred Arabian horses. Barabbas orders, "Give these men each a sword." Antipas gives the command with a nod. The four mount the horses and race out of Tiberias.

As the soldiers wait and watch with Antipas, Barabbas sees Tola and the Zealots wave a white flag from the specified mountaintop. Gripping and pulling Salome up from the floor by her hair, he holds the sword firmly against her throat and says, "One soldier leading my horse, Salome, and I shall walk to the edge of the city, is that clear?"

"No deal, Barabbas," answers Antipas, trying to get an advantage.

Not falling for any deal short of what he wants, Barabbas says, "Antipas, I shall have it my way or Salome and I die. I'll not let you have the pleasure of torturing me. I have gotten four men released. You've gotten nothing out of the deal. If you weren't going to let Salome live, you wouldn't have let the Zealots go. So don't play games with me. You know I will cut her throat. Now I'm walking out of here with Salome under my sword and a soldier leading my horse. When I see the road is clear, I shall mount and leave. I mean what I say, so don't test me."

With those promissory words, Barabbas walks forward with Salome. The soldiers step back out of the way. Antipas follows at a distance. Walking through the city with an Arabian horse, a sergeant leads and commands people to stand out of the way as the fugitive and hostage follow.

At the edge of the city, Barabbas stops and orders the followers to stop. "The sergeant, Salome, and I shall walk up the yonder hill alone. I swear that if nobody follows me beyond this point, I shall give Salome over to the sergeant and I shall ride away alone. Salome shall not be harmed. But if—"

Antipas interrupts: "Barabbas, I shall make you wish you were never born! We shall wait here as you say, but one day you will beg me to kill you, I promise!"

As Barabbas, Salome, and the sergeant walk halfway up the hill, Antipas orders a group of his soldiers to get ready to ride after Barabbas.

Realizing that Barabbas has done what was necessary to save his fellow Zealots and not believing he would have really killed her, Salome says, "Barabbas, take me with you. I love you."

"That is impossible. The soldiers of Antipas would catch us easily."

"Barabbas, I had rather die with you than live without you. But if you can't take me with you, one day I will come to you. Then we can spend our lives together."

"Salome, that is impossible. I'm a fugitive."

"Somehow, someway, we must be together."

"Listen . . . Salome, you're not an Orthodox Jew. Until I heard those four Zealots quote the Shema—'The Lord our God is one Lord'—I didn't realize how much that verse of Judaistic faith meant to me. Seeing those men of like faith in distress brought out the real, undeniable me. I now realize that for me to be happy, I must fulfill my calling. I am an Orthodox Jew and always shall be."

"What about me, Barabbas?"

"You're a good woman."

"I mean what about you and me?"

"Salome, forget us. As a fugitive, I am no good to a woman. Even if I weren't a fugitive, I am an Orthodox Judaist."

"What you're saying is that because of my birth, you can't marry me? Barabbas, I can't help that I was born to pagans!" Salome breaks down and weeps.

Reaching the hilltop, the sergeant lays the reins of the horse across its neck. Barabbas tells the sergeant to stand back. As he does, Barabbas shoves Salome to him and says, "I'm sorry, Salome. That is just the way it is—I was born an Orthodox Jew."

The sergeant holds Salome as she laments vehemently. Barabbas races the thoroughbred out of sight.

Nineteen days after his mother's death, Pasah stays in close company with Rosh, the gentle shepherd. The best graze and the milk of the ewes have made Pasah the model of a healthy lamb.

Rosh grows attached to the orphaned lamb. They spend the day together and snuggle during the night. The shepherd talks to Pasah as if he is his best friend. Giving his guttural call to gain the attention of his sheep, Rosh speaks, "Pasah, we must graze our way back home. We must be in Bethel on the ninth of Nisan. On the tenth day, my family and I must choose our best lamb to sacrifice for the Passover celebrated on the fourteenth day of Nisan. We must graze toward home so Keseb, the best-looking lamb, can be selected." Giving his call again, Rosh moves toward Bethel.

In the ruins of Ai, the poison-fanged viper knows the time is near.

7
Zealots & Shepherds

Two miles from Sychar, Jair and his group of Zealots meet with Barabbas and Tola. The Zealots are thankful that Barabbas rescued Tola and the others while Barabbas is thankful that Antipas' soldiers were easier to lose than the legionnaires of Pilate. During the celebration, Barabbas cannot help but remember the grief Salome displayed as he left her three days ago. He prays that somehow she will find solace.

The bastion of friendly Zealots offering smiles, congratulations, and handshakes cannot stop the war waged between Barabbas' heart and mind on the battlefield of love. The shepherd of his mind tells him that God must come first and that he must not entangle himself with the pagan Salome. The giant of his heart tells him of his love for the girl. The goliath champion of Barabbas' heart boasts as he adroitly pulls his sword of humanistic reason, while the seemingly feeble shepherd of his mind tactically loads his sling with the rock of religious belief. Releasing the centrifugal, revolving rock, the shepherd of the mind watches the hurled stone strike the forehead of the giant soldier. Then the shepherd of his mind runs to the fallen warrior and takes the sword of humanistic reason to claim victory. With the goliath man of the heart down, the prevailing shepherd of the mind makes a grave mistake—he neglects to decapitate the giant of the heart. The goliath warrior will rise again . . . wiser and stronger, for Barabbas loves the girl.

Jair speaks to gain the attention of the Zealots. "My fellow companions who are zealous for Jewish autonomy, we give thanks to Barabbas." The Zealots applaud and cheer. Raising his hand for silence, Jair addresses the concerns of the Jews. "I am not sure what we can do about the tax collectors' extortion. The Romans protect the publicans closely now, so I advise you not to bother them. The Roman government takes our money—and speaking of money, our funds are gone. We need money to operate. Without money, the Zealots cannot survive. Without Zealots, our traditions and beliefs cannot survive. We have to save our heritage."

A man near the front raises his hand and asks, "Well, how are we going to raise money? We're over taxed. With the extra charge of the collectors, there is no money left."

Another blurts, "One option is to rob Pilate as he transports the tax revenue from Jerusalem to Caesarea." The entire group chuckles at that suggestion.

"I don't consider suicide a reasonable choice for raising money," replies Jair. The Zealots sigh in agreement, and Barabbas raises his hand.

"Yes . . . Barabbas?" asks Jair.

"Robbing the tax revenue from Pilate might be a good idea."

Not wanting to embarrass the young Barabbas, the group refrains from laughing at his idea. Showing respect for the champion and newest member of the Zealots, Jair explains the security of the tax transport. "Pilate surrounds himself with his praetorian bodyguards. He transports the tax revenue from Jerusalem with an escort of at least a thousand infantry troops, fifty cavalrymen, and a dozen chariots. So . . . see?" Then, Jair says apologetically, "That's what we're up against."

"May I speak?" asks Barabbas.

"Go ahead," replies Jair.

Barabbas stands to take the floor and speaks. "Herod levies ridiculous taxes on the Galileans such as the poll tax, the land tax, and a tax on fishing rights, which he keeps and uses within his province. The revenues that Herod receives are not sent to Rome. However, the inhabitants of the royal provinces of Idumea, Judea, and Samaria have to pay the same types of tax as the Galilean province and more. The royal provinces under the imperial governor Pilate have to pay another despicable tax—a tax that goes to the imperial treasury at Rome. A required tax that causes one to commit treason against God—the temple tax!"

"Amen!" several shout.

"We pay tithe to take care of the Temple. In a sense, the Roman government taxes God and taxes us for believing in God. God gives salvation, but the government charges us for it."

The words of Barabbas arouse the enthusiasm of the Zealots. Some shout their approval. Jair and Tola receive the words with gladness when someone shouts, "You talk like a Zealot!"

Barabbas replies, "I am a fugitive, and that makes me a Zealot. Now listen to what I have to say. I think this missing ledger I told you about proves the misappropriation of the Jewish temple funds. If Caesar knew the tax funds were misused, he would probably remove Pilate."

"What good would that do?" asks one in the crowd. "Caesar would appoint another governor."

"That is true, but the next governor would have more

respect for the Jews and the Temple," affirms Barabbas. "This temple tax is a sin against God—please, hear me out. Caesar does not like uprisings, so if there were an uprising over taxes, then Caesar would investigate. Right now, the Herods and Pilate allow the tax collectors to extort more tax money than is required by the Roman government. The tax collectors pocket the extra money. The Herods and Pilate don't care as long as they get their share. That is why Tola's neck was on the chopping block three days ago. If we could steal the temple tax from Pilate, then Tiberius Caesar would investigate the tax system. I'm not saying that we can . . . but if we could take the temple tax back from Pilate, we would have funds, and Pilate would be under greater scrutiny."

Jair speaks up to defend his position. "We cannot afford the risk of robbing Pilate. This would be suicide for the Zealots. Without Zealots, there is no hope for an independent nation of Israel. We cannot risk losing lives and that is what it would take—a concerted effort of all the Zealots to go against the legionnaires."

"I suppose you're right," Barabbas concedes. "It is too great a risk to put the whole organization in jeopardy. Yes, to rob Pilate of the temple tax is too risky unless . . ."

As Barabbas pauses to think, Jair asks, "Unless what?"

"Unless one man can do it. One man is not a great risk to the Zealot organization."

"Indeed, one man is not a great risk *unless* that someone is *you!*" someone shouts to bring laughter to the crowd.

Barabbas defends his idea: "When the shepherd boy, David, went out to fight Goliath, he didn't respect the size of the giant. When Gideon fought the vast multitude of the Midianites, he did not regard the number of the enemies. When Shadrach, Meshach, and Abednego were thrown into the fiery furnace, they did not estimate the consequences. All these men and more were victorious. And we should not consider the size, number, or consequence of Rome's wrath."

Jair breaks the present silence of the meeting. "With all due respect for the convicting words of Barabbas, we must not be foolish. We must ask ourselves if our plan is practical and in the will of God. Sometimes ideas sound good, but no matter how they sound, we still have to ask if they will work. When Joshua's men went to the city of Ai to fight for the Lord, they were defeated because of the sin in the camp of the Israelites. We must not be foolish. Can one man or our whole organization challenge Pilate and win? I say not at this time. Eventually, with the help of the Lord, we shall overcome."

Realizing that he has challenged the authority of the group and considering that most of these men have children to support, Barabbas apologizes to the fellow Zealots because he sees their predicament. "I'm sorry, Jair and friends. I speak as an inexperienced fool. I know that I have spoken without wisdom. We can't jeopardize the only savior of Israel—the Zealots—at this time. Please forgive me."

After the apology of Barabbas, Jair adjourns the meeting.

Jair and Tola stand near Barabbas as Lud comes forward to hug Barabbas. Lud says, "Barabbas, come and stay at my house."

"Thanks, Lud. I would love to stay with you and Sarai until the Passover."

After a good night's sleep and eating breakfast with Lud and Sarai, Barabbas puts the bridle on his black Arabian stallion and rides south to a wide mound. The slope on the mound is gentle enough for a horse to gallop over except for one protrusion of layered flat rocks that juts out of the valley floor to make a cliff-like shelf. In the afternoon, this shelf of rocks provides shade from the sun and travelers usually stop to rest here. A few trees grow along the mound. Other than the few trees, the mound appears to be safe from ambush.

Barabbas sits and patiently watches the valley floor from

the shade trees. The mirage of heat coming from the ground to the north is broken by a lone rider. Barabbas mounts his horse and pursues the horseback rider.

The equestrian is shocked to see the approaching Barabbas. When the horses meet, the horseman dismounts as Barabbas shouts, "Javan!"

Barabbas and Javan laugh as they embrace each other. The two walk toward the shade of the protruding flat rocks on the valley floor.

In the shade, the two each sit on rocks previously used to form a campfire barrier. Barabbas tells Javan about his escape from the legionnaires and his escapade with Antipas; however, he does not feel strong enough to tell Javan about his love for Salome. Then, in turn, Javan tells Barabbas the good news about Joktan and Mary becoming friends and how Joktan got Logos for Mary.

After sharing their experiences and what they know concerning Barabbas' precarious situation, Barabbas tells Javan what he intends to do.

After hearing Barabbas' intentions, Javan argues with him. "Don't try it," Javan insists. "They'll kill you. You're crazy."

Barabbas speaks in frustration. "I don't have a choice. I'm a fugitive in my own country. What am I supposed to do, rot in this desert? There's a bounty on my head, and all I know to do is fight for freedom, not only for mine but also for all Jewish people. My life is worthless as things are now. The Romans have much to lose, and all I have is my miserable life to gamble with. And I do not act selfishly. I'll save the children of God, or I'll die for them."

Realizing the desperation of his friend, Javan apologizes. "I'm sorry, Barabbas. Is there any way I can help you?"

"I do need a favor or two if they are safe enough for you to accomplish."

"Tell me, Barabbas."

"First of all, I need you to take these two letters to my mother. Next, I need you to bring Logos to me on your next mail ride. I need him to help me get away when I take the temple tax revenue from Pilate. Tell everyone who has contact with Logos that you are thinking about buying a new horse to replace Logos on the mail run. Be sure to inform all the caretakers of the stables. Everyone who has dealings with Logos needs to think you are going to trade him for another horse. If they don't expect that you are going to trade him to some horse trader, someone might suspect you have made contact with me. Our contact is to be kept a secret among you, Mother, and me. Nobody else is to know, all right?"

"Sure, Barabbas. Your mother is going to be excited when I tell her about you. Should I tell her what you are up to?"

"Yes, it's fine. I told her about it in one of the letters. In fact, Mother is going to help me accomplish the task. There are specific instructions for Mother in the letter—instructions on how to help me. So be careful not to lose those letters; it could cause us trouble. I want her to know what I'm doing. I need her to pray for me. I need God's help. God has given me a plan."

"What is your mother going to do?"

"Ask her. You might be able to help her. You need to go now."

"But Barabbas, what's in the other letter? Is it secret material?"

"No, it's the Shema."

"The Shema? Everybody knows the Shema. I don't understand."

"Javan, it's not the words written on the paper which are important. It's the insignia that is important. The Star of David insignia will make the letter look authentic. The Shema is the key to change the course of our nation. It's the key to saving my life."

"This letter does not have the star of David insignia. It

doesn't have any insignia." Willing not to question what Barabbas is doing, Javan concludes, "I don't understand this, but I'll deliver the letters and I'll bring Logos in three days." The two shake hands. Javan mounts his horse and rides toward Jerusalem. Barabbas looks across the valley floor and realizes the dirt on which he stands may hold his blood in a few days. Barabbas makes a mental picture of the valley floor as he mounts his horse and rides back to Lud's house.

On the ninth day of Nisan, Lud, Sarai, and Barabbas arrive at the home of Salah, Lud's brother. Lud explains to Salah that Barabbas is going to celebrate the Passover with their family. Salah extends hospitable words: "I am pleased to have you celebrate the Passover with our family."

Seeking advice, Lud inquires, "Barabbas will disguise himself to enter Jerusalem. I don't want anyone to see him here. So what should we do?"

"Well, Rosh is bringing the flock here today. Barabbas can go to the sheepfold in the ruins of Ai. He could act as a shepherd for a few days, which would keep anyone from asking questions."

"That sounds like a good idea to me—what do you think, Barabbas?" asks Lud.

"That sounds great to me. I like that idea. I appreciate all you are doing for me. When the sheep come, I will go to the ruins of Ai."

Seeing something in the distance, Salah stands up and puts his hand above his brow to see the eastern horizon. Barabbas and Lud stand to see. "There he is—Rosh, my son." The three on the porch watch and listen to the call of the approaching shepherd. Salah calls for his wife, "Beeri! come . . . Rosh is here."

After celebrating and feasting at the return of Rosh, Lud and Barabbas offer to tend the sheep so that Rosh may sleep in his father's house for the night. Rosh is very appreciative, but he explains that he needs to be with his flock until the Passover: "I have kept these sheep for a year—waiting for the Passover. I can't leave them now at the last four days. After the Passover, I shall stay a little while with the family, but I now have to finish my job. I cannot risk losing the Paschal lamb—our sacrifice to God. Besides . . . tomorrow is the selection day of the Paschal lamb according to our tradition."

Barabbas asks, "May I go with you, Rosh?"

"Yes, if you would like . . . You'll have to sleep in the ruins of Ai."

"That's fine with me," replies Barabbas.

"Well, let's go."

"I'll walk out and look at the flock," says Salah.

"I'll go too," says Lud.

As the four men walk out to look at the sheep, Pasah runs to Rosh's side. Salah notices that Pasah looks good enough to be the Paschal lamb, for he is free of all blemishes, more than eight days old, and less than one year old. This observation prompts Salah to ask Rosh a distressing question: "Is this the Paschal lamb?"

"Oh, Father, you must look at the rest of the flock," exclaims Rosh.

Looking at the flock, Salah asks, "You mean to tell me there is a better lamb than this one?"

Rosh does not answer, for he knows the head of the household must select the Paschal lamb. Anxiously waiting, Rosh worries as Salah looks at the flock. *All the favoritism I have given Pasah has made him a model lamb—possibly the endangered Paschal lamb. What shall I do if my father selects Pasah? I can't bear to lose my companion!*

Finally, Salah steps back from Keseb to make a better inspection of the lamb. Pointing to Keseb, Salah proclaims, "This lamb is the only lamb better than the one that stands by you, Son."

Rosh smiles, lifts his eyes toward heaven, and says, "Thank you, Lord." Then Rosh looks to his father and says, "Father, you are the best judge of sheep I have ever known."

Salah replies, "I not only know sheep, but I also know you. So . . . what is so special about the lamb that has your affection?"

"He is an orphan. He goes where I go, sleeps where I sleep, and he comforts me all of the day. He is a friend who sticks closer than a brother. He's the lamb of my life."

Rosh tells the story of how Pasah's straying mother was devoured by the demon of darkness. Then he pauses to look at the reddening horizon and says, "Barabbas, are you ready to go?"

"Of course. I'm ready when you are . . ."

"We need to go. We have only about two hours of light left. I need to get the flock in the sheepfold at Ai."

Barabbas inquires about the sheepfold by remarking that he did not know that there was a sheepfold at Ai.

Rosh answers, "There is not a sheepfold there; however, I use the roofless rooms of the ruin to house my sheep for the night."

"I see."

Lud jokingly says, "See, Barabbas, you are learning to be a shepherd already."

Barabbas laughs at Lud's remark as Salah and Rosh embrace to say goodbye for the night. Then Salah and Lud go to the house as Rosh gives his call. The sheep follow Rosh and Barabbas toward the ruins of Ai.

Crossing over the hills toward Ai, Barabbas and Rosh talk about the life of a shepherd. As they walk within view of the ruins, Barabbas asks a personal question, "Have you ever thought of getting married?"

Rosh answers with a question, "Barabbas, do you think it is strange that I am not married?"

"Well, you are thirty years old."

"If I got married, who would keep the sheep? Would my wife roam from pasture to pasture with me?"

"No, Rosh. I mean why don't you get married and settle down? When will you stop being a shepherd?"

"Never, I think."

"You can't do this forever. You need a life too."

"Barabbas, these sheep are my life. I love them. Each has its own temperament, character, and personality. Each of them is different—some good and some bad. I love them all. I'll not forsake them."

"Rosh, they are mere sheep."

"And quite innocent," adds Rosh. "Unlike humans . . ."

"But you are willing to sacrifice one of them in a few days," argues Barabbas.

"According to the will of God," replies Rosh.

Barabbas doesn't argue with that reply.

Walking toward the ruins, Rosh breaks the silence with a personal question for Barabbas, "Have you ever been in love?"

Barabbas pauses to think for a moment. "Well, yes and no—I mean . . . I'm not sure. Yes, I was. I may still be."

"I know that love is hard to explain, but what do you mean, Barabbas?"

With sorrow in his voice, Barabbas whispers, "I love her, but she is a pagan. So innocent . . ."

"I see," sympathizes Rosh. Noticing the pain overtaking Barabbas, the gentle shepherd quickly changes the subject and directs Barabbas to help him lead the sheep to the fold. Heeding his gathering call, the sheep come in close to Barabbas and Rosh as they move near the sheepfold ruin.

The shadow of dusk falls as Rosh and Barabbas lead the way for Keseb and Pasah with the others close behind. Seeing the sheepfold of safety, Keseb and Pasah move ahead of the gentle shepherd and Barabbas. As the group comes near the pile of rocks beneath the tamarisk tree at the entrance of the sheepfold ruin, the camouflaged, sand-buried horned viper prepares his poison haemotoxins and anti-coagulants for his unsuspecting victims.

Feeling the vibration of the footsteps on him, the serpent pushes his heavily keeled scales against the dust of the earth to throw his broad, spade-shaped horned head into the air. With heat-seeking accuracy, the viper strikes.

Immediately responding, the sheep scatter; Barabbas jumps back with a jolt of adrenaline while the good shepherd leaps on the snake. Trying to stomp it with his heel as the serpent strikes, the faithful shepherd prays vehemently.

The viper lunges sideways to escape beneath the pile of rocks. With the sheep scattered, Barabbas runs to Rosh and asks, "Are you all right?"

"I think so," replies Rosh. Let's check the sheep, Barabbas."

Rosh begins to call the sheep when he suddenly stops and shutters. "I'm . . ." Rosh stops to vomit.

Barabbas runs to Rosh's side. The shepherd lies down as Barabbas finds the fang marks on Rosh's ankle. Barabbas makes a small incision and tries to suck the poison from the wound. Rosh cries out. "Barabbas, it's no use. I feel the fire of the venom around my heart. It's no use. Stop!" Barabbas stops giving aid when Rosh implores again. "Stop! Pray for me. Pray for me!"

Barabbas leaps to his feet and wails, "Oh! Lord God Jehovah, save my friend's life. Please! God, come and touch him personally. Oh! Jehovah, save him . . ."

Barabbas' prayer is interrupted by the sobering, calm words of the gentle shepherd, "Hear, O Israel: The Lord our God is one Lord: And thou shalt love the Lord thy God with all thine heart, and with all thy soul, and with all thy might."

Rosh begins to convulse, so Barabbas runs into the darkness of night to Salah's home.

Receiving the bad news and rushing the two-mile journey to the ruins of Ai, Barabbas, Lud, Sarai, Salah, and Beeri arrive and find Rosh sitting at the gate of the sheepfold. Salah and Beeri run to hug Rosh. Beeri cries out, "Thank God—you're alive!"

"I'm fine, Mother." Rosh looks to Salah and says, "Father, I'm well."

Barabbas looks Rosh in the eye and says, "That's impossible!"

Rosh retorts, "No, a miracle."

Everybody is puzzled, so Rosh begins to explain. "Barabbas, I lost consciousness—"

"I know," Barabbas interrupts.

Rosh continues to tell his story. "While I was dead, a man headed toward Jerusalem came to me and spoke with authority, 'Arise and learn the true meaning of sacrifice.' I immediately gained consciousness and felt no effects of the snake bite."

"Impossible," argues Barabbas. "I saw you. I cut your ankle. You were dying."

"That's what I'm telling you. Look at me. I'm whole. I was dead, and now I'm alive."

Barabbas bends to look at Rosh's ankle. "It's still there—the fang marks and my incision. This is incredible."

"Who was this miracle man?" Salah asks.

"I don't know. All I know is that he is like someone not of this world."

Beeri says, "This sounds like one of those miracles Jesus performs that I have heard about."

"Ridiculous," says Barabbas.

"Jesus?" questions Rosh. "I don't know him. But I would like to see him."

Barabbas captures Rosh's attention by saying, "Maybe Rosh was just dizzy from the excitement of the snake trying to strike the sheep. Maybe the snake didn't have much venom. Maybe—"

"Barabbas, you are wrong. I was dead! And now I'm healed!"

Barabbas realizes that he must believe the story as Rosh tells it. "All right, I admit you looked seriously ill to me. I thought you were going to die."

"I believe . . . I was . . ."

Changing the subject, Barabbas asks, "How did the sheep get in the sheepfold?"

"Believe it or not, the man called the sheep."

"I can't believe this. Those sheep won't come to any other call but yours. They know your voice. And I don't believe you could call them in past the place where the snake struck anyway," argues Barabbas.

"Barabbas, look at the proof. The sheep are in the pen. The sheep came to the miracle man. They seemed to understand him. They knew his voice, and he knew them each by name."

"Incredible!" snorts Barabbas.

Still mystified by the phenomenon of the miracle man, Salah interrupts, "Now . . . what did that man tell you?"

"He said for me to learn the meaning of sacrifice—the true meaning."

"I wonder what he meant," remarks Salah.

"I don't know—I know what he said, but I do not know what he meant," replies Rosh.

"Well, that's enough thinking for one night," says Salah. "Let's sleep on it, and maybe tomorrow, we'll understand. Rosh, you must come to the house for the night."

"I can't, Father. Tomorrow is the tenth—the selection day. You are to choose the Paschal lamb."

"Well, I'm staying out tonight with you," declares Salah.

"And I," affirms Lud.

"So are we," state Beeri and Sarai in unison.

Salah speaks aloud for the whole group. "We shall all

spend the night here at the sheepfold. This can be like old times. In the morning, I shall choose the Paschal lamb."

Ready to get involved with the celebration, Barabbas says, "I'll build a fire."

Early the next morning, Rosh feels something wet against his face. Opening his eyes, he sees Pasah lying beside him licking his face. "Pasah, my friend, I thank God that I am alive for your sake. You're my lamb."

Hearing the conversation, the group rouses one by one. Getting up, Salah announces to the group, "We do not have enough food for everybody to have breakfast here, so if everyone will get up, we shall choose the Paschal lamb and go back to the house." Stopping to clear his throat in an authoritative manner, Salah then adds another announcement. "By the honor and authority invested in me, I hereby commission Rosh with the responsibility to select the best lamb for the Passover sacrifice. Rosh is now thirty years of age, and he has proven his respect for God."

Everyone applauds as Rosh calls his sheep. One by one the sheep come from the sheepfold. Rosh calls the sheep by name as they emerge. When the stream of sheep stops, Rosh says, "Where is Keseb? He's the one I'm looking for."

Walking up to the ruined stone walls of the sheepfold, the group sees a pitiful sight—Keseb—dead—stiff with dried blood upon the fang marks made by Satan's serpent. All eyes turn to see the silent tears rolling down Rosh's face. Only one other lamb is suitable for the Passover.

8

Passing Over the Sacrifice

Multitudes of people come to Jerusalem to celebrate the Passover—a holiday not commemorating God's plague of blood, pestilence, natural disasters, or the terrible plague of death. But on this fourteenth day of Nisan, the Jews celebrate God's deliverance from Egypt and God's salvation for the firstborn of the enslaved Jews who had put the blood of a lamb on their doorposts and lintels.

More than commemorating the Passover by sacrificing a lamb, some believers ponder the unexplainable future and symbolism of the lamb prophesied by Isaiah: "He was oppressed, and he was afflicted, yet he opened not his mouth: he is brought as a lamb to the slaughter, and as a sheep before her shearers is dumb, so he openeth not his mouth." Some believers are even aware that the one brought as a lamb in Isaiah's prophecy is to bear the sins of many and to make intercession for the transgressors. Those people who know the scriptures well do more than celebrate the Passover of the past, but they look to the future—looking for the Lamb of God to come with deliverance from sin.

Standing on the Mount of Olives, on this fourteenth day of Nisan, Barabbas stops, looks, and takes a deep breath with his group before proceeding toward Jerusalem. Dressed like a woman, Barabbas wears a loose-fitting, long-sleeved, dark blue tunic with an ample fringe to conceal his feet, a shawl for an outer garment, and a flowing veil to cover the top of his head, temples, and mouth. Underneath the tunic hangs the Sword of Sacrifice.

Having passed through the garden of Gethsemane and across the Kidron Valley, Barabbas, Salah, and Lud approach from the east. Rosh is not with them, for he must enter the Sheep Gate in the north wall. Shepherds are not allowed in the Temple because the Jews consider them unclean. Passing through the Golden Gate, Barabbas sees Roman legionnaires and a familiar face—that of Antipas' executioner, Hema. Concealing his face as the devout women do upon entering the holy Temple, Barabbas passes through the gate to Solomon's porch without arousing suspicion to Antipas' emissary. *Seeing my enemies from this disguise is effective. But this is detestable to the Lord. Man should not wear a woman's apparel. God, I know that you see the necessity of my sin. This is the only way I can partake of the Passover and keep a watch for my mother's safety. Forgive me, Lord.*

On the north side of Jerusalem, Rosh leads Pasah past the Pool of Bethesda toward the Sheep Gate. He remembers the words of his healer: "Learn the true meaning of sacrifice." Rosh prays. *Father, forgive me for my selfishness, for I love this lamb. God, I can only imagine how Abraham felt as he climbed this mountain, Moriah, to sacrifice his beloved son,*

Isaac. But what did Abraham mean when he said to Isaac, "God will provide himself a lamb for a burnt offering." Himself? God Himself—a lamb? God, I wish that this Paschal lamb somehow could be spared like Isaac.

Reaching the Court of the Gentiles, Salah stops and informs his group, "I must go to the Sheep Gate to receive the lamb of sacrifice from Rosh. You go to the Court of Treasury and wait for me to pass through with our lamb. Afterwards, everyone knows we are to meet at my sister's home in the upper city?"

With a nod, Lud replies, "Yes, we all know where to meet."

After crossing the porch and the Court of the Gentiles, Barabbas passes the Roman soldiers and walks into the Sacred Enclosure. *Well, this enclosure protects me from the Romans, for no Gentiles are allowed here. Now all I have to be wary of are my Jewish brethren, especially the Sadducees. Caiaphas surely doesn't think I would come to the Passover. Furthermore, he is officiating, so I should not have to worry about him. The Romans don't know what I look like. I have it made! My disguise gives me the advantage.*

Barabbas and his group go into the Court of the Treasury and stand across the court from the treasury office. With less than an hour before the sacrifice begins, Barabbas watches from underneath his veil. *Mother doesn't have any idea that I am here. I wish I could find her in this crowd. There are Nicodemus and his family. And there! There goes Mother into the treasury office.*

Waiting at the Sheep Gate, the turbaned Rosh, wearing his fleeced robe of sheepskin, sees his father coming for the lamb. With one hand on his staff and the other caressing Pasah, Rosh tries to be strong. He takes his eyes off the lamb and looks to his approaching father. A lump, then a knot, begins to choke the sacrificing shepherd. Tears roll down his cheeks. "Oh, Pasah," Rosh cries, "if I could, I would take your place."

Aware of Rosh's personal sacrifice, the compassionate Salah approaches his son with a solution. "Son, please choose another."

Not wanting to extend the pain, Rosh pleads, "Father, take the lamb and go, for I must go back to my sheep."

"Rosh, this *is* one of your sheep. This is your most beloved. This Passover is the Passover for the lamb of your choice."

"No—not my will, but God's. He deserves our best. He requires our best. He's the only true, wise God—worthy is He. With all my heart, with all my soul, and with all my might . . ." Rosh implores a command, "Take the lamb and go, Father, please!"

Salah takes the lamb and grieves for his resolute son as he trudges up Mount Moriah toward the Temple.

Inwardly, Rosh cries. *Father, why have you forsaken me?* Shocked by the silent sound of his own words, Rosh cries again. *I do not mean that. I only wish that the lamb could be saved. I know that my family is suffering also.* Conviction falls on his broken heart, so with a contrite spirit he begins to weep and pray. "Oh, God, I am so sorry for my attitude. I know you are looking out for me even when I don't understand. Almighty God, create in me a clean heart and renew a right spirit within me. Hide thy face from my sins, and blot out all mine iniquities. Purge me with hyssop, and I shall be clean: Wash me, and I shall be whiter than snow. Open my lips and my mouth to show forth thy praise. Restore unto me the joy of thy salvation. Make me to hear joy and gladness." With those words, the peace of God, which passeth all understanding, comforts the shepherd's heart and mind.

Inside the treasury office, Mary talks with Seth, the treasurer. "Seth, this is my first time to visit the treasury office since Rabba died."

"You are welcome to visit any time, Mary."

"Well, I haven't really felt good about the idea until now."

"I understand."

"Do I hear the bleating of the sheep?"

"Yes, it must be time . . . I must lock the office and go watch."

"Seth, will you let me sit in here alone for a few minutes?"

Seth sees Mary's floating eyes. "Certainly. I understand. I'll step out to look for the first division of sacrifice. When they enter the court, I shall come for you so you can watch."

"Thank you, Seth. I appreciate the hospitality."

When the door closes behind Seth, Mary jumps up and runs to the bronze insignia box. She opens it and removes the Star of David insignia. Then she pulls the Shema letter from her tunic and lays it on the desk. The bleating of the sheep becomes loud as Mary tilts the desk candle over the seal of the folded letter parchment. Mary knows that Seth is about to come for her. *I must not be caught.* Pressing the insignia into the hot wax, she affixes the seal. Hearing the latch on the door move, Mary, without time to clean the insignia, quickly places it into the box. As Mary closes the lid, she looks up to see Seth staring at her. *Oh, my God, what am I going to do?* Nervously, Mary says, "I am just looking around—browsing. I'm sorry."

With an eye of curious suspicion Seth says, "You must leave now."

Seeing Mary safely exit the treasury office, Barabbas turns his attention to the first division of men who have come into the court with their paschal lambs. Silence falls on the crowd as the doors to the Court of Israel open. The thirty-man division marches forward to leave the Court of Treasury.

After the representatives and their paschal lambs come to

stand within the Court of Priests, the huge gates close behind them. Along the court up to the altar, the priests stand in two rows. Each priest in one row holds a silver bowl while the priests in the other row hold a gold one. Besides the priests with bowls are some with silver trumpets. As if someone had given them a cue, the priests put their trumpets to their mouths. With this action, Salah and the others pull their daggers and wait. In unison the priests blast their trumpets three times as Salah and the representatives slay their lambs. The blast of trumpets, which covers the bloody bleating, stops. The priests catch the blood of the slain paschal lambs in the gold bowls as the congregation sings a praise hymn—the Hallel.

The priests hand the bowls filled with blood to their colleague in exchange for an empty silver one. Receiving the bowls of blood, the priests pass them to Caiaphas at the altar. Caiaphas jerks each bowl of blood sharply at the base of the altar, spilling the blood in one jet. Orderly and impressively while continuing to sing the Hallel, the priests and the representatives perform their sacrificial duties in unison.

After hearing the blast of the trumpets, the solaced Rosh talks with God. "God, I give my beloved lamb without remorse, for You are worthy of my best. I know the true meaning of sacrifice, but is the sacrifice true? How can a lamb redeem a man from sin? Only a man can be a true sacrifice for man, and only You, God, can redeem us. God and man? We need a God man. Now that You have revealed the true meaning of sacrifice, God, reveal the true sacrifice to me."

After the pouring of blood on the altar, Salah and the others hang their slain lambs on the hooks along the court. They strip the skin off the lambs and remove the entrails to clean them. Then they take the fat, put it in a dish, salt it and place it on the fire of the altar for a burnt offering. With the completion of the burnt offering, Salah and his division leave as another division enters the court.

At sundown, only the lights of the trimmed lamps and the fragrance of the burnt incense remain in the Temple. The people have left to roast their lambs for the Passover meal. Meeting in groups not less than twenty and no more than thirty, the people prepare the bitter herbs, unleavened bread, and roasted lamb. Even Pilate and Herod Antipas, each having received a roasted lamb from Caiaphas, eat it for dinner.

At Mary's house, Nicodemus, Lazarus, and Joktan prepare to remove the paschal lamb from the oven. Nicodemus says, "Joktan, if you will watch to make sure that we do not touch the oven walls with the meat, Lazarus and I will remove it."

"Certainly, but why is it so important that the meat does not touch the walls?"

"Because the meat is considered to be defiled if it does, and we'll have to cut that part away. The paschal lamb must be handled according to God's instructions."

"Are there any other details I should know about?"

"Well, another rule is that this lamb of God's must not have a bone broken."

"Well, I have much to learn about being an Orthodox Jew. I don't fully understand this holiday."

"We'll teach you," replies Lazarus.

Lifting and pulling, Nicodemus and Lazarus remove the lamb suspended on the spit of pomegranate, which pierces from mouth to vent. Together, they place the roasted lamb on a platter.

Mary comes to look at the roast. "Mmm—that looks good. I have the bitter herbs and the unleavened bread prepared."

Joktan looks at Mary with excitement. "This experience is new to me, but it feels so natural. It's—fulfilling, somehow. It seems that I've always partaken, yet it is new." Pausing to chuckle at himself, Joktan asks, "I sound confused, don't I?"

"Not at all, I understand. After all, you *are* Jewish." Mary quickly responds while reaching for Joktan's hand. "Your ancestors were a part of the first Passover. And now you have come home to your national heritage and belief."

"And it feels good," proclaims Joktan.

In the upper city of Jerusalem, Sapphira, Salah's sister, sits with her group to dine. Following tradition along with the others, she places her left elbow on the table, rests her head in her left hand, and makes sure she has free movement of her right hand to feed herself. With Ananias, Sapphira's husband, seated at one end, and Salah and Barabbas in the middle, all bow their heads. Salah gives the first benediction of the Passover meal.

At Herod's palace, Antipas dines with Herodias, Salome, and Mizzah. The servants carve the roasted lamb that Caiaphas gave to Antipas. Drinking his second cup of wine, Antipas asks, "Do you know the significance of the Passover, Salome?"

"No, sir," she softly replies.

Herodias defensively requests, "Antipas, please leave her alone. She doesn't feel well."

"Herodias, I do not mean any harm. I simply wonder if Barabbas explained the Passover to her. If not, I am going to."

Denying the Jewish history she was taught as a child, Herodias says, "Darling, Salome knows that this Passover is a superstition of sort. God did not kill the firstborn of the Egyptians and save the Jews who had a lamb's blood on their doors. That's just a fable."

Antipas questions Herodias. "Think so? I believe it happened."

Not wanting to arouse the anger of Antipas, Herodias replies, "What do I know? You're the historian and theologian. Tell me."

Satisfied with her reply, Antipas eagerly begins to tell the Egyptian story of the Passover while Herodias silently analyzes the situation. *You're superstitious, Antipas. You're even afraid of John the Baptist! You have imprisoned him, but you won't put him to death even though he shames us by announcing that you and I live in adultery. Nobody else could get away with that. You give reverence to him only because of your religious fears. I'll not let this religious man ruin my position. When I get to the Machaerus castle in Perea, I'll see to it John is put to death. May the gods curse John with my plan!*

As Antipas continues to tell the Egyptian story, Mizzah notices that a Herodian servant enters the room. Mizzah's break in attentiveness prompts Antipas to ask, "What is it, Mizzah?"

"I'm sorry, my lord, but our spy has arrived."

Antipas looks to the Herodian servant near the door. "Come to the table, my servant. Tell us the news."

The servant comes forth and bows before Antipas. "My lord, I watched Barabbas' mother as I was ordered. The only people I saw go to Mary's house for the Passover were some of her family and friends. Barabbas did not show. I kept an eye on her all day except when she went into the treasury office. The treasurer left her alone in the treasury for a while."

"Hmm . . . that's strange. The treasurer is not supposed to let an unauthorized person have unattended access to the office."

"She was in there for only a few minutes, my lord. Barabbas was not there. I'm sure of that."

"Barabbas is too smart. He may not go to his mother. But I know—I would bet my life on it—that he is in Jerusalem. I know him, and I shall get him. Servant, go and watch again."

Seeing Salome bow her head in shame, Herodias asks,

"May Salome and I be excused?"

"Fine. I know that Salome languishes. This is no place for her or you. Mizzah and I have matters to discuss."

Each day for the next seven days, Caiaphas sacrifices two bulls, a ram, seven lambs of the first year for a burnt offering, a goat for a sin offering along with the usual daily sacrifices. On the fifteenth of Nisan, the day for cutting of the first barley sheaf, the disguised Barabbas gathers with the multitude of people going to a field outside Jerusalem just before sunset. The multitude watches as three men, each with a sickle and a basket in hand, gather some barley to offer in the Temple on the sixteenth. As the three men cite their traditions, Barabbas slips away from the group and heads for Lud's stable at Sychar. On the eighteenth, Javan delivers Logos and the sealed letter that Mary affixed with the Star of David to Barabbas. On the twenty-first, the Zealots meet near Sychar, and Barabbas tells of his plan. Tola and Jair agree to help him.

On the twenty-second day of Nisan, Pilate leads fifteen hundred infantry troops, one hundred cavalrymen, thirty-two chariots, and one wagon carrying the tax collected at the Passover celebration. Sixteen chariots are near Pilate to protect him. Each of these chariots has three men: a charioteer who controls the reins, a shield-bearer, and one of the praetorian guard with a bow, sword, and javelin. Behind Pilate are the cavalrymen with the wagon carrying the taxes collected at the Temple. Following the wagon are fifteen hundred infantry troops and behind them sixteen more chariots.

Thirty miles north of Jerusalem, Pilate and his troops, traveling in the second day of their journey toward Caesarea, enter the valley just south of Sychar. With the sun to their backs, Jair, Tola, and a few men watch Pilate's entourage. As Pilate nears the protrusion of flat layered rocks in the valley floor, Jair says, "All right, men, here is where it all begins. Pray."

As Pilate comes within fifty yards of the small shadow cast by the layered rocks, Barabbas approaches from the south riding an old, sweaty horse, appearing to come from Jerusalem. One of the charioteers turns around to stop Barabbas. "I have a message for Pilate," exclaims Barabbas.

The sergeant charioteer replies, "Give it to me."

"But—"

"Give it here," interrupts the sergeant, reaching to snatch it from Barabbas. "Wait here!"

Seeing the Star of David on the seal of the letter, the sergeant drives his chariot to the front of the formation toward Pilate. Barabbas stands still as Pilate and the troops keep moving forward. Barabbas worries. *Stop, Pilate. You are supposed to stop when I come on the scene. Stop! You are passing the shadow of the rocks. God, what am I going to do? I'm not close enough to the shade, and he has passed it. I just knew that he would stop to rest in the shade. Now he's traveled too far.*

After giving the letter to Pilate, the sergeant rides back to Barabbas as Pilate keeps riding forward. Upon returning, the sergeant asks Barabbas, "Boy, can you read the letter?"

"Yes, sir."

The sergeant climbs out of his chariot to search Barabbas for weapons. He pulls off Barabbas' turban. "You're bald—your head is shaved."

"I have taken a vow. I am fasting according to my religion."

While being frisked, Barabbas grabs his head as if he were faint. "What's wrong, boy?"

"I'm fasting, and I have been riding since the middle of the night to catch up to you. I'm worn."

The sergeant frisks Barabbas' body again for weapons. "You religious people will learn better, I guess. You Jews are peculiar—and dumb. Now mount your horse and follow me."

The sergeant climbs on his chariot and races toward Pilate, who is still leading the regiment forward. Barabbas follows with anxiety. *Pilate was supposed to stop at the shade of the protruding rocks. He has now gone too far. Well, my plan that God gave me calls for the shade so that is where I'm stopping.*

Passing by on the west side of the marching troops, Barabbas rides into the shade of the rocks and falls off his horse. The sergeant charioteer turns around to see Barabbas on the ground. "You stupid Jew!" the sergeant curses in a mumble, and rides forward to tell Pilate. "Sir, the boy suffers from fasting and exhaustion."

"Fasting?"

"Yes, sir. He's a religious Jew. Do you want me to drag him up here to you?"

"Whoa! Halt!" Pilate commands the charioteers. "At this rate, this could take all day. I'll go back." The whole regiment stops. Pilate rides back with his sixteen-chariot escort.

As Pilate rides back, Barabbas pretends to struggle to his feet. Stepping left and right, Barabbas, feigning dizziness, leans forward. Pretending to give attention to Pilate as he rides near, Barabbas straightens and then falls forward on the coals of an abandoned campfire.

"Give the boy some water," commands Pilate, holding the letter. The sergeant takes water and gives it to Barabbas. Barabbas sits on the edge of the campfire site with his feet resting in the ash.

Appearing to gain some strength from the water, Barabbas whispers, "I'm sorry, sir." With his voice gaining volume, Barabbas points to the letter in Pilate's hand and says, "Caiaphas gave me that letter for you last night. I rode all night to get here. He said the message is urgent."

Pilate cautiously hands the letter to Barabbas. The sixteen

praetorian guards gather around with Pilate. "The letter is written in Aramaic—the temple language. Can you read it?"

"Yes, sir. That's the reason Caiaphas sent me. He did not want some of your men to read it first."

"Why?"

"Security, sir."

Pilate and the praetorian guards look puzzled. "What do you mean?"

"Sir, before I answer that, Caiaphas told me to tell you that one of your praetorian guards is out to assassinate you."

Pilate instantly draws his sword defensively and moves to face his guards as one of the praetorian guards speaks forth to the governor. "Sir, this is a trick!"

Cautiously analyzing the situation, Pilate reasons with the guard. "Persis, I agree that this may very well be a trick. But I have a sealed letter from the hand of Caiaphas and a defenseless young man before me. Caiaphas has nothing to gain and this young man is harmless. Therefore, this is my plan: Men, if you are named as an assassin in the letter, this does not mean I think you are guilty. All sixteen of you have proven yourselves to be faithful, worthy praetorian guards. This is only an allegation, not an indictment. But for Rome's sake and mine, if you are named, lay your weapons down until I can investigate the allegations. If you don't relinquish your weapons, the others are to slay you. Understand?"

"But, sir," Persis persists, "I must warn you . . ."

"Enough!" shouts Pilate. "Frisk the boy yourself, Persis!"

Persis frisks and searches every inch of Barabbas. Finding nothing on him, Persis concedes, "Nothing—the boy is clean."

With Persis standing behind him and Pilate facing him, Barabbas straightens his clothes and looks at the letter. Feigning weakness, he sits on a rock with his sandals on the ashes and coals.

"Read it!" shouts Pilate, impatiently, flashing his sword

in Barabbas' face.

The guards step back out of the way of the threatening sword as Barabbas pretends to read the fake Aramaic letter from Caiaphas: "Governor Pontius Pilate, after your departure from Jerusalem, a young man came to me. Wanting me to perform a sacrifice for him so he would be clean of his sins, the young man confessed he was part of a group who planned to assassinate you. In his confession, he disclosed that one of your praetorian guards has plotted to murder you. I know this seems ridiculous, but I felt I needed to report this to you. His name—" Barabbas pauses to recall the name of the praetorian guard that Pilate conversed with earlier.

"Read it, boy!" Pilate threatens Barabbas with the point of his sword. "I'm tired of waiting."

Barabbas declares the name, "Persis."

Motionless and stunned, Persis pronounces, "That's a lie!" Frustrated, he starts to defend himself when he notices that the other fifteen praetorian guards are watching his weapons. Realizing he must put his weapons down, he carefully lays his sword on the ground. "I can't believe this is happening!"

Believing that Persis is probably innocent, Pilate steps past Barabbas to console the troubled, defenseless praetorian guard. All eyes are on Persis and the governor when Barabbas, back to back with Pilate, reaches into the coals and retrieves the hidden Sword of Sacrifice. Jumping up, turning, grabbing Pilate by the back of his collar, poking the sharp point to the governor's back, Barabbas shouts, "You're dead if you move! I'll push this sword through you, Pilate! Now tell your men to back away!"

Stunned, the vulnerable Pilate does not move or utter a word. The praetorian guards look helpless as Barabbas facetiously taunts them, "Go ahead . . . do something stupid and Pontius Pilate dies!"

"Back off, men! Do as he says!"

The whole army gives their attention to Barabbas. The closest archers in the infantry hold their bows ready to shoot. "Go on and shoot an arrow, but your aim had better be accurate and deadly!"

"No, don't shoot!" orders Pilate. "Put those arrows down!"

"Now, governor, send one man to drive the wagon carrying the temple taxes over the hill to the west. Tell him to leave it there and walk back."

"You can't get away with it!"

"If I didn't think I could, I wouldn't be here, would I? And if I didn't have enough courage to kill you, I wouldn't be here, would I? Now give the order." Barabbas convinces Pilate by firmly pressing the Sword of Sacrifice to Pilate's back.

"I don't believe you will do it."

"I killed Anak and Marcus," whispers Barabbas.

"Barabbas!" exclaims Pilate, stricken with fear.

"At the count of two, you shall die. One—"

"Apelles, drive the wagon over the hill and leave it!"

"Yes, sir," replies Apelles.

Watching Apelles leave, Pilate tries to reason with Barabbas. "Barabbas, you wouldn't kill me, would you?"

"You wouldn't kill my father, would you?" Barabbas replies.

"I didn't, Barabbas! I was as shocked as you were about Rabba's death."

"I heard Marcus say he paid Anak to murder my father."

"Yes, but Caiaphas and I didn't know Marcus was going to do that."

"Marcus did it to protect you."

"But if I had been in Jerusalem at the time, I would have handled the matter another way. I would not have murdered Rabba."

"So what was Marcus trying to cover up for you?"

Unable to answer the question without incriminating

himself, Pilate pauses, trying to think of an acceptable answer because he knows better than to tell the truth.

Barabbas refreshes Pilate's memory. "I overheard my father and Caiaphas discussing the fact that you withdrew money from someone else's account."

"Oh, that's common knowledge. I was reprimanded by Tiberius Caesar himself for taking the temple tax to build an aqueduct to Jerusalem. The Jews caused me enough grief by approaching Tiberius with their complaint."

"You must be doing it again."

"Oh, no. I learned my lesson. If I were caught doing that again, I would be banished. Tiberius will not tolerate my using the temple taxes again. I'm not that stupid."

"Pilate, you are doing something wrong. If not, my father would not have been murdered. The missing ledger supplies all the answers."

"A ledger?" Pilate pretends not to know what Barabbas is talking about.

"Don't play games with me. I know you have been looking for it. When I find it, Caesar will hear about it, I promise."

Having driven the wagon over the hill, Apelles returns, walking toward Pilate and Barabbas as Jair, Tola, and the other Zealots fill their bags with the money. Realizing this is a crucial time for persuading Barabbas not to kill him, Pilate says, "If you kill me, my troops will kill you. Then Tiberius will be angry with the Jews. Killing a Roman soldier is a serious crime, but if you murder his appointed governor, Caesar will retaliate with the death of many Jews. And the next governor will be instructed to be cruel and merciless toward the Jews."

"True, but if I can prove you are unjust toward the Jews, Caesar will be kind. And I'm going to find that ledger to clear my name, convict you, and gain a new governor who will favor the Jews by order of Tiberius."

With Jair, Tola, and the other Zealots racing away with the money, Barabbas tells the governor what he wants. "Bring me a horse."

Pilate orders Apelles to get Barabbas a horse. Receiving the order, Apelles does not bring one of the best horses. Barabbas doesn't argue. "Now, Pilate, tell your men to march out of this valley and over the next hill."

Realizing that Barabbas is not going to kill him because that would cause many deaths to the Jews, Pilate gives the order. "Men, march out of the valley and over the next hill." Pilate knows the horse Barabbas was given is substandard. He also knows that once the men march over the hill out of sight, they will quickly circle to capture Barabbas.

Having whipped the horses pulling the tax money wagon so that they stampede westward, Jair, Tola, and the Zealots take the money and ride northward toward Sychar. As the first soldiers go over the hill traveling northward, Barabbas pushes Pilate forward, jumps on his horse and rides southward. Then some legionnaires go west hoping to retrieve the tax wagon, some circle eastward hoping to surround Barabbas, and some who see Barabbas fleeing southward turn in their tracks to chase after him. With everybody racing west, east, or south, the Zealots safely travel north.

With less than a half-mile lead, on a tired and slowing horse, Barabbas races southward on the road toward Jerusalem. Possessing positive expectations, Pilate's legionnaires gain ground on Barabbas. With the distance growing shorter between the legionnaires, Barabbas rides west off the main road to a thicket of shrubs. He quickly dismounts and grabs the reins on Logos that is tied there.

Seeing Barabbas stop in the thicket, the legionnaires delight themselves until they see Barabbas emerge on the rested, spirited, black and white stallion. Leaving the cavalrymen behind, Barabbas and Logos disappear on the western horizon.

Barabbas & The Sword of Sacrifice

After sunset, Barabbas stops riding west and makes a looping trail to the east back to the road that Pilate is traveling. After creating a diversion in the road, Barabbas crosses and continues to go east. Then he loops northward to Sychar. Early the next morning with the first light of day, Pilate goes southward on the road back toward Jerusalem and finds his soldiers hunting Barabbas' trail. With all the trails people made going to and from the Jerusalem Passover, Pilate knows Barabbas could be in any direction. With no clue on which way Barabbas exited the heavily-hoofed road, Pilate takes the troops back to Jerusalem.

After the evening sacrifice, Caiaphas goes to meet Pilate. In the darkness of his unlit tribunal, Pilate makes it very clear that he must see their contact. "Caiaphas, I am tired of meeting with you. I want to meet with our contact. If he does not come, I will go see him."

"Governor, I talked with him today. He knew you would want to see him. He has agreed to meet us here tonight."

"Does he know that this Barabbas has robbed me? Or I should say that he has robbed us?"

"Yes. Your soldiers told us how it happened. All of Jerusalem knows about the robbery."

"I thought our contact had his dagger on the heart of the situation, Caiaphas."

"He'll be here any minute. I'm sure he has an explanation and a plan."

"Oh, yes, Caiaphas, what about that Star of David seal on the letter?"

"That Pharisee, Seth, didn't watch over the treasury the way that he should. He'll pay for that. Tomorrow I am meeting with the Sanhedrin. I'm calling for his resignation."

"Well, get a trusted Sadducee for a treasurer this time."

"I can't. Since I, a Sadducee, hold the position of high priest, the treasurer must be a Pharisee. Besides, we need a

Pharisee to be treasurer. If the Pharisees ever found out what we are doing, then they would have to take half the blame."

"What do you mean by 'if the Pharisees ever found out'? This plan is supposed to be foolproof."

"It is, Governor. I just mean that things look less suspicious if the Pharisees account for the money. If anyone is to take the blame, then the Pharisees can't say anything."

A dark and sinister silhouette appears. Pilate and Caiaphas look at their contact of darkness approaching the tribunal. "Greetings," says their contact.

"Good evening," returns Pilate in salutation.

"Governor Pontius Pilate, I apologize for the trouble and inconvenience which have come your way. I take the blame for it all. I guarantee that from now on you will not have any more trouble. I am about to rectify the problem."

"How?" questions Pilate in a tone of disbelief.

"Barabbas' mother is falling in love with me. She cooks for me, and I reward her for her kindness. With your help, Pilate, I gave Barabbas' black and white stallion to her. She trusts me. She even thinks that she has converted me to Judaism and that she is guiding me to her God. She is good bait. I have not yet pushed her for information; therefore, I didn't know about the robbery. But the time has come for me to make my move. After I catch Barabbas and get those ledgers, I have a plan to ruin her."

"Well, Joktan, what should I do?" asks Pilate.

"Just keep a bounty on Barabbas' head. I will do the rest. If Barabbas contacts Mary, I will know. If Barabbas gets the temple ledger and Sadoc's ledger, he will need someone to deliver them to Caesar. I'm going to volunteer to do that. After all, I do have shipping service to Rome, and I do have family with access to Caesar. Once I get my hands on those ledgers, I will destroy them. And I will tell you where to find Barabbas. I will set him up for a fatal fall."

"I can't wait," says Pilate.

"In the meantime, let's keep our plan at work. Money is power. Pilate, I am going to make you a powerful man as we all get wealthy."

"That sounds good," agrees Caiaphas.

Three days after the robbery of Pilate, Mizzah and six riders leave Jerusalem and travel east to ford the Jordan River at Jericho. Crossing the river and entering Perea, a region under Herod Antipas' jurisdiction, Mizzah and his men travel south toward Machaerus—the Black Fortress. They pass through the narrow, steep-walled gorge, then cross a narrow deep valley, about a mile wide, leading upward to a town on the shoulder of the Machaerus hill, surrounded by walls and fortified by towers.

Passing through the city gates, Mizzah and his men view the impregnable fort ahead, which is made of massive walls and flanked by towers 280 feet tall. They see storehouses and arsenals containing many kinds of weapons, but they do not see the sinister dungeon that incarcerates John the Baptist down in the hot darkness. Climbing near the peak of the conical hill, Mizzah and his men have a view from the highest point on the west of Machaerus. On the north, south and east, valleys too deep to be filled for siege purposes protect the fort.

From this pinnacle fortress atop the dungeon of darkness, Mizzah and his men descend 150 yards to the west. They reach Herod's magnificent palace resting on an oblong flat plateau. Arriving at the mountain palace and fortress, nearly four thousand feet above the Dead Sea, Mizzah enters to give Antipas the latest information about Barabbas.

Escorted through the torch-lit hall to the banquet room, Mizzah and his men stop and bow before Herod Antipas. Herod greets Mizzah: "Mizzah, I am looking to find the best room to have my birthday celebration. I think this room will hold all of my guests, don't you?"

"Yes, sir."

"Mizzah, you have brought good news, have you not?"

"How did you know?"

"Analytical sensitivity, I suppose. So . . . tell me the news."

"Well, my lord, when you left Jerusalem to come here, Pilate left Jerusalem headed for Caesarea. Traveling on the Way of Shur just short of Sychar, Barabbas robbed Pilate of the temple tax money. My informant told me that Barabbas was carrying a letter sealed with the Star of David, the seal of the Temple.

"You're joking," laughs Antipas.

"No, sir."

"How did you find this out?"

"After Pilate was robbed, he returned to Jerusalem and ordered the tax collectors to exact more money from the Jews. The legionnaires and the praetorian traveling with Pilate witnessed the incident. Now everybody in Jerusalem knows about it. Barabbas has become a hero to the Jews; however, Pilate proclaimed Barabbas to be a criminal guilty of insurrection and murder. Pilate is sending men all over Judea and Samaria from the Jordan River to the Great Sea to post 'wanted' signs. He has a description of Barabbas and a hefty reward posted all about Jerusalem. Barabbas may find difficulty hiding with a bald head, for he was shaven when he robbed Pilate."

"Go on. Tell me more."

"Pilate and Caiaphas had a closed meeting. Then the Sanhedrin had a meeting in which Seth, the treasurer, was removed from his job."

"Aha!" exclaims Antipas. "Remember when your spy told us about Mary being alone in the treasury office at the Passover?"

"Yes, I remember."

"I told you something was not right. Mary sealed that

letter and Seth's demise in the treasury office." Antipas pauses and concentrates intently for a moment and then listens as Mizzah tells more.

"I also found out that Barabbas escaped on his black and white stallion; therefore—"

"Therefore, someone is assisting Barabbas!" interrupts Antipas.

"Yes. His name is Javan, Barabbas' friend who is delivering messages and invoices to Joppa and Caesarea."

"If—" Antipas interrupts himself to think for a minute "if you and I surmise that Mary and this messenger boy, Javan, have helped Barabbas, then Pilate surely knows about their actions."

"But," Mizzah poses a question, "if Pilate knows, then why doesn't he arrest Mary and Javan?"

"That's simple. Mary and Javan are the keys to finding Barabbas. I guarantee they are being watched very closely, day and night. Pilate is not unskilled in matters like this. He is ignorant of the Jews and their traditions, but he knows espionage. Pilate is not going to disturb his bait."

"Well, that makes perfect sense. But explain one thing to me."

"Yes?"

"Why does Pilate seek advice from Caiaphas?"

"Well, Mizzah, that started when Tiberius appointed Pilate to be governor of Judea. Not knowing very much about the religious compunctions and traditions of the Jews, Pilate moved his headquarters from Caesarea to Jerusalem. Moving a multitude of troops bearing the image of the emperor on their standards offended the Jews. In return, the Jews were ready to fight to their death to have the troops removed. Pilate slaughtered many Jews at this time. Then in his palace on Mount Zion, Pilate hung golden shields inscribed with the names of Roman deities. And finally, Pilate offended the Jews by taking the revenue of the Temple for the building of an aqueduct."

"So how does Caiaphas get involved?"

"I'm getting to that. A group of Jews went to Rome to plead their case before Tiberius. Wanting peace, Tiberius ordered the removal of the offending shields and cessation of misappropriation of the temple revenue. With that order, Pilate became afraid of the influential Jews. Pilate could not understand why Tiberius defended the Jews. Pilate recognized that he needed help in dealing with them, so he went to Caiaphas for advice. Shortly after that, Pilate and his troops went back to rule from Caesarea. He keeps a smaller group of legionnaires at Jerusalem now. The only time that Pilate comes to Jerusalem is on holy days and then *only* to keep peace. Pilate is governor over the region, and Caiaphas is his advisor. Caiaphas' advice keeps Pilate in the favor of Tiberius."

"So when Pilate is away, Caiaphas advises Villus as he rules over Jerusalem," concludes Mizzah.

"Exactly," replies Antipas, pushing his fingers through his hair, concentrating. "Now, you said that Barabbas has shaved his head?"

"Yes, sir."

"And he is riding his black and white stallion."

"Yes, sir."

"And he is carrying that Sword of Sacrifice."

"Yes, sir."

"It looks as if Barabbas will have no place to hide. He must flee. And I think that I know where to find that weasel."

"You do?"

"No. I don't think I know. I am sure I know."

"Where, my lord?"

"Think, Mizzah. With a recognizable horse, sword, and head, Barabbas has to run. He will not go far because he needs to be as close as he can to Jerusalem without jeopardizing himself. He can't stay in the regions of Samaria,

Judea, and Idumea because of the Roman soldiers and the bounty hunters. He can't go to the regions Galilee and Perea because I am looking to arrest him. There is only one place to go."

"Where, my lord?"

"Decapolis."

"Yes, that makes sense." Mizzah pauses, then questions, "But Decapolis is so vast: it contains ten free Roman cities. We'll never find him there."

"Yes, we will. Barabbas is in or near Aenon or Salim."

"Why do you think that, my lord?"

"Because they are on the west side of the Jordan. They are out of Pilate's and my jurisdiction, yet they are still in the proximity."

"So is Scythopolis, my lord."

"But Barabbas is known in Scythopolis. He escaped from Exum and the legionnaires by making himself, his horse, and sword known there."

"Oh, yes."

"Aenon and Salim are small and out of the way. Wouldn't that be something to catch Barabbas there—in the same place where John the Baptist once baptized?"

"Yes, sir. Speaking of John Baptist, where is he?"

"In the dungeon."

"Which one?"

"The deepest and darkest . . . ten months of that hellhole have not changed his mind—yet!" says Antipas with disgust.

"What are you going to do with him?"

"I'm not sure."

"Execute him for defamation?"

"No. I haven't decided." Changing the subject, Antipas says, "I believe that Barabbas will flee because his fame has made him easy to spot. His head, his horse, and his sword will make him run—right into my trap."

"Do you think Pilate knows how to find Barabbas?"

"No. Pilate evidently thinks that the bounty will catch him. The governor will probably tighten security at the river fords, but Barabbas is too smart for that."

"Well, what are you going to do?"

"I am going to send two men to catch him."

"That's all—two? Barabbas just fooled Pilate and several hundred troops and you are going to catch him with two men."

"That's all it will take. Omar will set the snare. Hema, my executioner, will secure the prey. If I send more than two, Barabbas will see the trap. Furthermore, these two men are to capture Barabbas outside my jurisdiction. I can't officially send troops into Decapolis. But I can secretly send Omar and Hema to the stable at Aenon and Salim. They will pay the owner to help them. After Barabbas is caught, they can slip out of Decapolis without notice."

"How will they get back to Machaerus with him? You said that Pilate would surely tighten security at the river fords."

"They can go north into my Galilee region and ford the river on the way of Shur, and then they can come back to Machaerus on the king's highway. That way they will not have to cross at either of the fords at Jericho, where the legionnaires control the river."

"That sounds good if you're right. Aenon and Salim, you say?"

"Well, Mizzah, here's what you must do: Go back to Jerusalem and gather any new information, but in seven days come back here for my birthday celebration. I'm giving a great banquet for my lords, military authorities, and the chief men of Galilee . . ."

At Sychar, Lud climbs Mount Gerizim to tell Barabbas about the Roman soldiers who came to town. "Barabbas, you are not safe here. A band of soldiers came and posted a reward for you. They gave a description of you, Logos, and your sword. Traveling with the legionnaires are bands of bounty hunters. They are in Sychar asking the people questions, right now as we speak. It is just a matter of time before someone sees you or betrays us for the money."

"Thanks, Lud. I'll go to Jericho. I must be ready to cross the Jordan if the legionnaires come too close."

"If you do go there, remember Obal is a Zealot."

"Who?" asks Barabbas.

"Obal, the stable owner from Jericho, the tall old man you met at our last meeting."

"The skinny old man with a missing tooth?"

"Yes, he's the one."

"I'll remember that."

"Be careful. May God be with you."

9
John Baptist—
Dance of Death

Hope is born in the hearts of Jews across the land of Israel. They look for the hand of the Lord to deliver them from Roman rule. Against the impossible circumstances, dedicated Judaists encourage themselves by remembering God's deliverance. They are well aware that the greater the challenge, the more God is able to perform His miracles. Without doubt, they believe that the acts of Barabbas are miracles from God. With anticipation, the Jews look for a deliverer.

The Jews consider the use of insignificant men to perform the miracles of God: Joseph, a prisoner of Egypt, saved the Israelites during a famine; Moses, a baby who once floated helplessly in an ark made of bulrushes and pitch, delivered the Israelites from Egyptian bondage; Joshua and Caleb, two encouraging voices among multitudes of dissenters, led the children of Israel into their homeland; Ehud, a left-handed man, defeated the Moabites; Jephthah, the son of a harlot, defeated the Ammonites; and Josiah, an eight-year-old, turned the idolatrous Israelites to serve God. With these facts in their minds, the Jews give attention to Barabbas, who robbed the governor and his army guarding the temple tax money that belonged to God.

On the outskirts of Jericho, near the ford in the river, Barabbas watches the legionnaires scrutinize and question all the people crossing. *My shaved head, Logos, and the Sword of Sacrifice endanger me. I must rid myself of Logos and my sword, or I'll be seen. With Logos fatigued, I can't get away. There is only one thing left to do. God, please give me favor with the stable owner, Obal.*

After sunset, Barabbas, wearing his turban lowly on his forehead, walks into Jericho to the stable. Lifting his turban, Barabbas reveals himself to Obal.

Obal quietly leads Barabbas to the back of the stable. "Boy, you are in danger here. The legionnaires are guarding both fords here. There is a bounty on your head and a description of you on every post."

"I know. I need to get rid of Logos, and I need to borrow a pony from you. Can you keep Logos hidden until I return?'

"Gladly."

Barabbas leaves the hidden Logos in the care of the stable owner. At a landmark outside of Jericho, he rids himself of the Sword of Sacrifice. Then he camps for the night and rides toward Aenon the next morning.

Suffering through a night of uneasiness, Mary prays as the first light of dawn reflects off the towering Jerusalem Temple. "Most Holy God of all power, presence, and knowledge, please help my son. I don't know where he is. I don't even know if he is safe, but something tells me he faces great danger. Lord, let your love keep Barabbas. Help him, and comfort my apprehensive mind. Give me consolation of faith, I pray."

After making her request of God, an answer of optimism enters her mind: "God, I know that neither tribulation, nor distress, nor persecution, nor famine, nor nakedness, nor peril, nor sword shall be able to separate us from your love." Gaining confidence by her positive confession, she goes on to say, "Moreover, neither death, nor life, nor principalities, nor powers, nor things present, nor things to come, nor height, nor depth, nor any other creature shall be able to separate us from the love of God."

Realizing that she had the wrong perspective about her restless night, she knows that God has prompted her to intercede for her son—heaven and hell battle for his soul. With a different view about the ominous night of anxiety, Mary refuses to be pessimistic. She thinks on the goodness of God. "Lord, I thank you and praise you, for I have not heard that Barabbas is dead or imprisoned. I have hope, and I have confidence in your providence. I trust you with my son no matter what happens. God, you have given me health, wealth, and friends. Moreover, I appreciate my close friend, Joktan. He is very considerate, compassionate, and dear to my heart. He is a blessing to me. Thank you, God." With peace of mind, Mary seals her trust in a final word, "Amen!"

"Knock, knock!" shouts a familiar voice at the door.

It's Joktan. He always seems to be here when I need him. Mary opens the door. "Good morning, Joktan, my dear. What are you doing here this early in the morning?"

"Actually, I come by here every time I get the chance. Sometimes you are asleep, but this morning I saw that you were up. I just enjoy keeping an eye on you. You make my day brighter."

"You are too kind. I appreciate your consideration."

"The pleasure is mine. I hope you don't mind my keeping an eye on you."

"Oh, I am flattered by it."

Suddenly, Joktan's countenance falls as though he is stricken with conviction. With a serious expression on his face and a wrinkled forehead, Joktan pauses and then expresses his anxiety. "Mary, I can't lie to you. I am here early because of my concern for you."

"What do you mean?"

"I have noticed more eyes and ears around your neighborhood."

"What are you talking about?"

"You are under surveillance. Yesterday, I noticed two men about the street watching you and your house. So I came back before daylight to see what I could see. I was right. I witnessed a change of shift in the surveillance. There was a man at the apartment up the street watching your house through the night. Then before dawn, another came and took his place."

"The Romans are watching me to see if Barabbas is making contact with me, aren't they?"

"No, Mary, these are not Romans. They are Idumeans, Herodians. I followed the spy who was relieved from his surveillance duty. He went to Herod Antipas' palace in the Upper City. What does Antipas want with Barabbas?"

With fear in her voice, Mary whispers, "I don't know."

Slightly frustrated with Mary's answer, Joktan presses for an answer. "Mary, I have never done anything to hurt you. I have tried to bless you and help you as you have helped me find God. But for some reason, I cannot help feeling that you are keeping something from me. There are too many pieces of the puzzle missing. For instance, why was Seth relieved of his job as treasurer? Mary, I have a great deal of influence with the Romans and Jews, and I even have sales contact with Antipas. My family's commercial trading reaches Tiberius Caesar in Rome. But I can't help you or Barabbas if you can't tell me everything that you know. Let me help. I want to spend the rest of my life with you. I love you."

With sorrow in her voice, Mary cries, "You are more righteous than I! It's my fault. I'm sorry I have not shared. I have had contact with Barabbas."

"When?" whispers Joktan.

"Do you remember hearing about the sealed letter with which Barabbas tricked Pilate?"

"Yes, but—"

"I am the one who went to the Temple and got it," Mary interrupts with her confession.

"But how did you get it to Barabbas?"

"Javan carried it to him."

"Where is Barabbas now?"

"I don't know. I haven't heard from him since the Passover. I know that Pilate and the Romans are trying to capture him. But I have no idea what Antipas wants with him. Now that Barabbas is running from Antipas, there is nowhere left to run."

"You're right. Let's pray for him."

"I have been," affirms Mary. "Joktan, swear to me that you will keep my secret. Nobody knows except for you, Javan, and me."

"I swear. I'm sorry you had to bear this burden alone. Mary, I love you. Thank you for being honest with me. Now that we have no secrets between us, maybe we can help Barabbas. Let's think."

Seven days since his last visit, Mizzah returns to Machaerus to celebrate Antipas' birthday party. Arriving at midday, Mizzah gives Antipas the Jerusalem news. "My lord, the Jews in Jerusalem are excited, even euphoric about the exploits of Barabbas. Some even think of him as their possible messiah.

When they heard that the legionnaires were looking to arrest the shaven Barabbas, many young men shaved their heads to make it harder for the legionnaires to spot Barabbas."

"A messiah, eh?"

"Yes, sir."

"You mean to tell me I have a messiah in my prison?"

"What do you mean, sir?"

Taking pride in himself, Antipas replies, "Omar and Hema captured Barabbas at Aenon—just as I predicted they would. They brought him in this morning."

"How?"

"Just as I told them to do. They simply waited for him to arrive at the Aenon stable."

"Did Barabbas find the ledger?"

"I don't know. He isn't talking to me because he probably has figured that when I get the ledger, I'm going to kill him."

"Have you tried to persuade him?"

"Oh, yes, he's stubborn and in very bad shape right now, I might add. He appears to have some broken ribs and two broken fingers. I have learned from previous interrogations that once a headstrong suspect is beaten, he needs time to think about the situation. I'll talk to him later, and he *will* talk to me. Hema will not stand for a prisoner to be intractable. Besides, I think Hema hates the boy."

"Why?"

"Pride and jealousy. Barabbas rescued those four Zealots from Hema's ax. Furthermore, Hema seems to have an eye for Salome. If I'm not careful, Barabbas will never see the ax—Hema will beat him to death. Right now, I am not concerned. The ledger would be a great asset, but I'll not put up with any misbehavior from Barabbas."

"Well, what about Hema's feelings for Salome?"

"He is not in her class. She is a princess—a gorgeous princess."

"Very true," Mizzah agrees. "Are she and Herodias here?

I brought them the things that they wanted from Jerusalem."

"No and yes. They have gone up to the fortress dungeon."

"Dungeon!" exclaims Mizzah in surprise. "What for, may I ask?"

"Well, Mizzah, I almost hate to tell you, for I'm afraid that you will not understand."

"My lord, I am most curious if you will have patience with me."

"Well, they actually aren't going into the prison. I have arranged for Salome and Herodias to talk with Barabbas in the meeting room. Barabbas will be chained. But I am letting the two women talk with him privately."

"Why?"

"First of all, sometimes women can get more information out of a man than a man with a whip or an executioner with an ax."

"I see."

"No . . . that's not all. Herodias is teaching Salome the facts of life. Salome believes that Barabbas loves her. Herodias is going to prove that Barabbas doesn't." Antipas stops explaining to say, "Women's talk—I don't know how Herodias ever talked me into this. Maybe I will gain something from it, though."

At the upper level of the fortress dungeon, Herodias and Salome stop outside Barabbas' cell. Inside, Barabbas is chained to the wall. Hema stops to inform the first lady and the princess, "Don't get too close to the prisoner. If you need my assistance, I'll go in with you."

"No, Hema," replies Herodias. "You may go now. This meeting is private. Do you understand?"

"Yes, my queen."

Hema leaves the hallway as Herodias instructs Salome. "You may talk to him alone, but you must remember the rules. You must not let Antipas know I let you go in alone.

This boy is a Jew. He has never loved you; he only used you as a hostage."

"Mother, you're wrong. You'll see."

"No, sweetheart. You'll see what men are like, and when you do, you'll listen to me. So go in and find out, for he is secure. I will go down the hall so that you two can talk privately." After her final remarks, Herodias walks away.

Salome watches her mother walk to the end of the hall to wait on a bench. Taking a deep breath, Salome opens the door and is stricken with the horror of the bruised and swollen appearance of her love. "Oh, Barabbas," she cries as she runs to hug him.

As Salome cries on Barabbas' chest, Herodias pulls off her sandals and quietly walks to the door to eavesdrop on her daughter. Salome weeps for Barabbas.

"You must leave, Salome. You must not weep for me."

"Oh, Barabbas, my darling, I love you!"

"No! You mustn't, Salome."

"Why do you say such, my love?"

"Look at me," says Barabbas as Salome continues to hug him. "Let go and look at me!" shouts Barabbas.

Startled by the shout, Salome backs away with tears streaming down her face and asks, "What's wrong?"

"Look at me, Salome. Are you insane? Look at me! I'm a prisoner . . . and you're a princess."

"That doesn't matter. I love you, Barabbas. I love you!"

"I'm beaten and broken. There's no hope for me."

"Yes, there is—there's a way. I can talk to Herod. If I can't have you, then Antipas and my mother can't have me."

"Don't talk nonsense, Salome. You are so naïve. You believe too much too easily. What are you going to do—go to Antipas and suggest that he let me go? It's foolish to even think such. Antipas knows I will always be a Jew. He is not going to free me. I'm a dead man, and you know it."

"What about us, Barabbas?"

"No future. There is nothing you or I can do. The best thing you can do is to leave and forget about me."

"But what about us?" cries Salome again.

Barabbas pauses to think as Salome waits for an answer. *Salome is so naive. She'll never understand my love for her. If I tell her I love her, she will only hurt more; therefore, the best thing for me to do is lie to her. I must make her believe I don't love her.* Realizing Salome's hurt and the futility of a future relationship with her, Barabbas explains the situation. "Salome, I'm a prisoner, and you are a princess—"

"I don't care," she interrupts.

"I'm an orthodox Jew, and you're not."

"I love you, Barabbas," pleads Salome.

Realizing he is not being stern enough to attain his objective, Barabbas says, "Salome, if Antipas freed me today and a decision had to be made between having you and my beliefs, I would choose my God."

"I will follow you as you follow your God!"

"But Salome, this is not real. Antipas is going to kill me or let me die in this prison." Barabbas pauses to think of how to explain his reasoning. "Look, let me explain it this way: I would have killed you in Tiberias to save those Zealots. And even if I were free today, I would still hold you hostage for my country, my cause, and my God."

"Barabbas, I would gladly be a sacrifice for you. I love you. Don't you understand?"

Disgusted with himself and Salome, Barabbas painfully screams, "Curse you, Salome, you're a pagan! You would sell your soul for me! You are guilty of what I'm talking about. You don't love God—you love me. I can't love someone who doesn't love my God more than me."

"Barabbas, I can love your God more than I love you."

"Liar! You would say anything to get what you want. That's what is wrong with you—you get everything you desire just like your mother. Well, I'm not a treasure. If I could love someone, she would be a Jew—a devout orthodox Jew."

Salome screams, "I love you! I love you!"

"No, get it through your head. I've tried to be nice, but hear me and understand what I'm telling you. You are nothing to me! You are and always have been nothing but a convenience. I don't love you—I hate you! I hate you and all of you damned pagans!"

Swinging her hand with all her strength, Salome slaps Barabbas' face. "You'll suffer for what you have done, Barabbas."

"And you'll burn in hell for your pagan beliefs! You can't make me suffer. You can kill me, and I'll be better off."

Responding with anger after Barabbas' cruel remarks, Salome spits at him. "Cursed be your god! Aphrodite, goddess of love, will take revenge on you! And you will suffer all right—I have something to tell you that will make you wish you were dead."

"Tell it and get out!"

Hearing the conversation through the door, the pleased, Herodias prepares to run to take her place on the bench down the hall. Listening for Salome's last remark, Herodias hears Salome say, "Barabbas, when I leave, you'll never see me again, but before I go I want to share my misery—."

"Share and go away."

"You'll never see the baby I'm carrying for you. I'm pregnant with your offspring!"

Barabbas and the eavesdropping Herodias are shocked by Salome's disclosure. "For the past few weeks, the torture of knowing I am pregnant has been greater than what you have endured. Now it's your turn to suffer. Mother was right: You don't love me, and you never will. You think too highly of your God. Let your God comfort you now . . . if he can. Now I'm looking forward to . . ."

As Herodias runs down the hall to take her seat, Salome

marches to the door and Barabbas cries for her. "Salome, please don't leave! Please don't leave! Let's talk. I didn't mean what I said!" Barabbas begs, "Salome, please come back!"

As Barabbas' pleas echo in the hall, Salome storms past Herodias. Herodias follows her daughter, but stops long enough to speak to Hema. "Put Barabbas in the deepest cell of the dungeon and make him uncomfortable."

"My pleasure, my queen. I will make him wish he were dead."

"He already does. But while he is waiting, make him live in hell."

Entering Salome's bedroom, Herodias tries to console her weeping daughter. "Salome, I'm very sorry. I had no idea."

"Mother, you listened, didn't you?"

"No, my darling. You were talking very loudly. It echoed in the hall. The god of fate let me hear. I'm your mother. I'm sorry about your grief, but I needed to know. I can help you."

"You were right—Barabbas doesn't love me. He tried to lie to me after I told him I was pregnant. Oh, Mother . . ." Salome cries on her mother's shoulder. "Oh, Mother, what am I going to do? I'm ruined. Nobody will have me when people find out I am pregnant. I have been disgraced!"

"Wait a moment, Salome. I think I have a way to change the situation. You will not be disgraced. If you listen to me and do as I say, you will be honored and become a most powerful woman."

"How?"

"Come with me. Let's have some wine and plan your future. You're a woman now. You must learn the ways of a woman and trust the goddess of love. Aphrodite will take care of you."

"I will serve Aphrodite if she can save me."

"She can, my darling. She has already given me the plan.

You are favored by the goddess of love. Come, and I'll show you."

Deep down in the lowest part of the dungeon, Hema pushes the beaten Barabbas to the floor. As he slowly stands to his feet, Hema puts the handle of the lit torch in the holder mounted on the wall. Then he opens the cell and shoves Barabbas inside. Shutting the cell door behind the prisoner, Hema leaves the light in the holder in the hall.

"Welcome, young man," greets a middle-aged man of medium stature. "My name is Eon. Let me help make you comfortable. You seem to have some broken ribs."

"Yes, they're broken, but it is these fingers that bother me."

Eon examines Barabbas' fingers. "These two are broken. They need to be set."

"Can you do it?"

"Yes. But it will be very painful."

"It has to be done. Help me, please."

He feels Eon firmly grasp one of his swollen fingers and pull. Trying to push aside the thought of pain, Barabbas recites the Shema in his mind. Barabbas groans aloud with pain. Nearly passing out, he protests as Eon finishes setting the first finger. "Let's wait to set the other one. I can't take it."

"I'm sorry," Eon apologizes. "I know that was painful. However, there is something you should be aware of."

Nursing his finger, Barabbas asks, "What?"

"The torch that Hema left will go out soon. I need the light to see how to set your other finger."

"The guards don't keep it lit?"

"Not down here. We get a lit torch once a day—when they bring food. The rest of the time we are in utter darkness, so look around while you can. Now, what about that other finger?"

"Do it. I'll endure the pain."

Barabbas screams the Shema as Eon sets the finger.

Barabbas rests and gains some color in his face. Then he opens his eyes to take advantage of the light from the burning torch.

Seeing that his cell is secure, Barabbas looks into the cell across from his and sees a curious sight—a man wearing raiment made of camel's hair belted with a leather girdle. The wild-looking man is slim—the ascetic, fasting kind—rugged and rawboned. Barabbas turns and asks, "Eon, who is that?"

Eon replies, "Who are you?"

"I'm sorry . . . my name is Barabbas."

Pointing to the camel-hair-clad man in the other cell, Eon announces, "That's John the Baptist."

"I've heard of him. He's the one who told Herod that it is not lawful for him to have his brother's wife. It's she, Herodias, who hates John because she was taught truth as a child—being the descendant of Simeon, a former high priest."

"I perceive that you know her personally. Do you think it is conviction that makes her hate John the Baptist?"

"Conviction? No!" replies Barabbas. "She is so wrapped up in her pagan gods that I think God has let her believe a lie for her damnation."

"You are probably right. Every time Antipas and Herodias come to talk to John, Herodias gets so frustrated that she swears she will have his head."

"Why would they want to talk to him?" asks Barabbas.

"To see if he has changed his mind about exploiting their adultery. Herod wants John to condone their marriage or at least not say anything about their adultery. It is obvious that Herod doesn't want to execute John. I think Herod is afraid the people who reverence John will rebel. Furthermore, he likes to please the Jews, and most of them feel that John is a holy man. Besides, Herod wants to be their king."

Staring at the prostrate John, Barabbas asks, "What's he doing?"

"Praying."

"Has he always looked like that—the beard and scraggly clothes, I mean? It looks as though mildew is growing on him. Mildew is all over his clothes."

"He has been down here for ten months. Prisoners don't get clothes unless someone brings them. The jailor has allowed only two of John's disciples to visit him."

Seeing the disgusted, inquisitive look on Barabbas' face, Eon explains the conditions of the prison. "The heat in the upper cells keeps the prisoners dry, but down here in this pit of the earth's coolness and dampness, we hang between hot and cold. Notice that the humidity makes you hot but everything you touch is cool. It's like heat within and cold without. It's miserable here—like a cold sweat. Can you imagine what it must be like to have been incarcerated here for the past ten months? However, John never complains. Well, almost never."

"What do you mean by almost never?"

"I suppose I shouldn't say that John complains about the prison. I should say that I think he wasn't sure of his calling."

"What do you mean?"

"Well, you know that John has preached that Jesus of Nazareth is the Messiah and Lord?"

"Yes."

"John sent two of his disciples to ask Jesus a peculiar question: 'Art thou he that should come? or look we for another?' I couldn't understand why John asked such a question—especially when he had been so sure of Jesus prior to his imprisonment." Shedding his puzzled expression, Eon answers himself. "This prison, this presence of darkness, has a way of piercing one's mind."

Being curious about Jesus' reply, Barabbas asks, "Did his disciples ever return with a reply from Jesus?"

"Yes, they came back and told John about the miracles Jesus performed. Jesus told the two disciples to tell John that the blind receive their sight, the lame walk, the lepers are cleansed, the deaf hear, the dead are raised up, and the poor have the gospel preached to them."

"Is that all the disciples reported?"

"No, there was one other thing I did not understand. The disciples reported that Jesus said, 'Blessed is he, whosoever shall not be offended in me.'"

"That is a strange saying, Eon. I'll have to think about that."

The torch goes out. Omnipresent, dour darkness smothers the flame of sight as dew-like dampness drips, wrapping its blanket of slime around the prisoners. Demons seem to creep out of the walls like slithering vipers, ready to strike with their venom of claustrophobic discouragement.

Down the western slope, one hundred fifty yards away from the fortress dungeon, Herod Antipas' guests gather to drink wine and to enjoy the sunset entertainment—the jester. Herod's fool brings laughter to the lords, military commanders, and influential Galileans who have come to celebrate Antipas' birthday.

As darkness falls on the castle palace, the servants light the torches, lamps, and candles to lighten the lively banquet and party. Music and shouts echo across the mountainside, reach up to the mighty fortress, and ring down into the damp darkness of the dungeon where Barabbas listens with his fellow prisoners. Hearing the merriment and the orgy of revelry, Barabbas worries about Salome and cries silently as fear and pain chill him to the marrow.

After hours of entertainment, the party reaches its crescendo. Antipas has nothing greater to offer his satiated, intoxicated guests. Even at its climax, the celebration seems to require more—a finale. Realizing it is time to implement her deceitful plan, Herodias whispers to Antipas, "I know this may be improper for a princess, but your daughter wishes to dance for you."

Surprised that Salome wants to do anything for him, Antipas asks, "For me?"

"Yes, you, my darling. The heartbreak of Barabbas has brought her to her senses. She now knows the power of love and the love of power. May she dance for you and the others?"

Excited at the prospect of viewing the young maiden performing the sensual stimulus of body language, Antipas eagerly answers, "Yes." Then Antipas orders his herald to quiet the party. The herald takes a mallet and strikes the giant cymbal. The guests, not expecting more entertainment, seat themselves quietly to see and hear what Herod wants.

The musicians begin to play softly as the doe-eyed Salome stands in the middle of the open floor before Antipas. Covered by a shroud of sheer red material, her five-foot-six, maturely shaped, body enthralls the spectators. The sharp manicure of her nails, the shine on her soft olive skin, the blackness of her coal-colored hair, the deep Mediterranean-red color of her lips, the effervescent sparkle in her eye, and the seductively tantalizing, alluring curvature of her sensual pose bewitch the guests.

The volume of the music increases, and Salome begins to move and sway with the rhythm of the music. The musicians begin to play music of a faster tempo and an Egyptian beat. The body movements become more appetizing and aphrodisiacal and Herod becomes more enchanted.

Herodias whispers in Antipas' ear, "I told you . . . she dances for you."

Herod listens but never takes his eyes off Salome. "For me?"

"For you," affirms Herodias. "Salome is mine, and what is mine is yours. I give her to you in secret. The guests may watch, but only you can taste her fruit. She dances to invite you. She is a new woman. She wants to be close to you. Will you accept her? She waits to lie at your beckoning. She wants to know if you accept her greatest gift—her body. She gives her body to you—will you give her something to show your acceptance?"

"What does she want?" asks Antipas as he watches Salome, his niece, his stepdaughter.

With the determination and vengefulness of Jezebel, Herodias whispers, "I don't know. Why don't you ask her? The only thing I know is that she wants to please you."

"I *shall* ask her what she wants."

Satisfied, Herodias rises and says, "I shall go and prepare the bedroom for you and my darling. I will let your giving consummate the acceptance between you two in my absence."

"As you wish, my queen," replies Herod. "When Salome finishes dancing, I shall offer her the gift of her choice," says Antipas to Herodias as she leaves the banquet hall.

Tortured by the cheers and applause coming from the palace, Barabbas declares to the others. "It sounds as if Herod and his friends are having a wonderful time."

"Don't remind us," requests someone from the darkness.

"A wonderful time is not always quite so wonderful."

"What do you mean?" asks Eon.

Barabbas talks louder to drown the cheers of the palace guests watching the dancing princess. "When Belshazzar was king of Babylon, he made a great feast for a thousand of his lords. Looking for greater heights of pleasure, Belshazzar commanded his servants to bring the golden and silver vessels, which his father Nebuchadnezzar had taken out of the Temple of Jerusalem. Belshazzar, the kings, princes, his wives, and his concubines drank wine from these vessels."

"In the same hour, came forth fingers of a man's hand and wrote over against the candlestick upon the plaster of the wall of the king's palace: ME-NE, ME-NE, TE-KEL, U-PHAR-SIN.

"Seeing the strange handwriting on the wall, Belshazzar turned pale, and was so frightened that his knees smote one against another. He called his wise men, astrologers, and soothsayers to interpret the writing, but no one could interpret it. Then the queen told Belshazzar about the Hebrew named Daniel whom God gave interpretations.

"Wasting no time at this wonderful party, Belshazzar called for Daniel. Seeing the handwriting on the wall, Daniel said, 'This is the interpretation of the thing: ME-NE; God hath numbered thy kingdom, and finished it. TE-KEL; Thou art weighed in the balances, and art found wanting. PE-RES; Thy kingdom is divided, and given to the Medes and Persians.'

"In that night was Belshazzar slain, and his kingdom was divided between the Medes and the Persians." Finishing the history of the Belshazzar's feast, Barabbas tries to encourage himself and the others. "Therefore, fellow prisoners, God may disrupt Herod Antipas' feast."

"Yes, men, let's be optimistic for a change," agrees Eon.

A few mumbles and grunts come from the other prisoners as they lie down and once again lend an ear to the celebration at the palace. Suddenly in the midst of the noise coming from the palace, Barabbas and the others hear nothing—the peak of noise avalanched to silence. The silence is deafening. Able to hear their own hearts beat and their ears ring, Barabbas and the prisoners sense something wrong. The insidious silence of the stalker renders them hopeless and despondent.

Flushed from her dance and kneeling before the aroused Antipas, Salome, descendant of the Hasmonaean high priest, listens as Herod swears aloud with an oath for all to hear, "Salome, my princely maiden, ask of me whatsoever thou wilt, and I will give it thee. Whatsoever thou shalt ask of me, I will give it thee, unto the half of my kingdom!"

With haste, the drunken Salome sobers Herod and the guests with her request, "Give me here John Baptist's head in a charger!"

Silence falls on the assembly. This demand from the princess who is little more than a child stuns everyone. Knowing that Herod reveres John as a righteous and holy man, the assembly cowers so as not to stare at Antipas. Paralyzed by his own oath, Herod seems to take forever to answer. Herod's fear, conscience, and moreover, his superstition cannot stay John's execution, for he has sworn with an oath. Furthermore, the reaction from the cowering guests shows Herod that if John is not executed, the guests will perceive Herod's weakness of character. With every eye fixed upon him, Herod lifts his glass of wine, takes a big gulp of courage, and says to Hema, "Bring John the Baptist's head in a charger."

As the demons slither about the dungeon injecting their venom of despair, Barabbas hears John call on the name of Jesus. "Jesus?" questions Barabbas. "John, why are you calling on Jesus? I thought you were the chosen one—going about baptizing people."

Standing to his feet to give a careful answer, John expounds: "I indeed baptize you with water unto repentance: but he that cometh after me is mightier than I, whose shoes I am not worthy to bear: he shall baptize you with the Holy Ghost, and with fire: Whose fan is in his hand, and he will thoroughly purge his floor, and gather his wheat into the garner; but he will burn up the chaff with unquenchable fire."

Gratified to do his job, Hema carries his ax with pride. Reaching the dungeon entrance, he orders five guards to accompany him with a light. Descending into the dungeon, Hema marches with exhilaration to get the head of John the Baptist. He cuts off the head of hope as the light in the guard's hand shines on the horror-stricken faces of the prisoners watching the executioner's sharpened ax head. For a moment, each prisoner wonders if Hema is coming after him.

John's exposition about Jesus prompts the disbelieving Barabbas to ask more questions: "Who is Jesus? And you? And for what purpose?"

John expounds again: "A man can receive nothing, except it be given him from heaven. Ye yourselves bear me witness, that I said, I am not the Christ, but that I am sent before him. He that hath the bride is the bridegroom, which standeth and heareth him, rejoiceth greatly because of the bridegroom's voice: this my joy therefore is fulfilled. He must increase, but I must decrease. He that cometh from above is above all: he that is of the earth is earthly, and speaketh of the earth: he that cometh from heaven is above all. And what he hath seen and heard, that he testifieth; and no man receiveth his testimony. He that received his testimony hath set to his seal that God is true. For he whom God hath sent speaketh the words of God: for God giveth not the Spirit by measure unto him. The Father loveth the Son, and hath given all things into his hand."

With a giant echoing laugh, Hema interrupts the exposition of John. The light of the torch brightens the deepest cells. Barabbas, Eon, John, and others are gripped with fear when they see the ax. Seeing the shock on their faces, Hema laughs hysterically. He flaunts his ax and looks at Barabbas. With his baritone voice, Hema exclaims, "Now, I am come after a prize—a head!" Even though he knows his orders well, he toys with his victims. "Now—hmm," Hema scratches his head as if he is puzzled. "Whose head did

Salome request?" Hema pauses to give a frightening effect. "The princess danced so pleasingly for Herod and the guests that the king has granted her anything she desires."

Barabbas is knocked to his knees by his own fear. Horror strikes him like a piercing spear, tearing down his ability to think, move or breathe. Then, gasping for air as his heart starts beating again, Barabbas regains self-control. Realizing that Salome is angry with him, Barabbas closes his eyes and cries, "Hear, O Israel: The LORD our God is one LORD: And thou shalt love the LORD thy God with all thine heart, and with all thy soul, and with all thy might."

Showing his jealousy over Salome, Hema laughs resoundingly. "I wish Salome *had* requested your head. I would love to separate your body. You're so famous, you know. You can be sure that the first opportunity I get, I will kill you. You mark those words, Barabbas. Lover boy! The ax is too quick for you—I'm going to beat you to death. When you get to hell, you just ask Satan who it was that beat you out of your last breath."

Putting his face against the bars, Hema watches to see the reaction on Barabbas' frightened face. "Well, hero, Salome's exotic dance won her any request up to half of Herod's kingdom. Guess what she asked for?" Receiving no answer from Barabbas, Hema turns to John the Baptist. "Salome said, 'Give me here John Baptist's head in a charger.'"

Appearing unshaken with an expression of acceptance, John backs away from his cell door to show courtesy for the jailor. John vocies no argument or plea; he listens compliantly as the jailor gives instructions. John walks into the hallway as the jailor grasps John's arm.

As the jailor escorts John down the hall, Hema shouts, "Halt!" Puzzled by the order, the jailor stops. Pointing to the floor in front of Barabbas' cell, Hema announces, "I'm taking his head right here. I want Barabbas to watch. The hero, lover boy, missed seeing his Zealot friends die at Tiberias' palace. He'll see this execution!"

"There's no chopping block here," protests the jailor.

"I don't need it. I can take a head anywhere!" boasts Hema.

Realizing that Hema is going to take John's head right before their eyes, some of the prisoners hidden in the darkness curse Hema. Ignoring the curses and concentrating on his duty of decapitation, Hema instructs the guards.

Two guards cross John's hands behind his back. One on each side of John, they grasp and pull in opposite directions. Another guard, a tall, muscular, man, slowly pushes John backwards and orders him to sit on the stone floor. With his legs straight in front of him, a heavy-set guard sits on John's ankles. Then a strong-armed guard grabs John by the hair and pulls him backward.

Lying on his arms crossed underneath his back, the outstretched John looks heavenward. Hema and the guard holding the torch move to John's head, which is positioned before Barabbas' cell. Hema places his foot on John's neck. Restricting John's breathing, Hema intimidates Barabbas, "This is what I'm going to do to you!"

Sickened by John's poignant mistreatment, Barabbas pleads, "Don't be cruel to him because of your hatred for me."

Hema laughs and then teases in a higher tone, "Oh, I'm sorry, Barabbas, I thought I was standing on your neck. I'm sorry, Baptist. Please forgive me." Hema backs away and positions himself with his ax.

With a man sitting on his feet, a guard pulling on each arm, a guard pulling his hair, a guard holding a torch above his face, and an executioner aiming an ax for his neck, the helpless John concentrates on his last objective—a good witness for Jesus.

Hema asks, "Any last word?"

Barabbas expects to hear the Shema, but John the Baptist proclaims, "He that believeth on the Son hath everlasting life: and he that believeth not the Son shall not see life; but the wrath of God abideth on him."

Even though he is eager to swing his ax, Hema cannot resist giving his verbal retaliation. "John, you are a fool. Your belief in the doctrines of Jesus brought you to prison. Now you're foolish enough to proclaim Jesus to be your savior. Can't you see I'm about to take your head? Your belief in Jesus brings you death!"

Looking at John, Barabbas listens for John's answer. John is silent. Barabbas, wanting an answer, exclaims, "John?"

John does not rebut, retaliate, or explain, but he simply and profoundly answers, "I am not offended in Jesus."

The guards pull in opposite directions as Hema swings the ax upward through the space provided by the high ceiling. Barabbas grimaces and shudders as the executioner's ax reaches the peak of its velocity. John looks past the imminent and prevalent danger as the blade passes through his neck and bounces off the stone floor. The guard pulling on John's hair falls backwards as the head catapults to strike him in the chest. Blood spurts into Barabbas' cell and about the hall. Hema laughs when he sees the ghastly head—open-eyed with its mouth agape.

Hema grabs the head from the blood-splattered guard. Holding the bodiless head up against the bars, face to face with Barabbas, the executioner takes pleasure and pride in displaying his trophy. Staring at the terrifying sight, Barabbas steps back in retreat. Hema, amused by Barabbas' reaction, exclaims, "Take a good look, Barabbas . . . you're next!"

Barabbas turns away with nausea, horrified by the ruthless murder. *Oh, God, how terrible is Hema! May you judge him ever so severely. And all of this because of Salome's request? God, I know she didn't mean it. It was surely Herodias' deceit that caused Salome to make this request. Oh, God, forgive Salome, for she carries my child. Help me,*

God. I don't think I can bear this and live. Barabbas weeps bitterly in the loneliness of the ominous darkness.

At the palace where maidens are performing dances, Hema enters the banquet hall carrying a charger. As if he were offering the princess a gift, he servilely presents the charger to the drunken Salome. In her stupor, she refuses to touch it but instructs Hema. "Give it to my mother. It is the gift of my appreciation."

Hema carries and presents the charger to Herodias. She commands Hema to take the lid off the platter. Removing the dome of the charger and setting it aside, Hema lifts the head so Herodias can see its face.

Recognizing John's face and realizing her dreams have come true, the ambitious, incestuous Herodias smiles with delight at the long-awaited delicacy of the ghastly dish. Satisfied with the eradication of John's adulterous condemnation, Herodias choreographs the seductions of Salome for the rest of the night.

Eager to sleep with Salome, Antipas retires for the night while some of the other celebrities stay up to watch the dancers. Inebriated, while the seductive Salome dances in his head, Antipas goes to his bedroom to lie down. The mother of adultery, Herodias, greets Antipas with a kiss. "I'm so glad to have family unity."

"That was a deceitful trick: The seduction of Salome in exchange for John's head."

"Oh, my darling, things will be so much better now that that troublemaker is gone. In fact, things are already better. I am happier. Salome is wiser to the lusts of men. She respects you and realizes she needs you. What more can you ask for?"

Antipas walks across the room, falls across the bed, and says, "Well, she had better be worth it and make her promise good."

"She will, my darling," avows the incestuous Herodias.

"Salome waits at the door." Wanting to get Antipas' mind off John and her deceit, Herodias seductively tantalizes Antipas with an alluring description of her daughter. "Just picture who waits to come unto you, even at your door as I speak, an effervescent youth with love as fresh as dew, lips as red as wine, a figure that the majesty of mountains cannot match, skin like silk, hair as dark as night, a scent as sweet as honeysuckle, and . . ." Herodias pauses to present attention to the next description of Salome and then tells the ultimate lie which will hypnotize the unsuspecting victim. "And . . . a virgin, a princely maiden . . . ready to fulfill the lusts of your flesh. I have prepared her for you. You'll be pleased."

Herodias steps into the side parlor to tell Salome that Antipas is ready. "Come, Salome; he's ready. He thinks he is getting a virgin, so pretend to be one. Tomorrow he will be upset because he was deceived into executing John. For this . . . he will be angry with me. But if you sleep with him, I can act as if he did me some injustice for sleeping with you even though I helped in your seduction. He doesn't know it is he who is seduced. Salome, this is the way you must maneuver men. Aphrodite's love rules the ruler."

"Mother, explain the plan again."

"Salome, if you sleep with Antipas tonight, then I can make him think he is the father of your baby. Believing he is the father, he will take care of you. After you have slept with Antipas, I will come get you during the night. Then, before dawn, you will go and sleep with your visiting uncle, Philip II, tetrarch of Iturea."

"Is he expecting me?"

"Yes. I put the secret in his ear earlier tonight. He is mesmerized by your beauty. I told him you would come to him during the middle of the night. With any luck at all, he too will believe he is the father of your baby."

"What then?"

"In a few weeks, I will tell Antipas he is the father of your baby. He will not like that. He has suffered enough grief—thanks to John—about incestuous marriages. The Jews will not accept Antipas to be their king if they know his daughter is the mother of his baby. Then I will offer a solution to the problem."

"Herodias," calls Antipas from the bedroom. "Is there something wrong?"

Herodias gives an appropriate and teasing answer. "No, my love. You must wait for a virgin. Patience is the greatest part of the pleasure—patience."

Salome prays for help. "Aphrodite, help me—take control. Avenge my virginity, for Barabbas used me. Now I shall have pleasure in taking revenge."

"That's right, daughter. You are learning, my dear. Now use your knowledge and body. You have a long night before you."

"Thank you for helping me out of my precarious situation."

"Salome, you shall be Philip's queen one day soon."

Under the direction of her mother, Salome sleeps with her uncle and stepfather, Antipas, and before dawn she then sleeps with Herod Philip II, another uncle.

10

Prisoner of Freedom

For the guests, morning reaches the bastion of Machaerus four hours later than usual. Herod Antipas awakens at midday along with the princes, military commanders, and other influential men. The long night stole the fresh and crisp morning dew from the late risers. Many guests awaken with headaches, and a few experience the discomforts of dry heaves. Their lethargic movements carry them in search of something to calm their queasy stomachs. By-products of their indulgence—the rotten stench of alcohol in their nostrils and the nasty taste on their tongues—linger. The celebrations of the night past are now the regrets of their present future.

Opening his bloodshot eyes, Antipas is annoyed by the brightness of the sun coming through the window. Reaching his peripheral vision, the light magnifies the blinding pain as the annoying reverberation of voices coming through the corridor intensifies. The rotten, stagnant odor of spilled wine, now soured, causes Antipas' face to turn a ghastly pale green. Leaping up, unable to reach his parlor, Antipas vomits. More stenches saturate the air. Weak and dizzy from his abrupt rising, he lies back gathering his strength. *I need to get up, but I don't think I am able. That was some wild party. I lost my head with the wine.*

Antipas tries to retrieve his memory of last night from the effects of the alcohol. He vaguely recalls his regrets. *Ugh, John lost his head by execution. I hope that the gods aren't angry. My daughter—I slept with her. That was exciting, but what if I got her pregnant? That would be a nightmare. I surely hope that doesn't come to haunt me. Moreover, I hope that nobody suspects me of incest. I need to arise and face everyone.*

Suddenly, the clicking of sandals rushing toward his bedroom door breaks Herod's reflections of revelry.

"King Herod," calls Omar, "a messenger is here to see you."

"What is it?" asks Antipas through the door.

"Your army, my Lord," exclaims the messenger.

"Come in and inform me."

The messenger enters the bedroom with Omar. "King Aretas of Arabia attacked your troops who are stationed to the south. Many of your soldiers were killed. The others had to retreat in order to save themselves. The survivors are coming here to recuperate."

Receiving the tragic news, Antipas excuses the messenger. "You may go and prepare to receive my troops."

As the messenger exits the room, Omar asks, "What do you think?"

"King Aretas—my ex-father-in-law," exclaims Antipas with disgust, "is a formidable enemy seeking revenge for his daughter. He will not forgive or forget that I divorced his daughter to marry Herodias just as John the Baptist would not let me forget that I committed adultery with my brother's wife."

"My Lord, you shall surely rid yourself of Aretas as you did John," Omar speaks, trying to encourage the distraught Herod.

"I fear that while my military commanders and I were celebrating and having fun fulfilling our worldly desires, John's God weighed me in the balances—balances that found me lacking. That is, John's head weighed heavily in the balances. Nevertheless, the battle has just begun. I'll fight back. Neither John's God nor King Aretas can stop me, for I have the Roman Empire to back me."

Before sunrise the following morning, the incarcerated Eon is puzzled by the apparent mental anguish Barabbas is going through. "Barabbas, I can tell you are worried about more than the shackles. What's bothering you?"

Secretly worried about Salome's pregnancy and grieved about her dancing to have John the Baptist's head removed, Barabbas sighs, "Antipas will be coming soon. With my words, I can save my life or destroy it. At best, all I can do is delay my execution. I must convince Antipas that I have found the ledger."

Detecting despair in Barabbas' voice, Eon apologizes. "I'm sorry; I should mind my own problems."

"Eon, what are your problems? I mean . . . why are you in here?"

"Oh, nothing much. I ordered some goods for the keeper of Antipas' palace. When I delivered them, he refused to pay me full payment. So I took my case before Antipas, but the tetrarch ruled in favor of his keeper. Then I made the mistake of calling Antipas a crook. I figure I should be out in a week or two."

"How long have you been in?"

"A week, I think. It's hard to keep up with the days down here in this darkness. Anyway, when I get out of here, I won't cross the Jordan River to sell merchandise any more.

I'm staying in Pilate's jurisdiction. At least he is a fair judge. When standing in Pilate's judgement, all a person has to worry about is peer pressure. Pilate is a great judge, but he can't handle the outside influence—politics. I've watched Pilate's court."

"Eon, do you know a merchandiser named Joktan?"

"Sure, I know that crook."

"Crook?" exclaims Barabbas. "We must not be talking about the same man? The Joktan I know is a kind and generous man."

"There is only one Joktan—he's a crook."

In defense of Joktan, Barabbas says, "Eon, I worked for the man. I know him. He is a true friend. He gave me money when my father was murdered. He takes care of my widowed mother now."

"Well, think what you will, but I say he is a wolf in sheep's clothing. *I* won't do business with him."

Suddenly a flash of light and the crackles of flaming torches arrive at Barabbas' cell. Hema takes Barabbas from the cell and applies a pressure hold on him. Another soldier holds a flaming torch near Barabbas' face as Antipas enters the hall. Realizing that Hema wants to kill him, Barabbas prepares himself for an interrogation.

Without any greeting, Antipas immediately questions, "Do you know where the ledger is?"

"Yes, sir," agonizes Barabbas as Hema squeezes his hold.

"Where is it?" demands Antipas.

"Jerusalem."

"Where in Jerusalem?"

"I'll not tell."

Antipas grabs the torch from the soldier's hand and strikes Barabbas on the temple. Barabbas screams as the heat of the flame blisters his head. The smell of singed hair fills the hall. "Barabbas, I'll burn you alive." Antipas swings the torch again to singe the eyebrows and eyelashes off

Barabbas' face. "Now, answer me, or I'll blind you permanently."

"My mother has hidden it," Barabbas concedes. "She will not hand that ledger to anyone except me—to me in person, for she knows my life depends on it. If you will take me to Jerusalem, I will get her to trade the ledger in exchange for my life. That's all I can offer you."

Antipas steps back, and Hema throws Barabbas on the floor. Four soldiers stretch Barabbas out. Hema stands over Barabbas with an iron mask. Reaching down and putting the back half of the mask under Barabbas' head and flipping the hinged, front part over Barabbas' face, Hema locks the mask on the side. Barabbas' sight and breathing are limited to a few small holes in the mask.

The soldiers stand Barabbas to his feet before Antipas. "Barabbas, you think you are so smart. You think I cannot send you to Jerusalem—Pilate's jurisdiction. Well, you're wrong—you are going. This mask will conceal your identity."

"Herod, I can hardly see. How can I eat?"

"You can't."

"How will I ride?"

"I don't know. If you don't ride, then you will die. I really don't care. I'm not convinced you know where the ledger is, but I'll know soon." Turning to leave, Antipas shouts, "Bring him out!"

Outside the dungeon, Hema and Omar privately receive their instructions from Antipas. "Men, ride to the fords at Jericho and stay for the night with our stewards. Then go to Jerusalem and stay at my palace. If Barabbas doesn't take you to the ledger, kill him. If he finds the ledger, still kill him. I don't want him alive. Kill his mother too if she gets in the way. Do you understand?"

"Yes, my lord."

"Take no chances in dealing with Barabbas. If there is

any mischief in anything Barabbas does, kill him. Barabbas is deceitful and elusive. If he misbehaves before he gets to Jerusalem, that is a good sign that he doesn't know where the ledger is. You *may* have to kill him before you get there. I would love to have that incriminating ledger, but he may not even know where it is. He may be buying time.

"If you deal with his mother, you make sure you get that ledger in your hand before you let Barabbas go. Remember that you hold her son's life and she holds the ledger. What you have is more valuable to her than the ledger. She will deal according to your terms. Afterwards, kill him."

Antipas stops talking as a guard approaches with Barabbas locked in the iron mask. Then the guard shackles Hema's left wrist to Barabbas' right wrist.

Barabbas protests, "Can't I have breakfast or water? I'll die before I get to Jericho."

Hema jerks Barabbas around with the chain between their wrists and pulls him toward the water trough. Grabbing the back of the mask, the executioner pushes Barabbas' head underneath the water. Barabbas struggles to get free, but his efforts are useless. When Barabbas loses consciousness and his struggle, Hema jerks him out of the water and slaps him on the back. Barabbas coughs and snorts to get his breath. Hema asks, "Do you want more?"

While Barabbas clears his breathing passages, Omar says, "Hema, let's go." The soldiers put Barabbas on a horse. Then Hema mounts to sit behind him.

"We have to ride together on the same horse?" coughs Barabbas.

Hema replies, "Unless you had rather run."

Omar gives assurance to Antipas, "We shall return with our mission accomplished." The three men ride out of Machaerus.

Arriving at the ford near Jericho as the sun sets, Hema rides his horse into the Jordan River and dismounts. Then he pulls

Barabbas off with the chain shackled to his wrist.

Landing in the water, Barabbas sticks the front part of his mask into the river so he can get a drink. His head pounds with pain, having worn the hot, iron mask in the sun all day. The cool water feels good to the burn he sustained from Antipas' torch.

Despair clouds Barabbas' mind. *I don't know if I will make it. I think I had rather be dead. I don't know where to find the ledger, and I know that Omar and Hema are expecting me to go directly to it. They are not going to waste any time on me. God, help me!*

Exhausted from the ride and weak from lack of food, Barabbas begs, "Hema, Omar, please take this mask off so I can eat. I beg you. I can't make it any farther if you don't."

Hema shoves Barabbas' head under the flowing Jordan River and holds him there. Realizing the futility of struggling, Barabbas does not resist, for there is no fight left in him. After a minute of submersion, Hema pulls Barabbas out of the water and says, "Would you like anything else? Answer me!"

"No, sir."

"Lover boy, you will not get anything to drink until tomorrow morning, which may be your last. After your morning drink, we are going to Jerusalem. There you will get the ledger. When you hand it over, I will set you free, and if you don't, I am going to take great pleasure in killing you.

"As for tonight, you can watch me eat and drink. We will be staying with our stewards of the ford. One of them will watch you and me while we sleep to make sure you don't try anything. Meanwhile, you'll make a notable charm on my bracelet. You're stuck with me."

Early the next morning, Hema and Omar eat as the shackled, torturously masked Barabbas watches. Hema tantalizes Barabbas with the food. "Barabbas, this is good pork. Jew boy, I'll make a deal with you. I will take the mask off you and let you eat if you agree to eat pork, but if I take the mask off and you don't eat it, I will take your life. Do you accept the terms?" Hema grabs Barabbas and demands an answer.

Weak in voice, Barabbas replies, "My God doesn't allow me to eat pork."

Hema laughs, "Omar, did you hear that? I offered Jew boy food and he refused." Offended by the religious refusal, the powerful Hema grabs and holds Barabbas by the throat and says, "All you will get is water." Hema begins to choke Barabbas down. "You will regret not eating because of your superstition."

Unable to breathe, Barabbas falls to his knees. Tears roll down Barabbas' face and saliva seeps down through the iron mask onto Hema's squeezing hands. Seeing the mucous and tears on his hands, Hema releases and curses. In disgust and anger, Hema then knocks Barabbas to the ground and begins to kick him.

Realizing that Hema's kicks could be fatal, Omar shouts, "Hema, we have to take him to get the ledger!"

Reluctantly, Hema stops kicking and proclaims, "If Barabbas spits on me again, I will kill him."

Omar agrees, "Very well, Hema!"

Omar and Hema drag Barabbas from the abode of the stewards into the river. Barabbas plunges his masked head into the knee-deep, cool water to get a drink. Omar says, "Drink a lot because it is a long ride to Jerusalem." Barabbas drinks and drinks and drinks when Omar snickers, "You are going to drink the Jordan dry." But Barabbas doesn't stop; he keeps drinking. Finally, Hema impatiently jerks the shackle chain and pulls Barabbas from the water.

Hema says, "No more water for you. I'm not stopping every few minutes to let you relieve yourself. You'd better hold your bladder. Letting you relieve yourself is disgusting to me. You had better take heed. I'm tired of dealing with you. If I have any trouble out of you, you are dead. Antipas said I was to take no mischief from you."

Omar orders the steward to go get their horses from the stable. Hearing the order, Barabbas asks, "May we go to the stable?"

Omar curiously responds, "What for?"

"My horse, Logos, is there."

Curious about the horse, Omar asks, "The black and white stallion you had in Tiberias?"

"Yes, that's the one. I sold him to the stable owner. I couldn't keep him with Pilate's bounty description of me and my horse."

"What became of that fancy sword you had?" asks Omar.

"I sold it to a merchandiser," Barabbas lies. "I couldn't afford to be seen with it either."

Omar looks to Hema and says, "Let's see if he is telling the truth. I've done business with the stable owner many times. He's a harmless Jew. Let's go to the stable."

As the trio approaches the stable, Omar warns Barabbas. "If you say one word, Hema will kill you."

Omar goes and talks to the stable owner as Hema stands at a distance with the masked Barabbas. The owner and Omar go to the back of the stable for a few minutes and then return.

Receiving their horses from the stable owner, Omar and Hema help Barabbas onto Hema's horse. Hema then climbs on the horse to sit behind Barabbas. Omar mounts his horse and says to the stable owner, "I shall be back on my return to Perea to commandeer that stallion. Have him ready."

"Soon!" Barabbas blurts. Hema throws a sharp punch to silence Barabbas. Kicking their horses in the flanks, Omar and Hema quickly ride away.

Exiting Jericho, Omar asks, "Soon?"

Barabbas apologizes, "I'm sorry. I didn't mean to say anything. It just came out. I just meant I wanted the stable owner to get the horse ready soon. The sooner you leave, the sooner I am free."

Hema hits Barabbas sharply in the ribs as they ride together. "One more word out of you and you're dead! Do you understand?"

Before Barabbas gets a chance to answer, Omar interrupts, "Just before we get to Jerusalem, we will remove the mask to gag his mouth."

"Good idea," replies Hema.

About a mile out of Jericho, nearing a huge rock where the road forks, Barabbas, sore and beaten, makes a request. "I need to relieve myself."

"No," replies Hema. "We are hardly out of Jericho and you want to relieve yourself. I told you before we left that I was not going to stop every few minutes."

Omar agrees. "I'm tired of putting you on that horse. You shouldn't have drunk all that water. You'll have to hold it for a while."

A few yards from the huge rock, Hema screams in disgust as he feels something warm and wet underneath him. "You have urinated on me!" Hema, dragging Barabbas with him, falls off the horse.

Scrambling to get up from the road to beat Barabbas, Hema regrets that Barabbas is wearing the iron mask, for he wants to beat Barabbas' face to oblivion. "Curse you, Barabbas!" shouts Hema. "I don't need an ax to remove your head. I am going to wring your head from your body with my bare hands!"

Realizing Hema's emotional madness, Omar watches in silence, for he knows Hema will now grotesquely execute Barabbas.

Enraged with the power of furious demons, Hema loses his mind in vindictive anger as Barabbas lies addled on the narrow road. The frenzied executioner begins to kick as Barabbas tries to roll out of the way. His anger flaring in determination to brutalize Barabbas, Hema continues to pound away life from his prisoner.

Rolling into the huge rock of the road's fork, Barabbas realizes he can no longer avoid the stamps that have taken the breath from his body. Without any other options of refuge, Barabbas desperately tries to wedge his body in a slight recession where the rock meets grass at the ground level. Hema continues to stamp Barabbas from the angle the rock affords.

Tiring in his frenzy of brutality, Hema realizes that his stamps are not as effective with Barabbas wedging the front side of his body against the rock. Hema stops to rest and verbally terrorize Barabbas. "You fool! You can't crawl under a rock. I have you bound to me. The rock provides no cleft, no refuge—no hiding place!"

Continuing to terrify Barabbas, Hema prepares to pull Barabbas away from the rock. "I am going to pull you from the rock and wring your head off with my hands."

Omar speaks up: "Hema, for my sake, please don't do that here. I don't have the stomach for it. Please do it in private."

"Shut up, Omar! Antipas told me not to take any mischief from him. I'm going to tear his head off and anybody else's that tries to stop me!"

"Very well," says Omar, not wanting Hema's wrath on him. Omar backs away, for he knows how unmercifully grotesque Hema can be.

"Now, lover boy," calls Hema as he tightens the chain, "it's time to add to my collection of innovative ways to procure a head." Grasping the shackle chain with both hands, Hema heaves as he yanks with all his might to pull Barabbas away from the rock.

Giving no resistance to Hema's tug, Barabbas leaps to his feet, causing Hema to lose his balance in a backward stumble. As Hema is falling, the two opposing forces on the chain reach their extent of distance. With Hema's body suspended by the jolt of the chain on his left, shackled hand, Barabbas wields a surprise, which was hidden at the base of the rock—the Sword of Sacrifice. As if it were God's perfect timing, Barabbas swings the sword to slice off Hema's extended hand.

Omar is paralyzed with shock as he watches Hema try to stop the profuse bleeding of his gruesome, bloody stub. Barabbas climbs on the horse he was sharing with Hema and rides back to the stable at Jericho.

Obal greets Barabbas, "Logos is ready to go." Then he grins and says, "Soon? You should have said *very soon*."

"Thanks, Obal," says Barabbas as he mounts Logos.

As Barabbas rides southward, he is amazed at the events that have just happened. *Heavenly Father, I thank you again and again. God, I can hardly believe it. I was in the clutches of the enemy's hand, nigh unto death, and you delivered me again. God, I am learning to trust You, not myself. A few days ago when I was running from Pilate's bounty hunters, I found it hard to let go of Logos and the Sword of Sacrifice. I did not know that my loss of horse and sword was for my own good. God, You truly know what is best. Everything You do is for good.*

God, I need your help again. I can't stay in the cities of Pilate's and Antipas' jurisdiction. I must go to the wilderness—the stony, salty desert. I'm not familiar with this wilderness. Mortals dare not go there for the tales of its terrors. God, who can help me? Who would help a fugitive—a fugitive with a mask and a shackle chain? I'll starve or scorch if I don't soon get this prison off my head.

"The Essenes!" Barabbas shouts aloud. "Thank You, God." *The monastic Jews who live near the Dead Sea. Their hospitality for their brethren is well known. I know they don't have many dealings with the rest of the world, but I do know they cannot bear to see anyone suffer. They are a peace-loving group; they bear no weapons. But the problem is that the Essenes who live in the monastery are remote. They are so obscure, God. How will I find them in a land where I am a stranger? I suppose I'm just going to have to trust the Lord.*

Barabbas travels southward all day and stops at a small fresh-water stream that runs into the Dead Sea. The next day, he leaves his oasis to search southward for the monastic Essenes.

Going without water the next day, Barabbas tries to encourage himself and Logos. "Logos, we will die if we do not find water or help tomorrow. We could turn back to our oasis, but I fear we cannot make it. Logos, the fruit is out on the flimsy limbs, not on the trunk. We must trust God and get out on a limb. I don't feel that we can make it another full day. If God doesn't intervene, we will be food for the vultures tomorrow. If that is what happens, then may God get glory. I'm not turning back—I'm moving forward. There is nothing behind; it is ahead. Let's trust God with our last day and move forward. God didn't bring me this far to let me die in this hell." Barabbas wants to sing, but he is too exhausted and his tongue is too dry. Therefore, in his mind he sings a glorious hymn to God as he falls into a deep sleep for the night.

The next morning Barabbas awakens to a nightmare of reality—the scorching sun beats his body and heats his mask. Taking part of his clothing, he covers the mask and pulls the reins of a discouraged and reluctant horse.

By mid-afternoon, Barabbas can hardly go, but his spirit refuses to quit until he can physically go no farther. His body falls on the desert floor. The wayworn Logos kneels and then falls on his side as the vultures circle.

By late afternoon, the vultures land to pluck the flesh from the boy and his friend.

Two weeks after the fall of Barabbas, the black fortress of

Machaerus still stands strong with its muscle-bound legs of undulating hills and Herculean arms of impregnable walls. With keen eyes in the unassailable towers, the gargantuan presence surveys the rocky keep of the surrounding valleys and is unaware of the havoc that is hovering—a spreading cloud foreboding judgement.

A word of impending judgement drops from the cloud to capture the domain of the black fortress. Though condemnation falls, Antipas refuses to repent. Thinking he can elude judgement, the tetrarch goes about the routines of life.

Having eaten his breakfast, Antipas sits upon his regal throne to hear the news from his messenger. "Tell me of the affairs."

The messenger arises from his bowed knees to address Antipas. "My lord, since you left the region of Galilee, a man named Jesus has amassed many followers."

"Jesus?" questions Antipas.

"Yes, my Lord. A miraculous thing happened."

"Tell me."

"Jesus went to a desert place. When the people heard thereof, they followed him on foot out of the cities. And Jesus went forth, and saw a great multitude, and was moved with compassion toward them, and he healed their sick. And when it was evening, his disciples came to him, saying, 'This is a desert place, and the time is now past; send the multitude away, that they may go into the villages, and buy themselves victuals.'

But Jesus said unto them, 'They need not depart; give ye them to eat.'

And they said unto him, 'We have here but five loaves, and two fishes.'

He said, 'Bring them hither to me.'

And he commanded the multitude to sit down on the grass, and took the five loaves, and the two fishes, and looking up to heaven, he blessed, and broke, and gave the loaves to his disciples, and the disciples to the multitude. And they did all eat, and were filled: and they took up of the fragments that remained twelve baskets full. And they that had eaten were about five thousand men, beside women and children."

Antipas asks, "So with the women and children, this Jesus fed maybe twenty thousand?"

"Approximately, sir."

Fearfully curious, Antipas asks, "Is this Jesus trying to establish rule of my kingdom."

"I don't think so, sir, for he sent his disciples away in a ship and sent the multitude away also. Then he departed into a mountain to pray."

"To pray?" questions Antipas.

"Yes, my Lord."

"Sounds like John the Baptist. Then what happened?"

"Sir, I was told that when even was come, the ship of the disciples was in the midst of the sea, and he alone on the land. He saw the disciples toiling in rowing; for the wind was contrary unto them: and about the fourth watch of the night he cometh unto them, walking upon the sea, and would have passed by them. But when they saw him, walking upon the sea, they supposed it had been a spirit."

"A spirit?" asks Antipas, sounding some fear in his voice. A frightening thought flashes in Antipas' mind: *Could this be the spirit of John the Baptist?* Focusing his attention back on the messenger, Antipas asks again, "A spirit?"

"A spirit, my lord. The disciples saw Jesus walking on the water and were troubled. And immediately he talked with them, and saith unto them, 'Be of good cheer: it is I; be not afraid.' He went up unto them into the ship; and the wind ceased."

Seeing the dazed look on Antipas' face, the messenger pauses.

"Is there more?" Antipas asks with inner fear.

"Well, sir, from there, Jesus went to Gennesaret. And

whithersoever he entered, into villages, cities, or country, they laid the sick in the streets, and besought him that they might touch if it were but the border of his garment: and as many as touched him were made whole."

Antipas rises from his throne and says, "Excuse me." Racing into his parlor behind the throne, Antipas shakes with fear. Having heard of all that was done by Jesus, Herod is perplexed, for he had heard that John the Baptist was risen from the dead. *John have I beheaded: but who is this, of whom I hear such things?*

Gaining his composure, Antipas goes and sits before the messenger. "I desire to see this Jesus."

"Yes, my lord. I'll try to find him."

"Now, what about the affairs of Pilate?"

"My lord, Pilate and the Romans still search diligently for Barabbas. Pilate has raised the bounty for the capture of Barabbas."

"Does Pilate know that Barabbas went into the wilderness?"

"I don't think so."

"What about *our* search?"

"It has ceased in the wilderness. The trail was lost. The men think that Barabbas is dead. Wearing a shackle and the mask, the fugitive could not have survived."

"I'm not convinced of that. Keep an eye out for him, for he may still be alive."

"Yes, sir."

"What do the Jews say about Barabbas?"

"Most of them support the actions of Barabbas. They believe that God is responsible for his success, especially since Barabbas was able to rob Pilate and his army of legionnaires. Some even believe that he is their messiah. The majority of the Jews are ready to rally with Barabbas, except for the ones who believe that Jesus is the Messiah. I believe that the young Zealots would fight if Barabbas gave the word."

"Yes, the Jews are so foolish. They would do anything if they thought their God was involved with it. They do not consider the circumstances. One day I will have their devotion. I will be their king."

"Yes, my lord," agrees the messenger.

Antipas sees Herodias in the archway to the throne room. "Come, my darling; the messenger was just leaving."

"Thanks, my lord," responds Herodias to the invitation. She comes to sit next to Antipas. "Is there good news today?"

"All bad. Here's the list: Barabbas has not been found. In my absence, many of my subjects are following Jesus. Pilate and I don't have good relations. Furthermore, the Jews are willing to follow either Barabbas or Jesus. And *I* am not their king yet."

"You will be, my darling," Herodias encourages her husband. "Barabbas and Jesus are no contest for the mighty and vast Roman Empire. The next king for all of Israel will be you. You pacify Rome. You are kin to the Jews. And most of all, you are married to me—the descendant of a former High Priest—the very thing that the Jews are looking for. Think about our plan in marriage. We are the only couple that meets the requirements of Caesar Tiberius and the religious Jews. It's just a matter of time. You will be king of it all one day."

"You are very optimistic, Herodias. But there is one thing that bothers me."

"What?"

"I'm afraid that I should not have executed John."

"You are too superstitious, my love."

"Some say that John has risen from the dead. At the same time, Jesus is here performing miracles. What if—"

"If so . . . we will get rid of Jesus too," interrupts Herodias.

"Oh, no, I shall not. I executed one devout man. I shall

not execute Jesus."

"You are too superstitious. Jesus is a mortal."

"True, but—"

"Well," interrupts Herodias again, "I hate to bear bad news, but I must."

"What is it, Herodias? The bad news you bring certainly cannot jeopardize my kingdom."

"Well, believe it or not, it could very well ruin your relationship with the Jews."

"What do you mean? How?"

Herodias grimaces to say, "Salome is pregnant, I think."

"No, I can't believe it!" cries Antipas, knocking himself in the head with the heel of his hand. "Ever since I executed John, I have had nothing but bad luck!"

"Don't start that again!" exclaims Herodias. "Let's use our heads instead of our superstition. Get control of yourself, Antipas. We don't want the Jews to find out. They would never accept you to be their king. Incest does not gain their respect."

"If she is pregnant, what should we do?"

"The only thing I know to do is to find her a husband quickly. If she marries soon, then her husband will think that he is the baby's father."

"Will Salome go along with that?" asks Antipas.

"Yes, I have already talked with her."

"Who would be foolish enough to marry her so hastily?"

"Your half brother, Philip II, the tetrarch of Batanea. After Salome danced for the party, he could not keep his eyes off Salome. The next day I saw him watching her intently."

"What does Salome think of her uncle?"

"Now that she knows the way of Aphrodite, she is ready to gain power and riches with her love. She learned the ways of men when Barabbas spurned her. She is eager to inveigle Philip II into her web."

"You mean to tell me she is willing to have my baby and

pin it on Philip II?"

"Yes. Though she will be Philip's wife, she will always want to please you because you are the baby's secret father. Therefore, you will have some control of Philip's kingdom too. The situation is not a problem; it is an asset."

Antipas notices a panting messenger in the archway. "Come, my servant. What news do you have for me?"

"My lord, King Aretas has routed your southern army again. He may attack Machaerus tomorrow."

"He can't take Machaerus. This black fortress is invincible. We shall not only defend ourselves but we shall slaughter our enemy. Go and tell my commander to get ready."

Herodias says, "Antipas, let's leave the black fortress. Let's go home to Tiberias."

"Why?"

"We need to take Salome to visit her uncle Philip II."

"Oh, yes, you are right. We shall leave immediately and go to Tiberias and then to Batanea. But first, I must instruct my commanders. You and Salome get ready to depart. We shall leave soon."

Antipas rises and goes to meet with his commanders while Herodias meets with Salome.

"Mother, did he fall for our deception?"

"Yes, my dear. He thinks he is the father. He is glad you are going to try to marry your uncle and claim that he is the father of your baby. He doesn't know you have already slept with Philip II. All you have to do is tell your uncle he has impregnated you. He will gladly marry you. Salome, my daughter, you and I are going to have two kings in our laps. Imagine the power. Philip II will think he is the father, and Antipas will think he is the father. Only you and I know who the father is."

"Mother, what about Barabbas? He's the—"

"He is dead, Salome. He is dead."

Salome hangs her head as her heart aches. Herodias hugs

Salome. "Everything will be fine," Herodias answers Salome. "You just wait and see. You shall live in riches and power. Let's get ready for a wedding—yours!"

11
Essene Monastery— Qumran

While the bloom of spring is flourishing, the royal wedding of Philip the tetrarch and Salome the princess adorns the southwestern slope of Mount Hermon in the city of Caesarea Philippi. Wearing his royal garments, Philip II looks across his city of political prestige. Just as Antipas had built Tiberias in honor of Caesar, Philip II built the city of Caesarea Philippi in honor of Caesar and himself. That is, he enlarged an old city that was once a Canaanite sanctuary for the worship of Baal, a city that was once called Paneas by the Greeks because its cavern was dedicated to the worship of Pan.

Dressed in fine linen, adorned with rings of gold, silver and ivory, the stunning Salome looks to her groom, Philip II. Wearing the most expensive precious stones, Salome enjoys the opulence surrounding her. However, the greatest euphoria she experiences is the power she possesses. She is no more her mother's puppet; she is the queen of many cities—a tetrarchy. As her red lips sip the finest white wine, Salome receives immense gratification from her position on the throne. The warm feeling given by the alcohol takes all her cares away. Flushed by the wine and her pregnancy, Salome lives for the moment, as though wealth will keep her happy forever.

The royal attendants of the wedding think that nothing as important has ever come this close to the city, but only the day before, the greatest of all prophets prophesied there—Jesus. When Jesus came into the coasts of Caesarea Philippi, he asked his disciples, saying, "Whom do men say that I the Son of man am?"

And they said, "Some say that thou art John the Baptist: some, Elias; and others, Jeremias, or one of the prophets."

He saith unto them, "But whom say ye that I am?"

And Simon Peter answered and said, "Thou art the Christ, the Son of the living God."

And Jesus answered and said unto him, "Blessed art thou, Simon Bar-jo-na: for flesh and blood hath not revealed it unto thee, but my Father which is in heaven. And I say also unto thee, that thou art Peter, and upon this rock I will build my church; and the gates of hell shall not prevail against it. And I will give unto thee the keys of the kingdom of heaven: and whatsoever thou shalt bind on earth shall be bound in heaven: and whatsoever thou shalt loose on earth shall be loosed in heaven."

The bloom of spring, the anesthesia of wine, the appeal of opulence, and the prestige of power carry Salome to the heat of summer. As her belly spreads, Salome perspires as her life swells with boredom. The wine becomes sickening, the opulence becomes ordinary, the power becomes a burden of responsibility, and Salome becomes very unhappy. Though she possesses the desires of her eyes, she is empty in her heart and soul.

All summer a businessman named Holee searches diligently for Jesus. Coming from Bethlehem, Holee has something for Jesus—death. In grievous determination, he searches in Capernaum, Phoenicia, Decapolis, Magdala, Caesarea Philippi, and Galilee. Finally, Holee gives up his search, but on his way back to Bethlehem, he finds Jesus near Samaria.

Holee sees that disciples surround Jesus. Nevertheless, he doesn't mind losing his miserable life, for it has been torment for over thirty years. Holee desires to plant his dagger in Jesus' heart. Watching people approach Jesus, Holee makes a plan to get close enough to kill the simple man.

Seeing a group of three men approaching Jesus, Holee marches behind them. Putting his hand on his dagger, he watches the first man approach Jesus and say, "Lord, I will follow thee whithersoever thou goest."

And Jesus says unto him, "Foxes have holes, and birds of the air have nests; but the Son of man hath not where to lay his head." Hearing that reply, Holee grieves with guilt—guilt carried for over thirty years.

And Jesus says unto the second man, "Follow me."

But the second man replies, "Lord, suffer me first to go and bury my father."

Jesus says unto him, "Let the dead bury their dead: but go thou and preach the kingdom of God." Hearing that reply, Holee grieves for his dead son, who was murdered over thirty years ago.

And the third man says, "Lord, I will follow thee; but let me first go bid them farewell, which are at home at my house."

And Jesus says unto him, "No man, having put his hand to the plough, and looking back, is fit for the kingdom of God." Hearing that reply, Holee drops to his knees grieving for himself, his son, and time wasted. Jesus and his disciples move on.

As the weather cools and fall arrives, Salome's swollen belly spreads, and misery with it. The growth of the fetus adds daily, but Salome's misery multiplies. The wine and promiscuity have left her with the heavier weight of regret and heartfelt grief.

One hundred twenty miles south of Salome and her misery, a merchandiser and his servant lead a camel and two donkeys along the shore on the west bank of the Dead Sea. The servant looks to his master and asks, "Master Eon, are those caves on the horizon?"

"Yes, they are. There is a community there. We are going to trade with them."

"Master Eon, who are they?"

"They are a religious sect affiliated with the Essenes."

"Who?"

"Let me explain what I know about them. A group of Jews disgusted with the corrupt religious leaders of the Holy Temple in Jerusalem decided to move here many years ago. They came up with their own laws. Anyone who joins the sect must give up all his possessions. They have all things in common: money, clothes, food, and even expenses. They are bound to unconditional obedience. Entering the sect, each member is given three things: a pickaxe, an apron, and a white garment. They wear this garment until it is shreds. They are humble, modest, and honest. And when they eat, they eat only enough to satisfy their hunger; they never indulge. Look at them; they all are slim. They have no slaves, no swearing, and no spitting forward or to the right."

"Are you serious, Master Eon?"

"Yes. Here at Qumran, everybody works and worships God. This is the kind of society they have—no violence, no rape, no murder, and virtually no problems. With the exception of the rank, they are common. It takes three years to become a full member. The first year they are not allowed to use the community's special water. And until a convert has served his three years to become a full member, he is not allowed to eat with the full members in the community meals."

"You said something about special water?"

"Yes, they have diverse baptisms. They have to bathe before each meal. In fact, they have to bathe before they can write the name of their God."

"Why?"

"Devotion. They are afraid they may profane the name of their God."

"Write? What do they write?"

"They copy the scriptures to preserve them, so I have been told. They regard the scriptures as their greatest possessions. I suppose they hide the scrolls for fear that the world wants to destroy the word of God. Personally, I don't care what they do. I just want to trade with them."

"Master Eon, I have just one more question: Do they worship at the Temple?"

"No. They don't sacrifice animals, but sometimes they do send gifts of incense to the Temple. They consider their personal sacrifice to be more valuable than the sacrifice of animals. They do not anoint their faces with adorning potions, for they consider their natural complexion to be praiseworthy as God's creation. They present their bodies as living sacrifices to God."

"Master Eon, you are a knowledgeable man."

"I've been trading with people a long time. I have learned whom to trade with. These people of the Qumran may be poor, but they are honest. Wealthy people are apt to cheat you. Just six months ago, I was thrown in prison because the wealthy tetrarch, Herod Antipas, tried to cheat me out of my money. He got away with it too. He's the reason I stay west of the Jordan and south of Tiberias."

Nodding his head toward a man dressed in white garments, Eon says to his servant, "That is the Teacher of Righteousness."

"Who?"

"The Teacher of Righteousness—that is what they call the leader of their sect."

"Hello," greets the teacher.

"Hello, Teacher. I am here to see if you have any goods for sale, or if you need anything. I am going to Jerusalem for the Feast of Tabernacles."

"I do have some incense to trade and some to send to the Temple for the feast."

"Fine, Teacher, let me see what you have."

The Teacher of Righteousness turns and leads Eon and his servant toward a ground level cave.

Walking toward the cave, Eon sees a familiar-looking young man working in the field. "Teacher," calls Eon.

"Yes."

"Is that young man in the field the infamous Barabbas?"

"You must be mistaken," replies the Teacher of Righteousness.

"I don't think so. I know him very well."

The teacher looks at Eon to inquire, "You know Barabbas?"

"Yes, sir. I was incarcerated with him at Machaerus." Eon looks closer and says, "That is Barabbas."

"You are wrong," replies the Teacher to assure Eon. "Now come and inspect the incense."

Sensing that the teacher does not like his word being disputed, Eon does not challenge the issue of the young man's identity. "Well, it *has* been about six months since I last saw Barabbas, and at that time, I saw him only by torch light. Anyway, I wish Barabbas well. He is a friend of mine."

After Eon leaves with the precious incense, the Teacher of Righteousness talks to Barabbas. "Barabbas, a merchandiser named Eon came by earlier and thought he recognized you."

Stricken with anxiety, Barabbas expresses his concern. "I can't stay here and jeopardize the whole group. What do you want me to do?"

"Until we know for sure that Eon believes he was mistaken about your identity, you will be moved to the upper cave."

"Teacher, I can't do that—only full members are allowed there."

"We have no choice, Barabbas. Don't you want to study and copy the scriptures?"

"Oh, yes, Teacher, but what about Logos? If the legionnaires come looking for me, they will find him."

"I hadn't thought about that."

"I know what to do," suggests Barabbas. "Send Logos to Obal, the stable owner in Jericho. He will hide him for me."

"Good idea."

"Teacher, I appreciate the refuge you have given me."

"Don't thank me; thank God. If it hadn't been God's will for you to be here, you would have died in the desert. I believe God has a plan for you. Now go to the over-looking cave. If the Romans come for you, you will be able to see them and escape. If Eon tries to collect the reward from the Romans, we will know shortly, for he will be in Jerusalem for the Feast of Tabernacles."

On the fourteenth day of Tishri, the seventh month, Eon delivers the incense to the Temple from the Qumran sect. Then he sells and trades goods needed for the festival. Eon and his servant wander among the booths made of fresh branches of leafy trees of palm and willow. The booths are located on courts, streets, public squares, and roofs. Eon watches the people prepare to live in the booths, for they must dwell in them for the next seven days.

At sundown, the priests of the Temple blast their trumpets announcing the advent of the Feast of Tabernacles.

Then, immediately after midnight, the priests throw open the gates of the Temple.

On the fifteenth day of Tishri, the Jews celebrate, for this day commemorates the time when the Israelites dwelt in booths on their journey through the wilderness to the Holy Land. The Feast of Tabernacles gives the Israelites an attitude of thankfulness for the crops. Moreover, the Jews are full of expectancy, for the feast points to the harvest of all nations written about in the Book of Isaiah: "And in this mountain shall the LORD of hosts make unto all people a feast of fat things, a feast of wines on the lees, of fat things full of marrow, of wines on the lees well refined. And he will destroy in this mountain the face of the covering cast over all people, and the veil that is spread over all nations."

Arising early on the fifteenth of Tishri, Mary, Martha, and a joyous procession with music follow a priest to the Pool of Siloam. The priest draws water into a golden pitcher and starts back to the Temple with it.

Meanwhile, Lazarus and Joktan follow a procession to Motza, a place in the Kidron Valley, and gather willow branches to place on either side of the great altar. The members of the procession bend the branches over the altar of burnt offering to form a leafy canopy.

Hearing a threefold blast on the trumpets, the priest who went to the Pool of Siloam enters the Temple with the golden pitcher of water as another priest enters with a pitcher of wine for a drink offering. The brethren bring the pieces of sacrifice to the altar. Each priest pours his offering into separate silver basins, which run to the base of the altar. Then all the people shout for the priest with the water to raise his hand to show that he poured the water into the basin.

Joktan whispers, "Lazarus, why do the people shout for the priest to show that he poured the water?"

"Because approximately one hundred twenty years ago, Alexander Jannaeus, the Maccabean priest and king, poured the water on the ground to show his contempt for the Pharisees. When he poured it on the ground, the people pelted him. The people would have killed him if it weren't for his bodyguards. There were over six thousand Jews killed that day."

"I see," responds Joktan.

"Alexander Jannaeus favored political Sadducees just as our high priest, Caiaphas does."

The Levites begin to chant the Great Hallel. Caiaphas offers the sacrifice. Over the next seven days of the feast, the priests offer seventy bulls, fourteen rams, ninety-eight lambs, and seven goats.

On the twenty-first day of Tishri, the last day of the feast, Jesus stands and cries, saying, "If any man thirst, let him come unto me, and drink. He that believeth on me, as the scripture hath said, out of his belly shall flow rivers of living water." (But this spake he of the Spirit, which they that believe on him should receive: for the Holy Ghost was not yet given; because that Jesus was not yet glorified.)

Realizing that this is the last day of the feast, Eon looks to his servant and asks, "Do we have any frankincense and myrrh left?"

"Yes, sir."

"That's unfortunate, for we won't be able to sell it to anyone now that the feast is almost over. I'll have to sell it to the exporter."

Arriving at the Joktan's office, Eon goes inside. Joktan is looking over a scroll as Javan puts some papers in his mailbag. Eon speaks up to get Joktan's attention. "Hello, Joktan."

Joktan rises from his chair and greets Eon. "Hello, it has been a long time."

"Yes, it has. I was wondering if you need any frankincense and myrrh."

"Well, I don't need any locally, but I can export it if the price is right and only if it is quality."

"The quality is of the best. Here is a sample. See for yourself."

Joktan examines the rich viscosity of the pungent products. "I'll have to agree with you; I haven't seen incense with this quality in some time. Where did you get it?"

"From some poor people in the wilderness. They sent some for a gift to the Temple, and I bought the rest."

"Since there's no need for it locally, I will give you the market price of a lower quality," offers Joktan.

"That sounds fair enough to me," answers Eon as he remembers what Barabbas said about Joktan. *Maybe Barabbas was right—Joktan may be trustworthy. Barabbas did say that Joktan and the boy who runs the mail were his close friends.*

Joktan calls, "Javan, wait a minute. I need to make an invoice for this incense and send it with the mail."

Javan—that's the name of the man Barabbas told me about. "Joktan and Javan?" exclaims Eon.

"Yes," the two reply simultaneously.

"Do you two know a young man named Barabbas?"

"Yes!" Joktan and Javan reply again.

Eon asks, "Do you know where he is?"

Javan is silent as Joktan replies, "No, but we really wish we did. Barabbas is our friend. I love the boy and his mother."

"Do you know where Barabbas is?" asks Javan.

"Yes, I do."

With excitement Joktan and Javan burst aloud, "Where?"

"Well, at first, gentlemen, I was not going to tell anyone, for I think Barabbas is content with hiding. However, since you are his friends, I will tell you."

"Where?" the two exclaim again.

"At Qumran with the ones affiliated with the Essenes."

Javan screams and leaps with joy as Joktan begins to question Eon. "Are you sure?"

"Yes, sir. I shared a cell with Barabbas at Machaerus. I was freed, and I heard that Barabbas escaped."

"Well, what did Barabbas have to say for himself when you saw him at the Qumran?"

"I didn't get to talk to him. The Teacher of Righteousness didn't like the idea of my recognizing Barabbas, so I acted as if I had made a mistake in identity."

"Did you see him up close?" Joktan interrogates.

"No, but I know it was Barabbas. He was working in the field—plowing with a beautiful black and white stallion, which I thought was peculiar."

"Logos!" shouts Javan.

"You know the horse too, I gather."

Javan replies, "Best horse on the face of the earth."

With a tone of authority, Joktan asks, "Have you told anybody about Barabbas?"

"No, sir," answers Eon, shaking his head firmly. "Barabbas is my friend."

Javan declares, "I'm going to tell Mary and leave for Qumran."

"No, don't do that!" exclaims Joktan.

"Why?"

"We're not certain this is Barabbas. If it isn't, then Mary will be disappointed by false hope. We can't put her through that."

"You're right. Well, I'm going to Qumran to make sure this man with the black and white stallion is Barabbas. It has to be."

Nervously, Joktan exclaims, "No, don't go!"

"Why?" asks Javan, puzzled by Joktan's reply.

"Uh . . . " Joktan pauses to come up with a logical answer. "You must take the mail to Caesarea."

"Please, Joktan, let me go to Qumran."

Holding the invoice for the incense he has just bought, Joktan replies, "These invoices must reach the port at Joppa by tomorrow."

"But . . ." counters Javan.

With a big smile, Joktan interrupts, "If you will take the mail to Joppa, I will go and see if Barabbas is at Qumran."

"All right, I'll run the mail and see you in two days," replies Javan as he races out the door.

Eon turns and begins to leave. "Well, I must be on my way. Good luck, Joktan. Tell Barabbas I wish him well."

Joktan locks his office and hurries to the fortress of Antonia to tell Pilate that he has found Barabbas.

In the lower city, Mary gathers her personal things and moves out of the booth she has shared with Martha and Lazarus. Her obligation to dwell there for seven days ends at sundown. She is glad to get back home so that she can sleep on her bed.

Darkness falls on the Pilate's praetorium—the former palace from which Herod the Great issued death sentences to many innocent men, women, and children. With the three mighty towers in the northwest corner of the praetorium, the princes of darkness conspire. The power of politics, the passion for profit, and the rhetoric of religion converge at the *Bema,* the portable tribunal placed on the *Gabbatha,* the mosaic pavement in front of the palace. Pilate, Joktan, and Caiaphas discuss their collusion.

Joktan asks Pilate, "Who did you send to arrest Barabbas?"

"My best—Villus, Exum, Persis, and Apelles, all of whom have been fooled by Barabbas before. They will be successful this time. I sent a quaternion with each leader—a total of sixty-eight men. They will surround the community. Barabbas will not escape if he is there."

"Well there's no mistake; Barabbas is there," replies

Joktan in assurance. "With Barabbas out of the way, there are only two minor people we must deal with—Javan and Mary."

"And Jesus!" blurts Caiaphas.

"Jesus?" exclaims Pilate. "I'll have nothing to do with your religious matters."

"What about insurrection?" Caiaphas rebuts. "Jesus is amassing quite an army."

"An army? I would hardly call his followers an army. They are a peaceful group."

Caiaphas warns Pilate about Jesus. "It appears that way right now, but you just wait and see. If you are going to do something about Jesus, you had better do it now, for this is the last day of the feast. Tomorrow he may be gone. He travels like a fugitive—very hard to catch."

Joktan speaks up to mediate. "Listen! When Javan returns from the mail route and finds out I betrayed Barabbas, he will tell Mary I have used them. Then she will ruin my business and your prestige, Caiaphas. And ultimately, all three of us will lose profits."

"Killing them would raise riotous suspicion," declares Pilate.

Joktan reminds the other two how their problem began. "That mistake has already been made once. That's the reason we have this problem. If Anak and Marcus hadn't murdered Rabba, then—"

"Don't start pointing fingers!" Pilate orders authoritatively.

"I'm sorry," Joktan apologizes. "Let's focus on the problem. Mary is respected by the religious community. She can cause problems if she starts talking. We must get rid of her." Pausing for a moment to think, Joktan rubs his chin, then looks at Pilate and says, "I will come up with a solution."

"I may be able to offer some advice," offers Caiaphas. "What if Mary's own people murdered her?"

"That would be ideal, but how can that happen?" asks Joktan.

Pilate says, "Good night, gentlemen. I'm going to bed. I'll leave this problem in your hands. I will not be involved."

Early the next morning, Joktan goes to Mary's house and knocks on the door.

"Who is it?" calls Mary.

"Joktan."

Mary opens the door and lets him inside. Wearing only her nightwear, Mary turns to go to her bedroom, which is a room partitioned off by curtains. "I'll get dressed and be right with you."

Joktan apologizes, "I'm sorry, Mary, but I could wait no longer to talk to you. I know that you are exhausted from the Feast of Tabernacles." Mary pulls the curtain to her bedroom as Joktan says, "Mary, please lie down while I talk to you. I insist that you lie down and listen through the curtain. I want you to be comfortable while you hear me out. Then I will leave and you can go back to sleep."

"Well, all right," says Mary as she lies on her bed.

Joktan paces the floor as he talks to Mary. "Mary, I can't stand it any longer. I want to please you and make you happy." Pulling the curtains back to look at Mary, Joktan says, "What I am trying to say is that I love you, and I want to marry you."

Mary starts to arise, but Joktan grabs her shoulders, pinning her to the bed. Looking into Mary's eyes, Joktan says, "Mary, I love you. I need you. I want to be your husband." Then Joktan pauses, looks intently at Mary, and asks, "Haven't I been good to you?"

"Oh, yes, Joktan, you know that I love you, but—."

Joktan kisses Mary to interrupt her reply. When Mary slips her arms around him to embrace him, Joktan relinquishes his kiss.

Mary sympathizes: "I'm sorry I have taken so long in my decision about marrying you, but—"

Lying with Mary, Joktan interrupts Mary again with an aggressive kiss as he starts to undress her. Mary turns her head to one side to free her lips. "No, Joktan, don't!" Joktan kisses her again and proceeds further. As Joktan kisses her, Mary's door, which Joktan has unlatched, swings open quietly.

Unnoticed by Mary, Caiaphas, two scribes, and two Pharisees go inside to get a glimpse of the nearly naked couple.

Upon realizing Caiaphas is standing over her, Mary suddenly shoves Joktan away. Joktan rolls up in the blanket and covers his face with his clothes. Without ample time to cover herself, Mary pulls her nightclothes next to her body as she sits on the edge of her bed.

"Mary, what are you doing with this man?" demands Caiaphas.

Mortified with fear, speechless, Mary looks to Joktan, who has covered his face.

"You two are adulterers!" declares one of the Pharisees.

Caiaphas speaks to defend Joktan. "We know that Mary is a Judaist. Sir, what about you?"

"I'm a Roman citizen and know not your God," replies Joktan, keeping his face hidden with the blanket.

"What about you, Mary? Do you denounce your God and your faith?"

Aware that adultery is punishable by death, Mary answers. "Hear, O Israel: The Lord our God is one Lord: And thou shalt love the Lord thy God with all thine heart, and with all thy soul, and with all thy might."

"You have condemned yourself. You will die at the hands of the believers, for Moses in the law commanded us those such offenders should be stoned." Pronouncing her death sentence, Caiaphas looks to his men. "Seize her men, for she is under the Law of Moses. As for this man, he is not punishable by Roman law."

The religious men seize Mary and drag her away to stone her. Caiaphas and Joktan are left alone as Joktan puts on his clothes. Joktan looks to Caiaphas with a sigh of satisfaction and says, "That's the way of business! Some reap the benefits and some lose."

"What are you talking about?" asks Caiaphas.

"Death is part of business."

"You're wrong," affirms Caiaphas prophetically. "Death is part of the law, and everyone is under it."

Incensed by Caiaphas' words, Joktan retaliates, "You don't live like it."

"Not many people do. We Sadducees believe that men die like dogs. When we die, there is no judgement. Therefore, there's no punishment."

"Exactly!" affirms Joktan.

"Let me clarify my words," says Caiaphas. "I believe there is no heaven, but I *pray* there is no hell."

Fifteen miles east of Jerusalem at Qumran, the senior member of the Essenes looks out of the upper cave. "Barabbas, come and see."

Seeing the whole commune surrounded by Roman legionnaires, Barabbas says, "They'll soon climb up to search for me." Barabbas and the senior run to the other end of the cave where there is an opening just large enough for him to crawl out to the top of the plateau.

Hearing voices from the outside, Barabbas knows the legionnaires have found his escape passage. Barabbas looks helplessly at the senior member and says, "I'll have to surrender, for there is no escape."

The senior says, "Follow me." Turning and running down into the cave, the senior leads Barabbas to a soft dirt floor. "Help me dig!" demands the senior. Together, they dig out loose dirt from a small square hole capped off by short wooden planks below the dirt floor.

Pulling the planks up, Barabbas sees the opening below. "What is this?" asks Barabbas.

"This is the secret compartment where we store the word of God—the Dead Sea Scrolls. We place the scripture in jars and put them down here for preservation. You will also find that the Sword of the Lord is down there."

Without hesitation or further instruction, Barabbas lowers himself through the opening. Then the senior places the planks back in the hole and covers the opening with dirt.

Nine days later, Javan rides into the monastic community at Qumran. Approaching the Teacher of Righteousness, Javan asks about Barabbas.

Teacher replies, "Not many days ago, the Romans came here looking for Barabbas."

"Yes, but I was also told they did not find him. Do you have any idea where he may be? I must find him. I have very bad news for him concerning his mother."

Peering from the upper cave, Barabbas waves and yells, "Javan, my friend, I'll be down in a minute."

Excusing himself, the Teacher welcomes Javan to have a seat while waiting for Barabbas to come down.

When Barabbas reaches the floor of the ravine, he and Javan embrace each other. Stepping back to look at each other, Barabbas notices Javan's sad face. Barabbas says uneasily, "You have brought bad news, haven't you?"

Javan almost breaks down in tears, and Barabbas demands, "Javan, what is it?"

"Your mother."

"Tell me."

"On the last day of the Feast of Tabernacles, a merchandiser named Eon came to the Joktan's office. He thought Joktan was your friend, so—"

"What do you mean?" interrupts Barabbas. "Joktan is my friend, isn't he?"

"Just listen, Barabbas. Eon told Joktan and me that you were at Qumran. I was coming to find you, but Joktan told me he would go and find you if I would carry the mail. So I left with the mail.

"When I got back to Jerusalem, I was terminated from my job upon arrival at Joktan's office. So I ran to Mary's house to find out what was going on. She was nowhere to be found. I asked a neighbor where Mary was and she replied that Mary was in hell. Then I ran to the Temple to investigate. Nobody was willing to talk about Mary for fear of the scribes and Pharisees. However, as I was hunting information, I overheard a man named John tell an incredible story—a story about Mary."

"Tell it!" shouts Barabbas with anxiety.

"Mary was condemned for committing adultery."

"What?"

"Let me finish. After I left with the mail, Joktan evidently told Pilate where you were. I imagine that he wanted the bounty money. The next morning Joktan and Mary were caught in the very act of adultery by Caiaphas and some religious men."

"That's a lie!" shouts Barabbas.

"That's not the worst of it. Joktan denied the Jewish faith, but Mary positively affirmed hers with the Shema. Caiaphas condemned her to be put to death by the letter of the law—stoning according to the law given to Moses."

"No!" cries Barabbas, grimacing with fear.

"She's alive, Barabbas!" declares Javan. "Mary was dragged to the Temple to be condemned before the congregation. Guess who was there teaching the people—Jesus."

"So how did Mother escape condemnation?" asks Barabbas, for he knows that nobody can change a sentence of death pronounced by the high priest.

"This is the story that I heard John tell: The scribes and Pharisees brought unto Jesus a woman taken in adultery; and when they had set her in the midst, they say unto him, 'Master, this woman was taken in adultery, in the very act. Now Moses in the law commanded us, that such should be stoned: but what sayest thou?'

"This they said, tempting him, that they might have to accuse him. But Jesus stooped down, and with his finger wrote on the ground, as though he heard them not. So when they continued asking him, he lifted up himself, and said unto them, 'He that is without sin among you, let him first cast a stone at her.' And again he stooped down, and wrote on the ground. And they which heard it, being convicted by their own conscience, went out one by one, beginning at the eldest, even unto the last: and Jesus was left alone, and the woman standing in the midst.

"When Jesus had lifted up himself, and saw none but the woman, he said unto her, 'Woman, where are those thine accusers? hath no man condemned thee?'

She said, 'No man, Lord.'

And Jesus said unto her, 'Neither do I condemn thee: go, and sin no more.'"

Having retold the story as he had heard it, Javan says, "The people in the Temple let Mary go free, but on her way back home, people came out and taunted her. Her friends and neighbors threw rocks at her. Bloodied by the rocks hurled at her, she realized that if she didn't leave Jerusalem the people would kill her. So she went to Bethany to live with Martha and Lazarus."

With relief, Barabbas sighs, "Thank you, God!"

"But Mary is not the only one excommunicated that day."

"Who else?"

"The blind man who used to sit and beg at the Golden Gate."

"You mean the blind man that Bartimaeus used to sit with."

"Yes, that's the one—Blind Bartimaeus' friend."

"Here's the story as told by John: As Jesus passed by, he saw a man which was blind from his birth. And his disciples asked him, saying, 'Master, who did sin, this man, or his parents, that he was born blind?'

Jesus answered, 'Neither hath this man sinned, nor his parents: but that the works of God should be made manifest in him. I must work the works of him that sent me, while it is day: the night cometh, when no man can work. As long as I am in the world, I am the light of the world.'

When he had thus spoken, he spat on the ground, and made clay of the spittle, and he anointed the eyes of the blind man with the clay, and said unto him, 'Go wash in the pool of Siloam,' (which is by interpretation, Sent.) He went his way therefore, and washed, and came seeing.

The neighbors therefore, and they which before had seen him that he was blind, said, 'Is not this he that sat and begged?'

Some said, 'This is he.'

Others said, 'He is like him.'

But the blind man said, 'I am he.'

Therefore said they unto him, 'How were thine eyes opened?'

He answered and said, 'A man that is called Jesus made clay, and anointed mine eyes, and said unto me, 'Go to the pool of Siloam, and wash:' and I went and washed, and I received sight.

Then said they unto him, 'Where is he?'

He said, 'I know not.'

They brought to the Pharisees him that aforetime was blind.

And it was the sabbath day when Jesus made the clay, and opened his eyes. Then again the Pharisees also asked him how he had received his sight. He said unto them, 'He put clay upon mine eyes, and I washed, and do see.'

Therefore said some of the Pharisees, 'This man is not of God, because he keepeth not the sabbath day.'

Others said, 'How can a man that is a sinner do such miracles?' And there was a division among them.

They say unto the blind man again, 'What sayest thou of him, that he hath opened thine eyes?'

He said, 'He is a prophet.'

But the Jews did not believe concerning him, that he had been blind, and received his sight, until they called the parents of him that had received his sight. And they asked them saying, 'Is this your son, who ye say was born blind? how then doth he now see?'

His parents answered them and said, 'We know that this is our son, and that he was born blind: But by what means he now seeth, we know not; or who hath opened his eyes, we know not: he is of age; ask him: he shall speak for himself.'

These words spake his parents, because they feared the Jews: for the Jews had agreed already, that if any man did confess that he was Christ, he should be put out of the synagogue. Therefore said his parents, 'He is of age; ask him.'

Then again called they the man that was blind, and said unto him, 'Give God the praise: we know that this man is a sinner.'

He answered and said, 'Whether he be a sinner or no, I know not: one thing I know, that, whereas I was blind, now I see.'

Then said they to him again, 'What did he to thee? how opened he thine eyes?'

He answered them, 'I have told you already, and ye did not hear: wherefore would ye hear it again? will ye also be his disciples?'

Then they reviled him, and said, 'Thou art his disciple; but we are Moses' disciples. We know that God spake unto Moses: as for this fellow, we know not from whence he is.'

The man answered and said unto them, 'Why herein is a

marvellous thing, that ye know not from whence he is, and yet he hath opened mine eyes. Now we know that God heareth not sinners: but if any man be a worshipper of God, and doeth his will, him he heareth. Since the world began was it not heard that any man opened the eyes of one that was born blind. If this man were not of God, he could do nothing.'

They answered and said unto him, 'Thou wast altogether born in sins, and dost thou teach us?' And they cast him out.

Jesus heard that they had cast him out; and when he had found him, he said unto him, 'Dost thou believe on the Son of God?'

He answered and said, 'Who is he, Lord, that I might believe on him?'

And Jesus said unto him, 'Thou hast both seen him, and it is he that talketh with thee.'

And he said, 'Lord, I believe.' And he worshipped him.

And Jesus said, 'For judgement I am come into this world, that they which see not might see; and that they which see might be made blind.'

And some of the Pharisees which were with him heard these words, and said unto him, 'Are we blind also?'

Jesus said unto them, 'If ye were blind, ye should have no sin: but now ye say, We see; therefore your sin remaineth.'"

Ending his story, Javan says, "Being ostracized, this blind man moved to Bethany too."

"Prosis," declares Barabbas. "Prosis is the blind man's name."

"Yes, that's his name. He is a close friend of blind Bartimaeus. Now Prosis and Mary have something in common. They were saved by Jesus."

"Did you go to Bethany to check on my mother, Javan?"

"I surely did, and guess who came while I was there."

"Jesus?"

"Yes, he came to Lazarus' house. Lazarus, Martha, and Mary invited him into their home." Javan adds, "Mary almost worships the ground Jesus walks on. When Jesus came into the house, Mary sat at Jesus' feet and heard every word that came from his mouth while Martha was cumbered with serving. Irritated at serving by herself, Martha says, 'Lord dost thou not care that my sister hath left me to serve alone? bid her therefore that she help me.'

Jesus answered and said unto her, 'Martha, Martha, thou are careful and troubled about many things: But one thing is needful: and Mary hath chosen that good part, which shall not be taken away from her.'"

"Well, Javan, I am grateful to Jesus for saving my mother's life, but I heard that he claims to be God. Jesus has said, 'Before Abraham was, I am.' That is blasphemy, for there is only one God."

"Listen, Barabbas, I can only reply as Prosis did. "Since the world began was it not heard that any man opened the eyes of one that was born blind."

"Javan, you are falling for this heresy too. Has God lied? For four thousand years, God has taught us that there is only one. You had better remember the scriptures of Moses. We know Moses and his origin."

Javan replies by reciting the words of Prosis again. "You know Moses. However, herein is a marvellous thing, that ye know not from whence Jesus is, and yet he hath opened mine eyes."

Hating to sound like the religious Pharisees, Barabbas concedes, "I give up, for there's no hope for those tossed by every wind of doctrine."

"What are you going to do now, Barabbas, stay here?"

"No! I'm fighting back. The Romans and the hypocrites are going to regret murdering my father and ruining my mother. I'm going to join my fellow Zealots."

"Join them? Barabbas, they think you are their messiah."

"I might be," replies Barabbas. "The Teacher of Righteousness is not going to like it, but I must break my vow. I'll get my sword—the Sword of the Lord. I must go."

"Where are you going?"

"You are going to take me to Jericho to get Logos. Then I am going to Bethlehem."

"Bethlehem? Are you crazy? That is only five miles from Jerusalem—only five miles from your greatest enemy!"

"True, but out of Bethlehem shall come forth a ruler in Israel. It is the birthplace of our greatest king—David. And now I must fulfill my destiny."

Realizing that Bethlehem is dangerously close to Pilate and Caiaphas, Javan reminds Barabbas, "Romans and Jews want to collect the bounty on your head."

"The Lord sent Elijah to Zarephath, near Jezebel's birthplace. That's why I need to be in Bethlehem—the backyard of my enemy. From there, I can assist the Zealots."

"Who will house you there?"

"A man named Holee. He is a devout Zealot. He owns a run-down inn and a stable. The Zealots meet there often. I will be safe with Holee. Come. I must tell the brethren goodbye."

12

Men & Miracles

As the days shorten and the nights lengthen, the harsh wind of winter blows across Caesarea Philippi. Heavy gray clouds of discontent and discomfort hang over Salome as she importunes her gods for relief. She stares across the courtyard of her palace. Looking at the trees, she sees only the cold shadows of the naked branches. Her body is frozen with ennui and nostalgia.

Having suffered in the opulence of her lifestyle, Salome is miserable. Her feelings of barrenness are abruptly broken by the birth of her child. Still curled as though in the womb, the wet, wide-eyed newborn lies beside Salome.

Tetrarch Philip II takes the baby out on the balcony, lifts him up, and heralds, "A prince is born!" The whole city celebrates, for Salome has given birth. Antipas and Herodias are there to bestow gifts on their grandson. Philip and Antipas both think that the newborn is their offspring. Philip and Antipas exit the bedroom to leave Herodias alone with Salome.

Watching Salome nourish her baby, Herodias says, "Why do you seem so depressed, my dear?"

With a tone of regret, Salome answers, "You know very well why I'm miserable. Both of those men out there think they are my baby's father. I don't like living this lie. I'd rather be poor and live with someone I respect. I should tell them the truth."

"I wouldn't do that if I were you," threatens Herodias.

"Why not?" pleads Salome. "I'd rather be dead than to live like this."

"Oh, that would make things simple," Herodias says facetiously. "However, you need to consider someone else. What do you think Antipas and Philip would do to this fine baby boy of yours? If they knew that Barabbas is the baby's father, the tetrarchs would cut your baby into pieces . . . and you too. You'd better think about it. If you tell the truth, your baby will die. If you use your head, your baby will be a prince and will have everything he needs."

Feeling trapped, Salome says, "Please leave, Mother, I just want to be alone."

"Salome, we will be leaving for Perea tomorrow. King Aretas, the king of Arabia has declared war on us."

"See, Mother, we must reap what we have sown."

"Nonsense, Salome. The war is only retaliation for his daughter. Antipas divorced that poor loser. She did not know how to please her man."

"Just go, Mother."

In Bethlehem, where Samuel anointed David as future king, Barabbas lodges in the inn owned by Holee. Having been notified by Barabbas, Mary and Javan visit with him from time to time. While visiting with her son, Mary always gives testimony of the greatness of Jesus.

Barabbas, Tola, and Jair meet at the inn to discuss their plans as the leaders of the Zealots. Realizing that King

Aretas wants revenge, not the Machaerus fortress, Barabbas proposes that the Zealots join the forces of Aretas to seize it. "King Aretas would probably give us Machaerus if we help him seize the fortress."

"Since Machaerus is out of Israel, why do we want it?" asks Jair.

"Machaerus would give the Zealots a stronghold outside Pilate's jurisdiction. Since Pilate and Antipas are not friends, I don't think Pilate will be eager to assist him there. If we can set up an arsenal in Machaerus, we can then seize Masada, the fortress on the west bank of the Dead Sea. From that natural stronghold, the Zealots can take Jerusalem. The Jews will once again own what God has promised us."

"I don't think the Zealots are ready," declares Tola.

Barabbas agrees, "Not now, but in the spring at the Passover, we can rally all of our Zealots."

"Barabbas, the zealous people of Israel will follow you. They believe you are the arm of God. Let's get the message to all the God-fearing Jews. Our time will come at the Passover."

Later in the winter, when Antipas and Herodias are staying at the fortress of Machaerus, some Pharisees come to Jesus and say unto him, "Get thee out of Perea and depart hence: for Herod will kill thee."

Jesus replies, "Go ye, and tell that fox, behold, I cast out devils, and I do cures today and tomorrow, and the third day I shall be perfected."

The Pharisees go and tell Antipas what Jesus said. Upon hearing the message, Herodias looks to Antipas and asks, "What is the meaning of the message?"

Very aware of Jewish beliefs, Antipas answers, "Jesus says he does the works of God by casting out devils and healing people. I'm not sure what he means by the third day, but the phrase about his being perfected means he will become

God. Jesus has grandiose delusions. He says that he now does the works of God and that in the future he will be God. His claim to be God is the reason the Jews want to kill him."

Lazarus of Bethany becomes very ill. Mary and Martha send a message to Jesus, who is in Perea. "Lord, behold, he whom thou lovest is sick."

When Jesus hears that, he says, "This sickness is not unto death, but for the glory of God, that the Son of God might be glorified thereby."

When Jesus hears that Lazarus is sick, he abides two days still in the same place where he is. Then after that he says to his disciples, "Let us go into Judea again."

His disciples say unto him, "Master, the Jews of late sought to stone thee; and goest thou thither again?"

Jesus answers, "Are there not twelve hours in the day? If any man walk in the night, he stumbleth, because there is no light in him."

These things says he: and after that he says unto them, "Our friend Lazarus sleepeth; but I go, that I may awake him out of sleep."

Then say his disciples, "Lord, if he sleep, he shall do well."

Howbeit Jesus spoke of his death: but they think that he had spoken of taking of rest in sleep. Then Jesus says unto them plainly, "Lazarus is dead. And I am glad for your sakes that I was not there, to the intent ye may believe; nevertheless let us go unto him."

Then says Thomas, which is called Didymus, unto his fellow disciples, "Let us also go, that we may die with him."

In Bethlehem, Barabbas hears that his uncle is dead. Mary warns Barabbas not to come to the funeral, for the Romans and Jews are watching closely to see if Barabbas will come to the grave. Barabbas weeps for his uncle, Lazarus.

Then when Jesus comes to Bethany, he finds that Lazarus has lain in the grave four days already. Many of the Jews come to Martha and Mary to comfort them concerning their brother. Martha goes to meet Jesus while Mary is still at the house. Then Martha says unto Jesus, "Lord, if thou hadst been here, my brother would not have died. But I know that even now whatsoever thou wilt ask of God, God will give it thee."

Jesus says unto her, "I am the resurrection, and the life: he that believeth in me, though he were dead, yet shall he live: and whosoever liveth and believeth in me shall never die. Believest thou this?"

Martha says, "Yea, Lord: I believe that thou art the Christ, the Son of God, which should come into the world." Then Martha goes and calls Mary, "The Master is come, and calleth for thee."

As soon as Mary hears that, she arises quickly and goes unto Jesus. The Jews follow Mary. When Mary is come where Jesus is, she falls down at his feet and says, "Lord, if thou hadst been here, my brother had not died."

When Jesus sees her weeping and the Jews also weeping, Jesus groans in the spirit and is troubled. Jesus says, "Where have ye laid him?"

They say unto him, "Lord, come and see."

Jesus weeps.

Then say the Jews, "Behold how he loved him."

And some of them say, "Could not this man, which opened the eyes of the blind, have caused that even this man should not have died?"

Jesus groans again as he comes to the grave—a cave with a stone upon it. Jesus says, "Take ye away the stone."

Martha says, "Lord, by this time he stinketh: for he hath been dead four days."

Jesus says unto her, "Said I not unto thee, that, if thou wouldest believe, thou shouldest see the glory of God?"

Then, they take away the stone from the place where the dead was laid. And Jesus lifts up his eyes and says, "Father, I thank thee thou hast heard me. And I knew that thou hearest me always: but because of the people which stand by I said it, that they may believe that thou hast sent me." And when he has thus spoken, he cries with a loud voice, "Lazarus, come forth."

And he that was dead comes forth, bound hand and foot with graveclothes: and his face was bound about with a napkin.

Jesus says unto them, "Loose him, and let him go."

Prosis, the blind man whom Jesus healed, having witnessed Lazarus resurrected from the dead, runs to Jerusalem. Arriving at Solomon's Porch of the Temple, Prosis runs to the beggar's area near the Golden Gate. He grabs blind Bartimaeus by the mantle and announces for all to hear, "Jesus resurrected Lazarus from the grave of death!" Pulling blind Bartimaeus by the sleeve, Prosis shouts, "Come, Bartimaeus and all who are afflicted, Jesus is in Bethany!" Bartimaeus walks as fast as he can to Bethany. A multitude, hoping to find a miracle, follows Prosis.

Arriving in Bethany, Prosis and the followers find that Jesus is gone and that the miracle of Lazarus lives. Lazarus stands and gives testimony about the miracles of Jesus.

Then, the chief priests and Pharisees gather to council: "What do we? for this Jesus doeth many miracles. If we let him thus alone, all men will believe on him: and the Romans shall come and take away both our place and nation."

The Caiaphas answered, "Ye know nothing at all. Nor consider that it is expedient for us, that one man should die for the people, and that the whole nation perish not." And this speaks he not of himself: but being high priest that year, he prophesies that Jesus should die for that nation; and not for that nation only, but that also he should gather together in one the children of God that are scattered abroad. Then from that day forth they take counsel together for to put Jesus to death. Jesus therefore walks no more openly among the Jews.

Even though he does not find Jesus in Bethany, Prosis encourages Bartimaeus. "We are going to find Jesus. I'll not give up until you receive your sight. Bartimaeus, let's get some supplies and go to Perea."

"Perea?"

"Yes, it is obvious that Jesus could not stay here, for the Pharisees want to kill him. I believe that Jesus is going to Perea. If we seek, we shall find him. When we find him, we must be ready to seize the opportunity to worship him. Come, we'll find him. I have faith."

In Bethlehem, Barabbas and Holee hear about the resurrection of Lazarus. The news delights and puzzles Barabbas. Barabbas asks, "Holee, do you believe this is true? Can Jesus resurrect a man from the dead?"

"If anyone can, Jesus can," confesses Holee. "I'm not saying that Jesus did this miracle, but from my experience, I believe that if any man can do it, Jesus would be the one."

"What do you mean? Have you ever seen Jesus?"

"I have seen Jesus twice. The first time I saw him, I loved him. The second time I tried to kill him."

Noticing the solemn expression on Holee's face, Barabbas sits and inquires, "Please, tell me your story."

"About thirty years ago, my father died, and I inherited this inn. I was only twenty years old. My wife and I had a baby boy, Ephraim. He was a year old and was just learning to walk." A big smile brightens Holee face as he talks about his baby boy. "He was so cute. His hair was like that of fine silk; his grin of four baby teeth brought laughter to the inn. We three were one happy family.

"I had just buried my father when Caesar Augustus issued the decree that a census be taken of the Roman Empire. Everyone in Israel had to register in his own town.

This decree is what brought a man named Joseph and a woman named Mary to Bethlehem. They both were of the lineage of King David, who was born in Bethlehem, so both had to register here.

"That particular day my inn was full, and a spare room in Bethlehem could not be found. I was not prepared for the overload of work. My wife and I were trying to prepare the food, rooms, water, and linens. Business was good. We were taking in lots of money, but we were working day and night. The influx of people to Bethlehem caught us shorthanded.

"The sun began to set on the day that Joseph and Mary came looking for a room. Not having any, I told him that there was no room for them in the inn. Abigail, my wife, noting that Mary was pregnant, scolded me ever so tenderly for turning the pregnant woman away. I asked her what was I supposed to do, for there was no vacancy. She suggested the stable. So I offered Joseph and Mary a place to sleep in the stable. They graciously accepted the offer."

"Wait, Holee," interrupts Barabbas. "What does any of this have to do with your first encounter with Jesus?"

"Mary was the lady about to give birth to Jesus."

"Oh, I see," replies Barabbas. "I'm sorry. Please go on."

"Joseph and Mary settled down in the stable. Every time Abigail got a chance, she ran to check on the young couple. The next thing I knew Mary had given birth to a son, Jesus. She laid the baby in a feeding trough—a manger. Then the word of the birth went forth. The stable became a busy place. People from Bethlehem came to see the baby who was born in the stable.

"As the night progressed, some shepherds came to see Jesus. They said that they were abiding in the field, keeping watch over their flock by night, when the angel of the Lord came upon them. The glory of the Lord shined round about them, and they were sore afraid.

"The angel said unto them, 'Fear not: for, behold I bring

you good tidings of great joy, which shall be to all people. For unto you is born this day in the city of David a Savior, which is Christ the Lord. And this shall be a sign unto you; ye shall find the babe wrapped in swaddling clothes, lying in a manger.'

"The shepherd said that suddenly there was with the angel a multitude of the heavenly host praising God, and saying, 'Glory to God in the highest, and on earth peace, good will toward men.' After seeing Jesus in swaddling clothes, lying in a manger, the shepherds made known abroad the saying which was told them concerning this child. This brought more spectators by to see the baby, and my inn and stable became a popular place.

"Some of the visitors did not understand my predicament of not having a room for the child. Some scolded me as though I had turned the mother and child out. Others said business was just too good for me to have room and time for this glorious child. Fortunately, most people understood my efforts. Joseph and Mary certainly appreciated my help.

"Later, Joseph told me that Mary was a virgin. I didn't believe that nonsense. Nevertheless, I loved having Jesus around. This baby brought people together. It seemed as though this child had brought unity to Bethlehem, for many people pitched in to help the couple. This baby was a blessing to me and my family."

Suddenly Holee's countenance falls as a tear floats over his eye. "Then . . ." Holee pauses to clear his tearful eyes. "Then came that notable night—a dark night—when the silence was mistaken for the sound of peace. While everyone was asleep, the silence was broken by the hooves of Herod's horses. I leaped out of bed as soldiers kicked my door in. They came in my house with a torch and took my baby. They ripped Ephraim in two with a sword." Holee breaks down and weeps. Barabbas cries with Holee.

After gaining his composure, Holee goes on. "The whole

city was robbed of any child less than two years old. First, the inhabitants screamed with terror; then they mourned in grief. There was nothing we could do, for the king—Herod the Great—had given the order. I found out Herod had been told that Jesus would be king one day; therefore, he gave the order in an effort to kill Jesus. Herod failed, for Joseph, Mary, and Jesus escaped. Jesus was gone, and I was glad.

At one time, I thought Jesus was a blessing to me and my house, but Jesus was a curse to us. Jesus brought a curse of calamity on me. Abigail could not conceive again. She was stricken with unbearable grief that she could not overcome."

"Where is Abigail now?"

"She left years ago."

"Why?" asks Barabbas sympathetically.

"Well, here's the rest of the story. After losing our son, a little girl was abandoned in the streets. She must have been about two years of age. The people of Bethlehem brought her to us—Abigail and me. We named her Charisma, for she was a gift of grace, and God was the donor. We loved her, and she loved us. Charisma healed all of our past. She brought joy to our hearts.

Abigail nourished Charisma and cleaned her up except for one small spot—a blemish. Charisma had leprosy. Abigail and I would not give her up. Gradually eaten up, Charisma died." Holee's eyes fill with tears.

"Our lives never healed. The days became lengthy torture. I thought things could not get worse; then it happened—Abigail's blemish. She had contracted leprosy. Knowing I would not put her in the camp of the lepers, she left during the night. I searched, but I could not find her. Now, here I am without a reason to live. That's why I risk my life for the Zealots. I want to see Jerusalem enjoy freedom from the rule of the Herods and the Romans."

Wiping a tear from his eye, Barabbas asks, "What about the second time you saw Jesus?"

"Oh, yes, that is another story. Twelve years after the birth of Jesus, I heard about a remarkable boy named Jesus who had visited the Temple. I was told that this boy astonished the teachers of the Temple, but I never saw him. However, I knew that this boy was he. Again, Jesus was gone.

This past summer, I did search for and found Jesus near Samaria. It had been over thirty years, and there he was. I was going to kill him, but some strange events took place. Remember what I told you earlier about taking some grief for not giving Jesus a room to lay his head when he was born?"

"Yes, I remember."

"Well, as I approached Jesus with my dagger, I heard Jesus say to the man in front of me, 'Foxes have holes, and birds of the air have nests; but the Son of man hath not where to lay his head.' Immediately, I felt conviction. Jesus was born without a place to lay his head, and thirty years later, he still didn't have one.

"However, my sympathy for Jesus lasted for only a moment when the bitterness of my family's death placed my hand on my dagger again. With a mental picture of Ephraim's mutilated body, I moved closer to Jesus to kill him. Then I heard him tell the other man in front of me, 'Let the dead bury the dead.' Again, I was stunned, but not stopped.

With only one man between Jesus and me, I heard Jesus say, 'No man, having put his hand to the plough, and looking back, is fit for the kingdom of God.' That's when I was convicted by a revelation—I had wasted all these years with bitterness in my heart toward Jesus. Jesus did not bring a curse on me. I brought a curse on myself—my sin. If I had put the kingdom of God first, then this bitterness would not have robbed me of the past thirty years."

"That was quite some coincidence," Barabbas remarks.

"I mean the words that Jesus said just at the right time—words that saved his life and yours."

"Well, Barabbas, to be honest with you, I believe that things would have turned out differently if Jesus had been what I expected."

"What do you mean?"

"Before I found Jesus in Samaria, I expected to see a radical man with ulterior motives. I expected to see some militant type, but that is not what I saw at all. I saw a calm, humble man with love in his eye and longsuffering on his brow. He appeared to be a man of grief and sorrows—a man stricken, smitten of God, bruised and rejected of men. When I saw him, I could not help respecting him."

Prosis and blind Bartimaeus travel from Bethany toward Jericho. Prosis finds no one who has seen Jesus. Bartimaeus grows weary from the journey, especially when he hears the travelers and local inhabitants say they have not seen Jesus. Prosis still does not give up; he is determined to find Jesus.

Finally, after a slow journey, Prosis and Bartimaeus reach Jericho. Bartimaeus, exhausted from the fruitless journey, expresses his concerns. "Prosis, I appreciate your help, but we may never find Jesus. Since we don't have enough money to go much farther, shouldn't we go back to Jerusalem? Jesus *may* go back there."

"Oh, no, Jesus can't go back to Jerusalem. After the resurrection of Lazarus, the religious people would kill him. The next time Jesus goes to Jerusalem he will be put to death. Caiaphas and Annas are ready to stone him. Jesus is out here somewhere."

"I can't go any farther," declares Bartimaeus.

"I understand, Bartimaeus. Let's try another plan. Since the fords to Perea are here at Jericho, I'll get a room for you here. Then I will go across the Jordan to search for Jesus. If I find him, I will bring him or follow him until he comes back through here. Meanwhile, you may stay here in Jericho until I get back."

"That sounds like a good idea. And while I am waiting here in Jericho, I will sit by the wayside and ask for alms. Maybe I can collect enough to pay for my lodging."

"Great idea," agrees Prosis. "Let's get you a room so I may cross over to Perea. I'll be back in two or three days if I can't find Jesus."

On the third day of his stay in Jericho, Bartimaeus congregates with the beggars at the gate of Jericho. Being blind, he can't compete with the lame and deaf-mutes who sit at the front of the group. Feeling as though their territory is invaded by an outsider, the local beggars push Bartimaeus aside. Not having enough money left for his lodging, Bartimaeus hopes Prosis will return soon.

Realizing his hopeless circumstance, Bartimaeus is about to quit asking for alms when one of the locals says, "Here comes a group."

Bartimaeus decides to try asking for help one more time as another beggar says, "Here they come."

A cripple says, "Ah, this group coming is as poor as we are."

Recognizing the approaching group, another beggar agrees, "He's right, they don't have any money."

Hearing that, Bartimaeus thinks to himself. *There's no use. I'll wait until this group goes by; then I'll leave the beggars free to take all. I haven't received one piece of money since I got here. Even if the group coming had alms, the local beggars would beat me out of it. It's useless.* Bartimaeus waits for the group to pass by.

Bartimaeus hears the group arrive, and he hears the local beggars soften to their obsequious voices and beg for alms. As the group passes by, Bartimaeus hears the beggar beside him plead, "Jesus, give me alms."

Amazed at hearing the name of Jesus, Bartimaeus shouts with a loud voice, "Who passed by?"

The beggars answer, "Jesus."

When Bartimaeus hears that it was Jesus, he cries out with all his might, "Jesus! thou son of David, have mercy on me!"

The local beggars rebuke and scold Bartimaeus: "Be quiet, you're not going to get any money from him."

Knowing that Jesus has passed by, Bartimaeus becomes violent, screams, and wails aloud with all his might. "Jesus! Have mercy on me!"

Hearing Bartimaeus shout, some locals are about to silence Bartimaeus with blows. Hearing someone call upon his name, Jesus stops as all of heaven gives attention. Standing still, Jesus commands that Bartimaeus be called to him. The locals look to see if Bartimaeus will get any money from Jesus.

Bartimaeus wastes no time: he casts away his garment, arises and goes toward Jesus.

Jesus looks on Bartimaeus and asks, "What wilt thou that I should do unto thee?"

The locals think Bartimaeus will ask for money, but he, falling to his knees before Jesus, pleads, "Lord, that I might receive my sight."

Jesus says unto him, "Receive thy sight: thy faith hath saved thee." Immediately, Bartimaeus receives his sight. With eyes that can now see the beauty of the world, Bartimaeus follows Jesus and glorifies God.

With winter past, the blossom of the almond and peach comes, barley harvest begins in the Jordan Valley, and wheat forms its ear as the uplands become brilliant with vegetation and flowers. The birth of spring brings new hope to the Zealots. Tola's northern Israel Zealots and Jair's Judean Zealots are ready to follow Barabbas. Still hiding in Bethlehem, Barabbas makes his plans to rally the Zealots after the Passover.

Jair comes to Bethlehem to meet with Barabbas six days before the Passover. Jair says, "Barabbas, Tola sends word that he is on his way."

"Good," replies Barabbas. "I hope his Zealots will go along with the plans."

"I think they will, for they believe God has His hand on you, and He has. Who else has single-handedly stood up to the religious hypocrites and the Romans? You are blessed of God, Barabbas. Even though Tola and I are older and more experienced in leading the Zealots, we still are looking to you for the salvation of the Jews and their beliefs. You have an excellent plan."

"Yes, I believe my plan will work—if the Zealots will rally with me to fight against Herod Antipas at Machaerus. King Aretas has agreed to let the Zealots have Machaerus if we will help him seize it. Together, we should be able to do it. Then we will take the unguarded fortress of Masada from the Romans. Aretas will probably assist us with that too. We shall use Aretas' personal vendetta with Antipas to attain the freedom of the Jews in Israel."

"That is an excellent plan. Antipas' downfall—all because of his infidelity to his wife. Antipas shouldn't have taken his brother's wife, especially while he was still married to King Aretas' daughter."

"Jair, I don't think infidelity is the only cause. I think the execution of John the Baptist had something to do with it. John was a devout man."

"While you are talking about devout men, what do you think about this man named Jesus?"

"Jesus is a healer, and that's all—a man whose magical powers have gained him fame. He bothers me with his claim of deity. That's blasphemy! He deceives many."

"He bothers me too. He has quite a following . . . a following that used to be Zealots. Jesus has stolen our members and transformed them into a peaceful group. He teaches the people to love and pray for their enemies. He also teaches them to subject themselves to the Romans. We may find that we do not have enough Zealots to carry out our plans."

The thought of Jesus persuading Zealots not to resist the Romans frightens Barabbas. Without the help of the Zealots, Barabbas will never be free to live in peace. Worried about his freedom, Barabbas paces the floor and says, "If the Zealots don't rally together, we shall be slaves forever."

"I know," replies Jair as he prepares to leave. "Barabbas, I must go. Tola and I will meet with you before Passover."

Jesus goes to Jerusalem and enters the Temple. Casting out the people who sell and buy in the Temple, he overthrows the tables of the moneychangers and the seats of them who sell doves. Then Jesus teaches by proclamation. "Is it not written, my house shall be called of all nations the house of prayer? but ye have made it a den of thieves."

The scribes and the chief priests hear it, and seek how they might destroy him: for they fear him, because all the people are astonished at his doctrine. And when even is come, he goes out of the city.

With less than a week before the Passover, Jesus comes to Bethany to the house of Simon the leper to dine. Lazarus sits at the table with Jesus while Martha serves. With a revelation, Mary comes in with a pound of very costly spikenard, anoints the feet of Jesus, and wipes his feet with her hair. Simon's house is filled with the perfume of the ointment. Then Judas Iscariot says, "Why was not this ointment sold for three hundred pence and given to the poor?"

Jesus replies, "Let her alone: against the day of my burying hath she kept this. Verily I say unto you, wheresoever this gospel shall be preached throughout the whole world, this also that she hath done shall be spoken of for a memorial of her."

Judas Iscariot then goes to the chief priests to betray Jesus. When the priests hear it, they are glad and promise to give Judas money. Caiaphas instructs the priests to be careful in dealing with Jesus. "We must rid Jerusalem of Jesus before the Passover begins. He is amassing many followers. If we don't stop him, we will lose our prestige with our fellow Jews and the Romans. Keep a watch for him."

While Caiaphas prepares the Sanhedrin, Pilate prepares Villus, his commander of Jerusalem. "Villus, I brought fifteen hundred legionnaires with me from Caesarea to secure Jerusalem."

"Governor, do you think someone is threatening you?" asks Villus.

"No, not me nor my life, but someone might try to raise a tumult. Since I was robbed of the temple tax at last year's Passover, the Zealots may rally for an offensive against me."

"I understand your concern, sir."

"Villus, you make sure my Jerusalem soldiers and the Caesarean legionnaires are on the walls, at the gates, about the Temple, in the streets to report and stop anybody who causes an uprising. Tell them to report anyone who has any sizeable following. I won't be staying at the Fortress Antonia. I am staying in the palace that Herod the Great built by the three towers. My wife, Claudia Procula, is here with me to watch the Passover."

"Yes, Governor Pilate, you can count on me. Jerusalem will be a Roman stronghold. The appearance of the legionnaires should be enough to stop anyone from trying anything. Is there anything else, sir?"

"Yes. Watch for that young Zealot, Barabbas. He is the Jews' hero."

While Caiaphas plots against Jesus and Pilate secures Jerusalem, Herod Antipas instructs his Jerusalem ambassador. "Mizzah, I want you to capture Barabbas. He will use this Jesus of Nazareth for cover."

"How do you know?" asks Mizzah.

"Because Barabbas is clever. The Passover is near and Jesus will be here. Barabbas will be among the disciples of Jesus. Take Omar and our executioner to help you."

"Yes, sir. Is there anything else I need to know?"

"No. I'll be here in my palace if you need advice. I will be entertaining Salome and my grandson, Philip III, when they arrive. Don't mention Barabbas around my daughter."

"Yes, my lord."

13

Revelation: God or Man

Bringing his sacrificial lamb to Mount Moriah, Rosh observes the people preparing for the Passover. Surrounded by and interwoven with merchandisers, he refuses to buy anything. *This holy place has become a marketplace, and man has made this holy celebration a stench in the nostrils of God. However, I must not dwell on the negative. God, help me find inspiration.* With that prayer, Rosh runs into a whirlwind of power and contention on Solomon's Porch. He sees two men empowered with boldness.

Rosh listens as a man named Bartimaeus testifies how he was healed of blindness. After Bartimaeus sits down, Prosis announces his miracle. "I was blind from birth, but Jesus gave me sight. I once sat at the gate begging for alms, but now I am here to testify about Jesus—the Messiah."

"You have been excommunicated!" shouts one of the

priests. Pointing at Prosis, the priest announces, "This man is no longer part of our Jewish fellowship!"

Upon hearing of the excommunication, the crowd of onlookers moves away, for they do not want to be ostracized by the Sanhedrin. The priest walks up to Bartimaeus and Prosis and says, "Men, if you know what is good for you, you will leave."

"We've already been excommunicated and have nothing to fear," replies Bartimaeus.

"Yes, you do, Bartimaeus. You still live here, and we know where you live. I know that Prosis has moved to Bethany among Lazarus and friends. I suggest you move too. If you are preaching here when darkness comes, I pity you. So if I were you, I would not be in Jerusalem when the sun goes down."

Prosis retaliates, "Darkness has already come in the hearts of men, so should we obey God or man?"

Tola comes to Bethlehem and tells Barabbas some bad news. "Barabbas, this Nazarene named Jesus has diminished our efforts to rally the Zealots. Some Zealots want to wait and see if Jesus will set up an offensive against the Romans."

"You know that Jesus isn't going to fight," replies Barabbas. "We are going to miss the opportunity of a lifetime if we don't capitalize on the help of King Aretas."

"Jair and I know that, but it does not change the fact that some Zealots are mesmerized by this Jesus."

"Well, where is this Jesus now?"

"At the moment, I don't know, but tonight he is planning to eat the Passover in an upper room. I can tell you exactly how to find it." Realizing the risk involved, Tola asks, "You aren't going to enter Jerusalem, are you?"

"I went into the Temple for the Passover last year disguised as a woman. I don't see why I can't do it again."

After the sun sets on Jerusalem, Barabbas finds the upper room where Jesus washes his disciples' feet. Disguised as a woman, he watches Jesus and the disciples leave the upper room. In darkness, Barabbas follows Jesus and his disciples out of Jerusalem to Gethsemane. *I wish Jesus would separate himself from his disciples. I can't afford to let anyone see what I am about to do. God, I don't want to do it, but for your children to be free, I must. I must kill Jesus! With Jesus thwarting my plan to establish a theocracy, God, you will never be our ruler. So God, help me. I need Jesus to be alone, for if the Jews find out that I killed him, then the Zealots probably won't follow me.*

Barabbas believes his prayer is answered, for Jesus immediately separates himself from his disciples by going a little farther to fall on his face and pray. Barabbas pulls off his disguise of women's clothing. Wearing only a linen cloth, he maneuvers in the darkness to position himself near the place where Jesus is praying.

Pulling the Sword of Sacrifice, Barabbas watches Jesus agonize, praying earnestly. His sweat falls to the ground as great drops of blood. *Holee was right: This would be easier if Jesus weren't a humble man. However, this is a necessity. I am doing this for God.* Holding the Sword of Sacrifice with both hands, Barabbas stands over Jesus. Thrusting downward with the sword, Barabbas suddenly sees the chief priests, scribes, and elders coming. Stopping short of killing Jesus, Barabbas backs away into the bushes to watch. *Maybe God will spare me from killing Jesus. God spared Abraham from sacrificing his son, Isaac. Maybe God was testing me. God, I would do anything for the cause. If the Jews will condemn Jesus, and the Romans will execute him, I will gain the support of all the Jews—united for one cause. I am the beneficiary of Jesus' followers.*

Barabbas watches as the multitude of men come with swords and staves to capture Jesus. Upon their arrival, Peter swings his sword and cuts off an ear from the servant of the high priest.

Barabbas is no longer hidden, for the multitude has invaded the bushes to surround Jesus. With only a linen garment and his sword, Barabbas doesn't move as he watches Jesus with the onlookers. Jesus speaks to Peter. "Put up again thy sword into his place: for all they that take the sword shall perish with the sword." The multitude watches as Peter puts up his sword; then all eyes turn to Barabbas, holding the Sword of the Lord.

The young men grab Barabbas by his linen clothes. Casting the linen cloth away, Barabbas runs with his sword in his hand. Running naked into the darkness, Barabbas falls into an ambush—Mizzah, Omar, and an executioner.

While Barabbas is carried to Antipas, the mob holding Jesus enters Jerusalem. With the fury of demons, the mob sees Bartimaeus giving testimony of the goodness of Jesus. One of the priests threatens Bartimaeus, "We'll be back for you after we get rid of this devil!"

Jesus is brought before the high priest. Caiaphas illegally proceeds to try Jesus, for it is unlawful to try a man at night. Jesus has no defense attorney to represent him. The prosecution is biased, for they seek false witnesses. The judge is prejudiced, for he previously said that Jesus should die for the people. Finally, the most egregious illegality of the trial is that the defendant, Jesus, is beaten while he is being tried. Wanting Jesus to be put to death under Roman law, Caiaphas decides that Jesus should be tried by Pilate.

At his palace, Antipas laughs at the shackled Barabbas. "You are predictable. Several days ago, I told Mizzah and Omar where they could find you. I don't suppose you will try to convince me that you have the ledger, for you should know I don't care. I know it is forever lost. So you are worthless to me; however, I did enjoy the challenge of outwitting and capturing you *again*. This feat is something our Roman governor could not do. So tell me how it feels to know I am going to execute you at dawn."

Suddenly, Salome enters the room. "Father, I want to talk to Barabbas alone."

"What do you mean? What are you doing up at this hour? Where is Philip II?"

"He's in bed asleep. I knew you would capture Barabbas if he were in Jerusalem. I have been keeping an eye on you. Now please, let me talk privately with Barabbas."

"I shouldn't let you talk to him without Philip's permission."

"Well, there are some things that should be kept a secret," answers Salome, as she widens her eyelids at her incestuous stepfather. "Some things should be kept a secret if you *know what I mean!*" Salome gives Antipas the eye to make him understand that she has not disclosed their incestuous relationship.

"As long as it is kept a secret. I will grant you a few minutes to talk to him, but he will remain in shackles."

Alone with each other, Barabbas and Salome resolve not to blame each other, for they both know this is the last opportunity to see each other. Salome weeps as Barabbas asks about his son. "What is my son like?"

"He is beautiful. He looks just like you. If only—"

"Salome, I'm sorry about—about everything," interrupts Barabbas.

"Our premarital sex has ruined three lives—yours, our innocent baby's, and mine," confesses Salome. "I feel sorry for our baby. He has to live a lie that he'll never know. Unfortunately, we have to live with it too. If I tell the truth about who his father is, Antipas or Philip will kill him."

"That is why I have told no one," replies Barabbas. "I want my son to live. I realize that as a fugitive, I cannot provide for my son."

"I can't provide a good environment for our child," replies Salome. "Though I have wealth and power, it is an awful environment to raise our baby. I am bringing him up the way I was raised. It is most miserable."

"Salome, I wish it were possible to raise my son in the humble commune at the Qumran. Life there was so peaceful, for they have no weapons. The people hoard no money. They study the scriptures of God and love each other. The members are true brothers, although many are orphans."

Salome and Barabbas apologize and share griefs of love—knowing that this will be their last time together. As dawn comes, Salome kisses Barabbas goodbye. She holds him close for a moment as the tears roll down her face. Barabbas realizes that death will be easy, but the present regrets of the past are unbearable. *Dying is easy, but leaving my son is torture. I want to live for my son. Giving up my only son—there is nothing harder.*

Salome goes straight to Antipas. "Antipas, if you execute Barabbas, I will tell all of Jerusalem that you slept with me. Then they will never accept you as their king even if you get the opportunity."

Not surprised at Salome's request, Antipas makes a deal with her. "Salome, if you will swear by the gods that you will never mention that I slept with you, I will not execute him."

"I swear I will never tell anyone that you slept with me."

At dawn, warming his hands by the enemies' fire, Peter denies the forsaken Jesus three times. Then the chief priest and officers of the Sanhedrin bring Jesus to the gates of Pilate's palace. These religious men stop at the gates, for they will be defiled if they enter the residence of a Gentile.

Pilate comes to the gates and learns that the most prominent religious men of Jerusalem desire the execution of Jesus. The governor asks, "What has this man done to deserve death?"

Realizing they have no accusations to warrant the execution of Jesus, the religious men falsely accuse him. "We found this fellow perverting the nation, he forbids to give tribute to Caesar, and he says that he himself is a king. He causes insurrection."

Pilate takes Jesus and examines him privately. Aware that Jesus has done nothing wrong, Pilate announces to the religious men, "I find no fault in this man."

Angered by Pilate's findings, the religious mob argues with Pilate: "Jesus stirs up trouble throughout all Jewry from Galilee to Jerusalem."

Not wanting to put an innocent man to death and not wanting to offend the religious leaders, Pilate searches for a way out of judging Jesus. "You said that Jesus stirs up trouble throughout all Jewry from Galilee to Jerusalem? Since Jesus is from Galilee, I will send him to Herod Antipas, tetrarch of Galilee. Antipas is here in Jerusalem for the Passover. He is the judge of Galileans."

When Jesus arrives at Antipas' palace, Herod is exceedingly glad, for he has desired to see Jesus for a long time. Antipas has heard about the miracles of Jesus. The tetrarch questions Jesus with many words, but Jesus answers nothing. Antipas marches around Jesus and glares at him. "Soldiers, look at this pitiful excuse of a man! He has no following; his *own* disciples have forsaken him." Antipas stops marching and laughs at the calamity about to befall Jesus. "Some people think this man is a threat to my kingdom. He is a joke. I appreciate Pilate for giving me the opportunity to meet this insignificant wanderer. He healed the dumb; yet he himself cannot speak. I am disappointed with this Jesus, for I was expecting a formidable enemy."

The remarks of Antipas prompt the executioner to ask, "Shall I execute him?"

"No," answers Antipas. "I'll send Jesus back to Pilate after I teach him who is Lord."

The chief priests and scribes stand and vehemently accuse Jesus. Herod and his men of war mock him, array him in a gorgeous robe, and send him again to Pilate.

Suddenly, Antipas has an idea. "Guards, take Barabbas to Pilate." *I am keeping my promise to Salome, for I will not execute Barabbas. However, Pilate will. The Jews will hate Pilate for it. If Salome asks why I sent Barabbas to Pilate, I will tell her that Pilate ordered me to. Pilate sent Jesus to me, so I am returning a like favor: I am sending Barabbas to him. Pilate should appreciate that.*

The soldiers and religious men escort Jesus and Barabbas to Pontius Pilate. The legionnaires take the two prisoners to stand on the *Gabatha,* a mosaic pavement in front of the palace. Pilate delights to see Barabbas arrive with Jesus. "Well, what a nice surprise!" exclaims Pilate. "Antipas has sent me a present—the notorious Zealot, Barabbas."

Standing at the gates overlooking the *Gabatha,* the chief priests and scribes murmur. "Jesus was here to be tried first."

Hearing the impatience of the religious men, Pilate ascends to the *Bema,* a portable tribunal placed on the *Gabatha.* Pilate pronounces Barabbas' fate: "You shall be crucified today for murder and insurrection."

Two legionnaires bring a cross and prop it on Barabbas' shoulders. Pilate laughs and says, "Barabbas, after I settle this issue about Jesus, we shall hang you on that cross." Barabbas stands in shackles, holding up his cross as the religious crowd watches.

Coming down from the tribunal, Pilate walks to the gates and announces, "Jesus has done nothing worthy of death." Seeing the angry religious men, Pilate tries to pacify them. "Before I release Jesus, I will scourge him."

The voices of the Sanhedrin demand that Pilate must crucify Jesus. Caiaphas incites the crowd to chant: "Crucify him. Crucify him! Crucify him!"

Disgusted with Caiaphas and the bloodthirsty men, Pilate

comes up with a solution. *I know what I'll do. I'll put the religious men on the spot. Since it is the custom for me to pardon a condemned criminal in honor of the Passover, I shall offer to release Barabbas. Barabbas is a threat to Caiaphas' life. That ought to change the high priest's mind and allow Jesus to be released. I'll put the decision on Caiaphas and his religious puppets.*

Raising his hands for the crowd to be silent, Pilate asks, "Whom will ye that I release unto you? Barabbas or Jesus?" Expecting the crowd to answer that they want Jesus to be released in honor of the Passover, Pilate ascends the *Bema* to sit on the Judgment Seat.

Realizing that many in the crowd are Zealots at heart, Caiaphas surprises Pilate with the chant, "Barabbas! Barabbas! Barabbas! Barabbas!"

Pilate raises his hands to silence the crowd. The crowd does not stop their chant. "Barabbas! Barabbas! Barabbas!" Finally, Caiaphas waves his hands and the crowd quietens.

As silence deafens the crowd, the footsteps of a woman echo across the mosaic pavement. Pilate's wife, Claudia Procula, marches to the tribunal and warns her husband, "Have thou nothing to do with that just man, Jesus, for I have suffered many things this day in a dream because of him."

Stricken with fear, Pilate feels the pressure of judgment. Hoping to free Jesus and avoid a riot, Pilate asks again, "Whether of the twain will ye that I release unto you?"

The religious crowd starts their tumultuous chant again, "Barabbas! Barabbas!"

Realizing the crowd is becoming uncontrollable, Pilate raises his hands to silence the crowd. Still hoping to free Jesus, Pilate asks, "What shall I do then with Jesus which is called Christ?"

"Crucify him!" shouts the mob.

Realizing that Jesus is innocent, Pilate pleads, "Why, what evil hath he done?"

Having no appropriate answer, the Jews cry out, "If thou let this man go, thou art not Caesar's friend: whosoever maketh himself a king speaketh against Caesar."

Pilate is overcome by his fear of Caesar. Peer pressure dictates to Pilate as the religious crowd goes into frenzy with their chant. "Crucify him! Crucify him! Crucify him! Crucify him!" Realizing that insurrection is imminent, Pilate yields to the tumultuous mob.

In an effort to be blameless for crucifying Jesus, Pilate calls for water and ceremonially washes his hands before the mob as a sign. "Crucify Jesus and free Barabbas," Pilate commands.

The legionnaires take the cross from Barabbas and place it on Jesus. Then they whip and lead Jesus into the Praetorium as Barabbas runs to freedom. The soldiers clothe Jesus with purple and place a plaited crown of thorns on his head. Bloodied from the blows and the scourging, Jesus still stands in silence as the soldiers hit him on the head with a reed and spit on him. Taking turns, the legionnaires bow their knees and mock: "Hail, King of the Jews!"

Following Jesus to the mount of Golgotha, Barabbas holds Mary close as she watches the legionnaires nail Jesus to the cross that was meant for her son. Watching in silence, Barabbas sees many physically afflicted people who have come to Mount Calvary—a mount so slight that even the crippled can climb it.

The physically afflicted grieve because their only hope of physical healing dies before them. The lame, deaf, dumb, and a severely cancered leper come to mourn like empathetic dogs that lick the wounds of their masters. Though the religious men threaten the leper's life, the leper comes in violent determination to worship Jesus.

The religious mob continues to mock Jesus as he dies on the cross. In return, Jesus prays, "Father, forgive them, for they know not what they do." Then at noon, darkness comes over all the earth.

Three hours after noon, the veil of the Temple is rent in twain from the top to the bottom. Now no separation between God and man exists, for Jesus is dead. It is finished. Feeling the earth quake, Barabbas and Mary run to their house in Jerusalem.

Fearing that something dreadful is about to happen, everyone runs for cover with the exception of the legionnaires assigned to watch over Jesus and the leper who continues to worship Jesus.

Arriving at their house, Barabbas and Mary go inside and find that their home has been ransacked. "I haven't been here for some time," Mary apologizes, gesturing toward the mess. "I have been living in Bethany, you know."

"Mother, I know that, and you will have to live with Uncle Lazarus and Aunt Martha a while longer until the animosity subsides." Looking at their scattered belongings on the floor, Barabbas says, "It seems someone was looking for the temple ledger. I wish I knew where it is."

Mary begins to cry. Barabbas consoles her, asking, "Mother, what's wrong?"

"Jesus—Jesus is dead."

"I'm sorry, Mother. He was quite a man."

"He was more than a man, Son."

"What do you mean?"

"Jesus saved me from the mob who wanted to stone me. He died on a cross meant for you. He has preached the gospel to the poor, healed the brokenhearted, preached deliverance to the captives, healed the blind, and set at liberty them that are bruised. He raised your uncle from the dead. Jesus is the resurrection—he is God."

Barabbas gasps, "Mother, that's blasphemy!"

"No, Barabbas. It is not blasphemy, for Jesus *is* God. I

don't know if anybody else has a clue about who Jesus is, but I have a revelation. Not long ago, I anointed Jesus with spikenard for his burial. Jesus made reference to his death often, but it seems that nobody listened. But I did. Jesus said he would be in the heart of the earth for three days and three nights. Then Jesus will rise again in immortality."

"Mother, that's ridiculous. Jesus is dead."

"He died for our sins, but he said that he will rise in three days. The sacrificing of lambs is meaningless now, for Jesus is the flesh of God."

"Wait a minute," argues Barabbas. "You're wrong. What about the Shema—one God?"

"Barabbas, listen to me," pleads Mary.

Wanting to understand his mother, Barabbas assures her: "Mother, I really want to understand you. I'm listening."

Mary begins, "First, there is only one God."

"Right," asserts Barabbas. "God has taught the Jews for all time that there is one indivisible God, and that there is no God besides him."

"That is my point. The one, indivisible God whom we know has a plurality of roles, manifestations, attributes, titles, and relationships to mankind. The Father is a designation for God and so is the Son. Jesus is the Son of God—the incarnation of God."

Confused, Barabbas asserts, "Jesus is mortal and God is immortal and eternal—God can't die."

"Let me explain," Mary demands. "When the fulness of the time was come, God sent forth his Son. The Son was begotten, made of a woman. Jesus called himself the son of man and the Son of God. Jesus was flesh—the son of man. Jesus was God—the Son of God. The flesh made of woman was not eternal, for it was made about thirty years ago of a woman, Mary—Jesus' mother. The flesh died on the cross, but the deity did not, for God cannot die. Deity is immortal—eternal. The flesh of God was the sacrifice for sin.

However, the Word of God existed from all eternity in the mind of God. The Word was God. And Jesus is His name—a name above *every* name.

"For thousands of years, the Jews have wondered about the name of God. Now, through the Son of God we know his name—Jesus. That which was from the beginning, which we have heard, which we have seen with our eyes, which we have looked upon, and our hands have handled, of the Word of life—Jesus. Barabbas, can't you see that the one God that the Jews know has been manifested in the flesh? And one day *every* knee shall bow, of things in heaven, and things in earth, and things under the earth shall bow at the *name* of Jesus."

"Then what is the difference in the Son and the Father?"

"The title Father refers to the Jews' God, but the title Son refers to the Father as manifested in the flesh. The title Son refers to humanity as well as deity. No man hath seen God at any time; the only begotten Son, which is in the bosom of the Father, he hath declared him. Isn't that wonderful that God made himself lower than angels and robed himself in flesh and came down so that mankind may know Him and know His name?"

"Mother, I don't understand. All I know is that there is one indivisible God. It seems to me you are saying there are two Gods."

"I'm not saying there are two Gods, Barabbas, for there is only one God." Mary suddenly remembers a better way to explain her understanding of Jesus. "Jesus said unto the disciple, Thomas, 'I am the way, the truth, and the life: no man cometh unto the Father, but by me. If ye had known me, ye should have known my Father also: and from henceforth ye know him, and have seen him.'" Mary stops to ask Barabbas a question, "Who did Thomas know and see speaking to him?"

"Jesus," answers Barabbas as he scratches his head trying

to sort the information. "I don't know about all this, for Jesus claims to be God."

"Exactly," explains Mary. "The disciple, Philip, made this request: 'Lord, shew us the Father, and it sufficeth us.'"

"Jesus answered Philip in affirmation, 'Have I been so long time with you, and yet hast thou not known me, Philip? He that hath seen me hath seen the Father.'"

"Mother, that's blasphemy, for Jesus claims to be the Father."

"That's right," Mary explains. "The prophet, Isaiah, wrote: 'For unto us a child is born, unto us a son is given: and the government shall be upon his shoulder: and his name shall be called Wonderful, Counselor, The *mighty* God, The *everlasting Father*, The Prince of Peace.'"

"The everlasting Father?" Barabbas questions. "This child born cannot be Jesus, for Isaiah said that this child's increasing government and peace shall not end. Jesus is dead and his government is over."

"You just wait and see," argues Mary. "He will rise again in three days. In his death, Jesus is immortal."

"That makes no sense," rebuts Barabbas. "First, you say there is only one indivisible God. Then you say that Jesus is God."

"Let me explain. God is omnipresent. Our God is in heaven and in Jesus Christ simultaneously. The one indivisible God—our Father, robed himself in mortal flesh and came to us so that we could see God and know his name. That's what is wrong with the Jews—they don't understand that the one indivisible God remained in heaven and came in the flesh at the same time. The son of man—the flesh—prayed to the Father even as the Father was in him. Jesus had all of the quality of God, for the Spirit was given to him without measure. Jesus is God! Nevertheless, God is not constrained or restrained to the physical body of the Son, for God is omnipresent."

"Mother, your theology is unorthodox and unrealistic. Let me explain how things are in our present real world. Now that Jesus is dead, the Zealots and I will inherit the followers of Jesus. They will fight for our cause. At the end of these fifty holy days, at Pentecost, I will have enough followers to launch an offensive for Jewish autonomy. The Zealots believe the hand of God is with me. And I have to admit it is miraculous that I'm still alive. I didn't set myself up as their leader, but God has spared me to do this job."

"Yes, Barabbas, God has blessed you, for He bore your cross."

Suddenly the door swings open and Javan comes in to greet Mary and Barabbas. "Hello. It's good to see both of you here at home again. I can hardly believe it." Javan looks at Barabbas with gladness. "You're free—pardoned by Pilate himself."

"Yes, we were just discussing how God has delivered me from all of my foes," replies Barabbas, remembering how his troubles started. "It seems as if it were only yesterday when you delivered that message from Caiaphas."

Javan's countenance falls as he says, "If I hadn't delivered that message to Rabba then, he might be alive today."

"Oh, no," Mary disagrees. "It was only a matter of time. Rabba knew too much for his enemies to let him live."

"She's right," Barabbas affirms. "I just wonder what was on that ledger. I know that Father took it, but it has never been found. I remember Father leaving Caiaphas' house and going toward the Temple."

"That's right," agrees Javan. "I remember."

"How did you know that?" asks Barabbas.

"Know what?"

"That Father was going to the Temple when he left Caiaphas' house."

Javan answers, "I heard Rabba tell Bartimaeus that he was going to lock the treasury office after he went to see what Caiaphas wanted." Javan jumps to his feet, yelling, "Oh, my! Oh, my!"

Barabbas grabs Javan by the shoulders and shouts, "What is it, Javan?"

"The day I delivered the message to Rabba at Bartimaeus' apartment, I remember that Rabba promised Bartimaeus he would return to the apartment after he locked the Treasury. If Rabba saw Anak—his murderer—following him that night, I suppose he could have decided to leave the ledger at Bartimaeus' apartment."

Barabbas, Mary, and Javan race to Bartimaeus' apartment but find it has been ransacked. Bartimaeus' furniture has been burned in the street.

Mary kneels near the ashes and cries. "The religious mob who crucified Jesus said they were going to stone Bartimaeus if he didn't stop witnessing for Jesus. Bartimaeus loved him very much."

Barabbas rummages through the few remains in Bartimaeus' apartment and doesn't find the ledger. Disappointed and angry, Barabbas says, "I have no doubt that the ledger was here, but it is gone now."

"So is Bartimaeus," exclaims Javan.

Seeing the ashes of Bartimaeus' belongings, Barabbas is aware that it is too dangerous for Mary to be in Jerusalem. "Mother, we need to go to Bethany. You need to stay with Uncle Lazarus and Aunt Martha until the animosity dissipates. Jesus has riled the Jews."

"I must attend to my Lord Jesus," replies Mary.

"Joseph of Arimathea is doing that," says Javan. "Caiaphas has asked that the Romans guard Jesus' tomb."

"What for?" asks Barabbas.

"Because Jesus said that he would rise again," answers Mary.

"That's enough of that nonsense," says Barabbas. "Let's hurry to Bethany before dark."

Arriving at the well-lit house of Lazarus, Barabbas and Mary open the door and are shocked to find Bartimaeus there. Bartimaeus hands Barabbas two scrolls. Bartimaeus says, "When the mob brought Jesus to be tried, I knew I must leave Jerusalem, for they threatened to stone me. As I packed some of my personal belongings from my closet, I found these ledgers tucked away. After I examined them, I knew I should give them to you. Rabba must have left them there the night he was murdered."

Barabbas takes the ledgers and examines them. "Look! Here is the insignia of the Temple. Here is where Father appropriated money for items needed in the Temple. Look at whom the Temple buys from . . . Joktan—that snake. He was charging four times the market for his items. And look—some of these items needed for the sacrifice were never delivered, but Joktan was paid."

Mary interrupts, "Rabba must have noticed that Joktan was robbing the Temple, but how does Caiaphas fit in?"

"Caiaphas is the one who actually ordered the goods from Joktan, but Rabba looked responsible. Father was the one who affixed the temple insignia on the ledger. He must have found that Caiaphas was helping Joktan steal from the Temple."

Barabbas examines the other scroll that Bartimaeus gave him. Barabbas says, "Let's see," as he peruses it. "Ah, ha! This ledger is Sadoc's—the moneylender. Sadoc is the man Father and I borrowed the money from for my horses. Father worked for Sadoc part time. Look at this—here is Joktan's insignia. Joktan was depositing his money in Sadoc's usury."

"What does that have to do with anything?" Mary asks.

"Look right here and you'll understand. Joktan did not withdraw the money he deposited. The insignia shows that Pilate withdrew the money."

"What does it all mean?" asks Mary.

Barabbas explains. "Caiaphas got Father to appropriate

treasury money to buy merchandise from Joktan. Father affixed the insignia without knowing that Caiaphas was paying exorbitant prices for the merchandise from Joktan. Caiaphas was helping Joktan steal the tithes from the Jews. Joktan kept part of the money and deposited the rest in Sadoc's usury. Then Pilate withdrew the money from the usury after the lending period."

"Why?" asks Mary.

"Caiaphas was laundering the money to buy his position as high priest. He paid exorbitant prices to Joktan so that Joktan could deposit Pilate's share in Sadoc's usury. Then Pilate withdrew his share. All three were doing well. Joktan and Pilate were receiving their share of the money, and Caiaphas was allowed to buy his position. Caiaphas looked perfectly innocent on the temple ledger. If anybody ever found out, then Father would look like the guilty one, for it was his insignia. And when Joktan cleaned his money up by filtering it through Sadoc's usury, Pilate was paid indirectly by Caiaphas. Pilate, Joktan, and Caiaphas looked innocent of wrongdoing until Father got both ledgers. There is nothing wrong with Caiaphas ordering goods from Joktan. There is nothing wrong with Joktan depositing money with the lender. And there is nothing wrong with Pilate receiving money from Joktan. But there is something wrong with Caiaphas giving God's money to Pilate. The Jews will revolt. Once before, Tiberius reprimanded Pilate for taking funds from the Temple. When Caesar sees this, Pilate, Joktan, and Caiaphas will be called in for questioning."

"I see!" exclaims Mary. "Caiaphas is stealing the tithes and giving them to the Romans, not God."

"Exactly," replies Barabbas, grabbing the ledgers. "Mother, I must go to Bethlehem." Barabbas kisses Mary and tells her goodbye.

With Salome in her palace, Mary with her family, and Jesus in the grave, Barabbas arrives at Holee's run-down inn.

Inside the inn, Barabbas finds Tola and Jair planning tactics. Barabbas asks, "Where's Holee?"

"He and his wife are packing to leave," answers Jair.

"His wife?" replies Barabbas.

Holee and a woman come from the back of the house. Barabbas stands in awe as Holee introduces the beautiful woman with him, "Barabbas, I would like for you to meet my wife, Abigail."

Staring at the woman's beautiful complexion, Barabbas says, "I thought she was dead—I mean I thought she had leprosy."

"I did," Abigail answers, "but Jesus healed me. Today, while my God hung on the cross, I was healed. I took my spotted, blemished, sinful self to Calvary. I worshiped Him for who he is, not for my healing, and look at me now! My God is real! Jesus brought newness of life in me today."

Holee says, "Barabbas, this may sound out of character but I have made up my mind to go to the commune of peace—the Qumran. I am tired of fighting God. Abigail and I will live the rest of our days in peace to study the scriptures, which testify about Jesus."

Barabbas hands Holee the two scrolls he received from Bartimaeus. "Take these ledgers to the Teacher of Righteousness in Qumran. Ask him to place these with the Dead Sea Scrolls."

"I don't understand," Holee insists.

Jair demands, "Don't we need those?"

"Not at this time. Let's wait and see how our offensive goes. With the followers of Jesus and my plan, we should have enough manpower to take Machaerus. But if we run into trouble with our offensive against the Romans' Masada, I can use these scrolls as security and blackmail. Pilate would make concessions to get these incriminating ledgers." Barabbas looks to Holee and says, "If anything happens to Jair, Tola, and me, get the letters from the Teacher of

Righteousness and send them to Caesar. These ledgers prove that Governor Pilate stole some of our tithes."

"I see," says Tola. "If we fail, the Jews can use these ledgers to explain that our attack is founded by injustices to our religion. Caesar doesn't allow that."

"Right," affirms Barabbas. "If we send the ledgers now, Tiberius will appoint a new governor. If we make an offensive against a new governor, we could not claim that he treats us contrary to the law. Our proof is against Pilate."

Holee takes the ledgers, hugs Barabbas, and says, "Goodbye."

"What about the inn?" asks Barabbas.

"You can have it. I don't need these things any more. I have what I need: I have a God who knows me." Holee takes his bags and carries them to the door. "Oh, yes, Barabbas, don't forget Logos. He's in the stable."

"Thanks, Holee. May God be with you."

Barabbas sits at the table with Jair and Tola, explaining his plans. "We must persuade all of our countrymen to come to Pentecost. At Pentecost, we will distribute the weapons you bought with the temple tax money that I took from Pilate. Let all of Jerusalem know something great is going to happen at Pentecost. That gives us fifty days to get the word out."

"What will we do then?" asks Jair.

"Since the two rulers have become friends, Antipas has agreed to celebrate Pentecost with Pilate. After Pentecost, Herod Antipas is going to Machaerus. We Zealots will be waiting for him. With my plan, we should be able to capture him on his way. When we arrive on the outskirts of Machaerus with Antipas, King Aretas will gladly receive us and help us take Masada. With Masada as our fortress, we can stand against Pilate."

"God has been with you so far, Barabbas," declares Tola. "We will continue to follow you."

When the day of Pentecost is fully come, Jair and Tola pass their plans among the Jewish brethren who have come from all over the world. Many are Parthians, Medes, Elamites, dwellers of Mesopotamia, Judea, Cappadocia, Pontus, Asia, Phrygia, Pamphylia, Egypt, Libya, Cyrene, strangers of Rome, Jews and proselytes, Cretes and Arabians. With the exception of approximately one hundred twenty followers of Jesus, Barabbas gains support from the Jews.

Antipas and Pilate meet early in the day, for they have heard that the Zealots are rallying with Barabbas. Pilate orders his legionnaires to bring Barabbas to the palace for questioning.

Hidden among the multitudes on the streets, Barabbas becomes aware that his support is greater than he had imagined it could be.

Suddenly, there comes a sound from heaven as of a rushing mighty wind, and it fills all the house where the followers of Jesus are meeting. There appear unto them cloven tongues like as of fire, which sits upon each of them. They are all filled with the Holy Ghost, and they begin to speak with other tongues as the Spirit gives them utterance.

Barabbas races with the multitude to the house where the disciples of Jesus are meeting. The Jews are all amazed and in doubt, saying one to another, "What meaneth this?"

Others mocking say, "These men are full of new wine."

But Peter stands up with the eleven disciples, lifts up his voice and says unto them, "Ye men of Judea, and all ye that dwell at Jerusalem, be this known unto you, and hearken to my words: For these are not drunken as ye suppose, seeing it is but the third hour of the day. But this is that which was spoken by the prophet Joel: 'And it shall come to pass in the last days, saith God, I will pour out of my Spirit upon all flesh: and your sons and your daughters shall prophesy, and your young men shall see visions, and your old men shall dream dreams.'"

Peter continues to preach as Tola nudges Barabbas and asks, "What is happening here?"

"I'm not sure, but I don't think this is going to help our cause. He preaches that Jesus is alive. Let's listen to him."

Peter concludes the whole matter with convicting words: "Therefore let all the house of Israel know assuredly that God hath made that same Jesus, whom ye have crucified, both Lord and Christ."

Now when the multitude hears Peter, they are pricked in their heart and say unto Peter and to the rest of the apostles, "Men and brethren, what shall we do?"

Then Peter says unto them, "Repent, and be baptized every one of you in the name of Jesus Christ for the remission of sins, and ye shall receive the gift of the Holy Ghost. For the promise is unto you and to your children, and to all that are afar off, even as many as the Lord our God shall call."

And with many other words, Peter testifies and exhorts: "Save yourselves from this untoward generation."

Then the ones who gladly receive Peter's words are baptized. Three thousand souls are added to the following of the apostles. The ones baptized continue steadfastly in the apostles' doctrine.

Barabbas is very angry because the multitude has forsaken the Zealots. He tries to dissuade the apostolic converts by questioning their actions.

As the twelve disciples baptize the multitude, Barabbas questions them. "What good is dipping someone in water?"

A disciple answers Barabbas with a question, "What profit is sacrificing a lamb?"

"God told us to," retaliates Barabbas.

"Not any more. The sacrificing of lambs cannot cover sins any longer. Only the blood of Jesus can cover sin now. You must repent and be baptized for the remission of sins. If you want your sins remitted, then you must be baptized for the remission of sins. That is God's plan through Jesus Christ." Ignoring Barabbas for the moment, the disciple takes the next man in line for baptism and asks, "Have you repented?"

The man answers, "Yes."

"I now baptize you in the name of Jesus for the remission of sins," asserts the disciple.

Wanting the apostles to leave Jerusalem, Barabbas questions the twelve disciples of Jesus, "What makes you an authority in the holy city of Jerusalem?"

They answer, "God has chosen us to take the gospel to the world. Furthermore, in the wall of the New Jerusalem, there are twelve foundations and in them are the names of the twelve apostles of the Lamb."

The exchange of words between the apostles and Barabbas catches the attention of some legionnaires. Realizing that Barabbas is the one arguing with the disciples, the legionnaires arrest him.

At his palace, Governor Pilate gives a feast for Antipas, Philip II, and their families. Herodias and Salome are enjoying the feast with their husbands when a messenger comes and whispers something to the governor. Pilate makes an announcement. "My friends, we are going to have an infamous guest. I'm sure everyone has heard of Barabbas."

Antipas is delighted that the legionnaires have brought Barabbas for questioning. Pilate watches as the legionnaires bring Barabbas before him and the guests. The legionnaires shove Barabbas to his knees. Salome's heart beats with love as she gazes on the father of her baby.

Pilate starts interrogating Barabbas. "It has been brought to my attention that you are rallying the Jews. You aren't trying to amass an army, are you?"

"Governor Pilate, I appreciate the pardon you gave me seven weeks ago. I assure you I am not doing anything illegal."

"Liar! The word is on the lips of every Jew that you are crazy enough to attempt insurrection."

"Governor Pilate, that is not true. I have no army. Just ask your men on the streets. The disciples of Jesus have amassed an army."

Pilate looks to Villus for an answer. "Villus, what are the present affairs in Jerusalem?"

Villus stands in attention and answers. "Governor Pilate, Barabbas tells the truth. Thousands of Jews have joined the apostles of this Jesus."

"Are they antagonistic toward Rome?"

"No, sir," answers Villus. "Quite the opposite—the apostles teach their followers to obey the moral laws of the land."

Turning to Barabbas, Pilate threatens him. "Barabbas, I *will not* tolerate your causing a riot."

"Sir, if you will let me go," Barabbas swears, "I will leave before morning. I will go to the wilderness to live in peace."

Not wanting to lose the confidence of the Jews by taking back his promise—the pardon of Barabbas, Pilate proclaims a final proposal. "I will give you until morning to be out of Jerusalem. If you are here at dawn, you shall die. You may not come back to Jerusalem for a season."

"Thank you, Governor," replies Barabbas as he looks at Salome one last time. "If God allows me, I shall leave tonight. I ask to take only one person with me—my blood kin."

Holding back the tears, Salome watches Barabbas leave. Then she leaves the feast without giving an excuse.

Aware of Salome's sorrow, Herodias follows Salome back to Antipas' palace. Antipas makes an excuse for his wife and daughter. "I'm sorry, Governor Pilate, Salome hasn't been feeling well."

Salome's husband, Philip II, speaks up to apologize for his wife. "Salome hasn't been away from our child before. I think she is worried about him."

Satisfied with the absence of Herodias and Salome, Pilate

relaxes and enjoys the feast with Antipas and Philip II.

At Antipas' palace, Herodias scolds Salome. "That was a stupid thing to do! You can't just leave the governor's party without some good excuse. This feast is an important political breakthrough. The Herods have just gained his friendship."

"Mother, I don't care about political gains. I don't care about anything but my baby. I only regret that he has to live the kind of life that is forced upon me."

Sick of participating in this argument, Herodias grabs Salome and draws her near. Gritting her teeth and looking Salome in the eye, Herodias sums up all the options to end the debate. "Well, there are only two ways out for you. If you tell the truth, your baby dies and possibly you too, or if you commit suicide, your baby will be raised in your stead. Now that's it! Like those choices?" Salome stares in silence.

Herodias releases Salome and adds, "I suppose there is one other choice—you could murder your son." With that ruthless remark, Herodias turns and leaves to go back to Pilate's feast.

Salome walks down the stairs alone, for most of the servants have gone to bed. She pours herself a glass of wine and considers her options. Then she wanders into the palatial room and sits on Herod's throne. Gulping down the last of the wine, Salome lowers her glass to slide it under the throne chair. Her glass makes a jingle as it bumps against something metal underneath the chair. Reaching under the throne, Salome finds the Sword of Sacrifice.

Holding the sword up before her eyes, Salome knows what she must do. Raising the sword and placing the tip on her navel, Salome cries as she attempts to commit suicide. Realizing she can't kill herself, she aborts her attempt and decides to pour herself another glass of wine.

Having finished the second glass, Salome hides the sword in her tunic and goes to the nursery. Finding her baby asleep, Salome dismisses the nursemaid. "I shall sleep with my baby tonight. You may go." After the nursemaid leaves, Salome takes her child and carries him to the balcony that overlooks Jerusalem.

As the midnight hour passes, Salome lays her baby on the ledge of the balcony. Regretting what she is about to do, she takes the Sword of Sacrifice from her tunic. Raising the sword, she drops it over the balcony ledge. Breaking down in tears and mourning profusely, Salome kisses her baby goodbye. "I love you, but I can't let you live in this hell."

Holding her baby in her hands, Salome stretches her arms out past the ledge of the balcony over the street. Then, with a broken heart, she releases her baby boy. Realizing that her baby has fallen from her hands, Salome looks down at the street. There she sees that he is gone forever.

Turning her back from the street, Salome puts her hands over her face in silence. Suddenly she turns and leans over the balcony, shouting, "What will you call him?"

With the Sword of Sacrifice dangling from his belt and his baby boy in his arms, Barabbas looks up at Salome. "His name shall be Ephraim," Barabbas answers. "He shall live in peace and learn of the one true God." Barabbas rides Logos out of Jerusalem.

Obeying the apostles of Jesus Christ, Rosh repents and is baptized in the name of Jesus Christ for the remission of sins.

Two days after Pentecost, Rosh calls his sheep toward the ruins of Ai. Having received the Holy Ghost, Rosh leads the way for his sheep.

Near the shade of a tamarisk tree, feeling the vibration of the ground camouflaging him, the horned viper waits until Rosh steps over him. Suddenly, the serpent springs his broad, spade-shaped head up from the sand to expose his large venom glands and tubular fangs.

Rosh feels something strike the calf of his leg. Immediately he knows the serpent of sin has injected the lethal, fiery mixture of venom. Rosh does not panic. With faith and confidence, he turns and looks at the puzzled serpent. The serpent of sin strikes the shepherd again. Full of the Holy Ghost, Rosh calmly takes up the serpent of death and speaks to him. "O death, where is thy sting? O grave where is thy victory? The sting of death is sin; and the strength of sin is the law. But thanks be to God, which giveth us the victory through our Lord Jesus Christ."

Twisting and squirming, the serpent wrestles free, falling to the ground. Then, the serpent of sin sidewinds, trying to get away. Rosh steps on the viper's tail to stop him. The viper strikes Rosh again. Then, with his heel, Rosh crushes the sin serpent's head.

Reaching Qumran with Ephraim, Barabbas greets the Teacher of Righteousness. "Teacher, I know it is against the commune's rule to take me back, but I need refuge."

"Barabbas, the commune is under new law."

"New law?" echoes Barabbas.

"The law of liberty in Christ Jesus," answers Teacher.

"What?" exclaims Barabbas.

"Jesus Christ," Teacher replies.

"He's dead. I saw him die on the cross—mine!"

"He isn't dead," affirms Teacher.

"I suppose you are going to try to convince me you have seen him too."

"No, Barabbas. I have searched the scriptures and they testify of Jesus. I trust the scriptures, not my personal feelings."

"What do you mean?" asks Barabbas.

"Barabbas, you know with what great care the commune has preserved and reverenced the scriptures. We painstakingly and meticulously copy the scriptures and preserve them in the caves. However, we don't reverence the paper or the script, but we reverence what they say."

"So?"

"So what I'm trying to tell you is that when I heard that Jesus rose from the grave, I knew it was real. I had a revelation—Jesus is God manifested in flesh."

"What?" exclaims Barabbas, stepping back for fear that lightning might strike Teacher for blasphemy. "What about the Jewish beliefs of the past? For four thousand years, God has taught us there is only one God. My father lived and died believing in one God. You are forsaking the Jewish traditions."

"Exactly, Barabbas, there is only one God. But beware lest any man spoil you through philosophy and vain deceit, after the rudiments of the world, and not after Christ. For in Him dwelleth all the fulness of the Godhead bodily. I admit I did not know who Jesus was while he was alive, but at his death, burial, and resurrection, the revelation came to me. Then your friends, Holee and Abigail, came and brought the miracles of Jesus."

"Holee and Abigail? Are they living here?"

"Yes, Barabbas, but let me finish before you change the subject. Forget about Jewish traditions and look at the scriptures. They hold the truths we must live by. Jews must live by them too. The scriptures tell of Jesus' lineage; Micah prophesied that Jesus was to be born in Bethlehem; Daniel prophesied the time of His birth; Isaiah prophesied that Jesus was of virgin birth; Jeremiah and Hosea prophesied of his life; Isaiah, Psalms, and Zechariah prophesied Jesus' death and resurrection; and many other scriptures testify that Jesus is the Son of God."

Suddenly, Holee and Abigail arrive to see Barabbas. They are excited to see him again. "Barabbas, come and stay with us," begs Holee. "You need to rest. Come to my house—you may stay as long as you want . . .."

Pointing to Ephraim, Barabbas says, "Thanks, but I have my son with me."

Abigail yells with joy when she sees the baby. She runs and picks him up and cuddles him in her arms. Loving the baby, she asks, "What is his name?"

"Ephraim," Barabbas softy replies, watching a tear roll down Abigail's face.

Adoring the child, Abigail holds him close and softly cries, "Ephraim."

As Barabbas departs for Holee's house, the Teacher of Righteousness says, "Barabbas, I pray that you will receive the revelation of who Jesus really is."

After enjoying the hospitality of Holee, Barabbas lies down for the night as Abigail sings a hymn for Ephraim. Barabbas falls into a deep sleep and is raptured in the vividness of an ethereal dream:

A door opens in heaven: and the first voice which I hear is as a trumpet talking with me. "Come up hither, and I will shew thee things which must be hereafter."

I immediately am in the spirit: and, behold, a throne is set in heaven, and one sits on the throne. He who sits is to look upon like a jasper and a sardine stone, and there is a rainbow round about the throne in sight like unto an emerald. Round about the throne are four and twenty seats, and upon the seats I see four and twenty elders sitting, clothed in white raiment. They have on their heads crowns of gold. Out of the throne proceed lightnings and thunderings and voices. There are seven lamps of fire burning before the throne. Before the throne there is a sea of glass like unto crystal.

In the midst of the throne and round about the throne are four beasts full of eyes before and behind. The first beast is like a lion, and the second beast like a calf, and the third beast has a face as a man, and the fourth beast is like a flying eagle. Each of the four beasts has six wings about him, and they are full of eyes within. They rest not day and night, saying, "Holy, Holy, Holy, Lord God Almighty, which was, and is, and is to come."

When the beasts give glory and honor and thanks to him who sits on the throne, who liveth for ever and ever, the four and twenty elders fall down before him who sits on the throne, and worship him who liveth for ever and ever, and cast their crowns before the throne, saying, "'Thou art worthy, O Lord, to receive glory and honor and power: for thou hast created all things, and for thy pleasure they are and were created.'"

I look at my judge before me. I recognize him, for he is the same judge that I dreamed about over a year ago. I speak to him. "Righteous Judge, I remember you from my past. A year ago, sin condemned me, but you saved me from Satan and his hell. You served my sentence. I was sentenced to die a death that Satan and his demons devised. You were unmercifully mocked, ridiculed, slapped, punched, kicked, beaten, whipped, flogged, and finally crucified. You were my savior."

Lifting his nail-scarred hands, the righteous judge speaks for all to hear. "Yesterday I was your savior. Today I am—I am, your judge."

Barabbas awakens in a cold sweat of fear. Jerking his clothes on in a scramble, he calls for Holee. Holee and Abigail come to see what all the noise is about.

Holee asks, "Barabbas where are you going at this time of night?"

"To the cave where the scriptures are stored." Barabbas looks to Abigail for help. "Will you care for Ephraim while I go to the cave?"

"I will be glad to—don't worry about him," affirms Abigail.

Barabbas climbs to the cave where the sacred scriptures are hidden. The senior member refuses to permit Barabbas access to the scriptures. Barabbas pulls his sword and forces the senior to let him through. Holee follows behind Barabbas with a light as the senior runs to inform Teacher.

Reaching the compartment above where the Holy Scriptures are stored, Barabbas digs up the planks and lowers himself down to the sealed jars. Finding the jar with the Book of Isaiah, he breaks the seal on the jar and unrolls the scroll. Barabbas begins to read as Holee holds a light.

The Teacher of Righteousness and the senior arrive as Barabbas finds what he is looking for. Barabbas reads aloud: "For unto us a child is born, unto us a son is given: and the government shall be upon his shoulder: and his name shall be called Wonderful, Counsellor, The mighty God, The everlasting Father, The Prince of Peace." Barabbas pauses as Holee and Teacher watch in silence. "The scriptures call this Jesus the everlasting Father, and there is only one Father. Then Jesus must be . . ."

"Say it," implores Teacher. "Go ahead and search the scriptures; for in them ye think ye have eternal life: and they are they which testify of Jesus Christ."

Barabbas unrolls more of Isaiah and reads aloud again: "Who hath believed our report? and to whom is the arm of the Lord revealed? For he shall grow up before him as a tender plant, and as a root out of a dry ground: he hath no form nor comeliness; and when we shall see him, there is no beauty that we should desire him. He is despised and rejected of men; a man of sorrows, and acquainted with grief: and we hid as it were our faces from him; he was despised, and we esteemed him not. Surely he hath borne our griefs, and carried our sorrows: yet we did esteem him stricken, smitten of God, and afflicted. But he was wounded for our transgressions, he was bruised for our iniquities: the chastisement of our peace was upon him; and with his stripes we are healed. All we like sheep have gone astray; we have turned every one to his own way; and the Lord hath laid on him the iniquity of us all. He was oppressed, and he was afflicted, yet he opened not his mouth: he is brought as a lamb to the slaughter, and as a sheep before her shearers is dumb, so he openeth not his mouth. He was taken from prison and from judgment: and who shall declare his generation? for he was cut off out of the land of the living: for the transgression of my people was he stricken. And he made his grave with the wicked, and with the rich in his death; because he had done no violence, neither was any deceit in his mouth. Yet it pleased the Lord to bruise him; he hath put him to grief: when thou shalt make his soul an offering for sin, he shall see his seed, he shall prolong his days, and the pleasure of the Lord shall prosper in his hand. He shall see of the travail of his soul, and shall be satisfied: by his knowledge shall my righteous servant justify many; for he shall bear their iniquities. Therefore will I divide him a portion with the great, and he shall divide the spoil with the strong; because he hath poured out his soul unto death: and he was numbered with the transgressors; and he bare the sin of many, and made intercession for the transgressors."

Barabbas stops and declares, "My God—He's Jesus—the Righteous Judge in my dream."

"Right," the Teacher affirms, realizing that Barabbas has received a revelation.

With tears in his eyes and gratitude in his heart, Barabbas whispers: "Jesus gave me refuge when I was a fugitive. He raised my uncle from the dead and rescued my mother from the penalty of the Law."

The Teacher adds, "Crucified for our sins, Jesus died for humanity."

"Teacher, He did more than that for me. He bore my cross and died on it. Now I must take up my cross and follow Christ." Barabbas falls to his knees and prays, "Jesus, forgive me, for I am a sinner."

A few months after his conversion, Barabbas recognizes the

silhouette of a young woman riding toward the commune. Fear grips Barabbas as he wonders what Salome is doing in the Qumran. *She is coming for Ephraim. God, please don't let this happen. I want to raise my son in the fear and admonition of the Lord.*

Barabbas walks out to meet Salome as she dismounts. "Salome, what brings you here?"

Trembling, Salome answers, "My son—and *you.*"

"What do you mean?"

"Barabbas, I know that I have mistreated you, but I still love you."

"You must not say that, for you are married."

"There is something that you do not know about, Barabbas."

"Tell me."

"I could not tell the truth about our baby, for Philip would have killed you and Ephraim. Therefore, Philip imprisoned me in the palace at Caesarea Philippi. He brought in harlots who practiced strange religions to satisfy his desire. One night while enjoying a drunken orgy, the harlots fell down and worshiped Philip as if he were a god. In his drunken stupor, Philip boasted of deity. At that moment, he fell dead before their eyes."

"How did you manage to come here alone?"

"After Philip's death, Herod Antipas and Herodias came and met with Vitellius, president of Syria, to secure the throne for me. On the day that I was to be crowned the tetrarch, I abdicated the throne. I gave it all up to come here. Antipas and Herodias were very disappointed, so they did not bother stopping me as I rode away alone."

Seeing curiosity on Barabbas' face, Salome tells the rest of her story. "When I heard how Philip was stricken down, I knew there was only one true God—your God. I have forsaken riches and power to share my life with you and Ephraim."

Realizing his prayer has been answered, Barabbas says,

"I'll always love you, Salome." Barabbas hugs Salome and seals his promise of love with a passionate kiss.

Jair comes to the Qumran and tries to persuade Barabbas to lead the Zealots in revolt, but Barabbas refuses. Understanding that Barabbas is Christian, Jair reminds him that there is only one God. Barabbas retorts, "Yes, there is only one God and I know who he is. You keep looking for someone else, but my God has already come to mankind. God was manifest in the flesh, justified in the Spirit, seen of angels, preached unto the Gentiles, believed on in the world, received up into glory. That which was from the beginning, which we have heard, which we have looked upon, and our hands have handled, of the Word of life. And the Word was made flesh, and dwelt among us. No man hath seen God at any time; the only begotten Son, which is in the bosom of the Father, he hath declared him."

"Well, since you are not going to help us fight, will you give us those ledgers that incriminate Pilate?" asks Jair.

"Certainly, I'll get them for you." Barabbas climbs to the cave that houses the scriptures and takes the ledgers back to Jair.

"Thanks," Jair says gratefully.

Barabbas hugs Jair and prays for him. Then Barabbas hands Jair the Sword of Sacrifice. "Jair, you may have this sword if you will listen to me." Jair nods his head with agreement. "The night I watched the mob take Jesus away, I heard Jesus give this warning: 'Put up again thy sword into his place: for all they that take the sword shall perish with the sword.'"

Seven years pass after the suicide of Judas, the one who sold Jesus for thirty pieces of silver. During these years, Pilate cannot seem to overcome the remembrance of his mistake—pandering to his peers to murder the innocent man, Jesus.

The Jews go to Vitellius and complain of Pilate's brutality. Vitellius sends Pilate to stand before Caesar Tiberius.

When Pontius Pilate arrives in Rome, he finds that Tiberius is dead and Caligula is on the throne. With indisputable evidence presented against Pilate, Caligula banishes the governor to the Lake of Lucerne in the remote mountains.

At Lucerne, Pilate lives in despair and remorse, but he refuses to repent. Overcome by his failure to do what he knew was right, Pilate decides to end his mortal misery. Trying to escape this hell, he plunges into the dismal lake. Though the Lake of Lucerne swallows Pilate, the local shepherds claim to see him occasionally rising from the lake in the early morning fog. They claim that as Pilate rises from the smoky mist of the lake, he continually washes his permanently bloodstained hands in this lake of torment.

Seven years pass after Herod Antipas beheaded John the Baptist. Having silenced the voice of one crying in the wilderness, Herod Antipas cannot seem to attain the political success he desires. He becomes jealous of his nephew, Agrippa I, who receives a kingdom from Caesar. To add insult after injury, King Aretas defeats Antipas' army.

With his army destroyed, Herod requests assistance from Tiberius, so Caesar sends Vitellius to punish Aretas. While Vitellius is on his way, Tiberius dies and Caligula calls Antipas to answer allegations made against him.

Discovering that Antipas is cooperating with the king of Parthia against the Roman Empire, Caesar Caligula banishes Antipas to Lyons, Gaul. Then Caligula confiscates Antipas' estate and awards it to Agrippa I. Antipas is stripped of his idols—power and political prestige. Eating insects and what he can find, wearing the skin of an animal, Antipas lives like the man who once cried in the wilderness—the one whom he executed—John the Baptist.

Thirty-six years after the crucifixion of Jesus, the Zealots rally the Jews to fight against Rome. After fours years of fighting, the Romans begin to seize Jerusalem. Titus, son of the Roman emperor Vespasianus, surrounds Jerusalem. After many days of the siege, the Jews within the walls of the holy city begin to starve. The people become so desperate that they eat the corpses of their starved children. Finally Titus takes Jerusalem and fulfills the prophecy that Jesus made forty years prior: "The days shall come upon thee, that thine enemies shall cast a trench about thee, and compass thee round, and keep thee in on every side, and shall lay thee even with the ground, and thy children within thee; and they shall not leave in thee one stone upon another; because thou knewest not the time of thy visitation." Seizing Jerusalem, the Romans tear the Holy Temple down to the ground so that not one stone is left upon another.

With Jerusalem destroyed, only 960 surviving Zealots are left to take refuge at Masada—the natural fortress, which was fortified by Herod the Great. Under the direction of Eleazar, son of Jair, the Zealots try to secure themselves up on the steep mount.

Masada is approximately 1900 feet long, 600 feet wide, and 1400 feet high. Its plateau is topped with surrounding massive walls, towers, buildings, a system of cisterns that even provides a pool for swimming, a bathhouse, preserved food supplies, fertile ground for crops, and two palaces that Herod the Great had built. With its steep sides, this fortress has only two ways that anyone can reach the plateau without great difficulty. One way is from the direction of the Dead Sea. Another is the way called the *Serpent*, named appropriately for it often winds perpetually back into itself. Other paths to the plateau lead the climber to dangle above destruction or to a dead end.

With Herodium, Machaerus, and Jerusalem taken by the Romans, the remnant of zealous Jews fortify Masada. Silva, the Roman commander of the Tenth Legion, builds a wall around the fortress so that none of the rebellious Jews can escape. However, Eleazar ben Jair does not plan to run away. With enough armor and weapons to equip 10,000 men, the 960 men, women, and children defend themselves against Silva and the Tenth Legion for more than two years.

With time and much labor, Silva's legionnaires manually pile dirt on the White Promontory, a pile of rocks about 450 feet below the top of the western wall. Reaching the top with the bank of earth, the legionnaires use the battering ram to break down the wall. As the wall crumbles, Silva sees that the Zealots have built another wall behind it. The legionnaires batter the second wall, only to find that it gets sturdier as they pound at it.

Noting that this second wall is made of timbers, Silva suddenly realizes how to destroy the wall. He orders his men to throw burning torches to it. With the wind blowing the wrong way, the legionnaires find that the flames blow back on them. Suddenly, without an explainable cause, a south wind comes to save the efforts of the legionnaires—the wall begins to burn. Silva and the legionnaires wait in the darkness for the sun to rise.

Eleazar and the others know the morning will bring death, torture, and slavery. Realizing their fate, Eleazar passionately but reasonably tries to persuade the Zealots that their only alternative is to commit suicide. Feeling compassion for the men, women, and children, some disagree.

Eleazar gives another speech. "Today we enjoyed our last Passover. God has blessed us to fight from the beginning to the last. We are the fortunate ones. However, tomorrow each man shall be tortured unto death or shall remain a slave to the Romans. Each man shall hear his wife and children scream as hundreds rape each one. Therefore, let us die with dignity and preserve our freedom."

Knowing Eleazar is right about the torture and death, the

men agree. Distressed and miserable, the men tenderly embrace their wives and take their children in their arms. With parting kisses and tears in their eyes, the men take their swords and slay their families. Then the men choose ten men by lot to slay the rest.

With the corpses of their loved ones lying about, ten men are left. Then the ten draw lots again so that one man may slay the rest.

The lot falls on Eleazar ben Jair. He draws his magnificent sword—the Sword of Sacrifice—and sacrifices the other nine who are lying with their respective families. He presses the tip of the sword against his abdomen and stops to think. *Jesus was right. Of the Temple, not one stone is left upon another. All they that take the sword shall perish with the sword. Here I stand with the Sword of Sacrifice to finish my fate.*

Clasping the sword firmly, Eleazar cries aloud, "Hear, O Israel: The Lord our God is one Lord: And thou shalt love the Lord thy God with all thine heart, and with all thy soul, and with all thy might!"

At 2676 feet up on the Mount of Olives, a humble, meek man stands. With piercing black eyes, dark skin, coal-colored hair, the son of a Hasmonaean princess and a zealous warrior, Ephraim looks at the dirt beneath his feet. *On this mountain, the people once spread their garments before Jesus and shouted praises to God.* "Hosanna to the Son of David: Blessed is He that cometh in the name of the Lord; Hosanna in the highest." *It was here that Jesus wept over Jerusalem. It was here that Jesus taught the Olivet Discourse—the sermon of the signs of the times and the end of the age. It was here that Judas delivered Jesus into the hands of His enemies. It was here that the men of Galilee stood as they watched the resurrected Jesus ascend to heaven. And it will be here on the Mount of Olives that Jesus will one day return.*

Holding the Holy Scriptures—the true Sword of the Lord—quick and powerful, sharper than any two-edged sword, able to pierce even to the dividing asunder of soul and spirit, Ephraim looks to the top of the world. From the summit of Mount Olivet, Ephraim looks to Mount Calvary—the mountain so slight that all humanity can climb—a mountain of love, blessing, and hope. Then Ephraim looks at the destruction of the Temple—with not one stone upon another. He sees the Romans and the Jewish slaves.

Moved with compassion for all humanity, emboldened with power from above, Ephraim draws the attention of the victors and the slaves. The whole world seems to hear the message one more time. The message from above will not go away. "Repent, and be baptized every one of you in the name of Jesus Christ for the remission of sins, and ye shall receive the gift of the Holy Ghost."

Printed in the United States
92619LV00001B/25-54/A